Y0-DJO-147

He made no move to follow her but leaned against the dune relaxed and thoughtful. "Why have you cut off some of your lovely long hair, your hair that blew in the wind out on Cape Cod Bay?"

She turned to look at him in utter astonishment. "You saw me, out on the water?"

"Not as I wanted to see you. Your lovely body was covered with wet cloth."

"But you couldn't possibly have . . ."

"My telescope has never been so lucky."

"You must have been very far away or I . . ."

"Close enough to remember everything." He followed and, with strong, confident hands, drew her back beside him.

Sarah understood at last that she was power-less to order her body on its way. Her entire person identified with this man who seemed a part of the fresh freedom of the sea. She had found another being like herself.

"Are you a mist maiden?" he asked. "When I was a boy, I used to listen to the old sailors' tales. They warned me against mist maidens—to see one is an omen of doom. Suppose I hold a mist maiden—like this . . . What then?" His flexible voice descended to a vibrant hypnotic note. "I accept the omen and . . . I take."

Sarah's body, long cheated by neglect, flared in response to this perfect equation of man, time and place . . .

*Also by Nancy Bruff:*
*CIDER FROM EDEN*
*THE MANATEE*
*THE COUNTRY CLUB*

# DESIRE ON THE DUNES
## Nancy Bruff

LEISURE BOOKS ⚬⚬ NEW YORK CITY

A LEISURE BOOK

Published by

Dorchester Publishing Co., Inc.
6 E. 39th Street
New York City

Printed in the United States of America

# Chapter one

A cresting wave
carves the Mist Maiden
of spume and the wake
left by a dream.
To see her once is forever,
in the moon shadow lying.

At the end, in the hour
of our mortal peril,
we will see her again
drawing her nets
woven of fog and time
in the surf shadow calling

to hold us in her fragile cave
beneath the curve of a wave,
for a lifetime in a moment
before we become what we must,
in the wind shadow drifting.

**W**here did you meet this silly bastard?" Zenas Mayo leaned back in his fishing boat. He and his daughter Sarah gave each other wary smiles.

Zenas squinted up at the gulls that had followed their little boat out into Cape Cod Bay. "Let me think . . . Wellfleet bristles with the masts of whalers."

"Father, *every*thing isn't whaling nowadays. This is 1803. We have pleasure boats, and even freebooters. Times have changed while you weren't looking."

"By Christ, if it's that young fop on the racing sloop . . .!"

Sarah was silent.

"He looks as narrow as a razor clam and I'll wager he's got a soul to match." Zenas peered into her eyes, nodding with triumph.

"You have seen him!" Sarah cried.

"Hahhhh!" Zenas gave a laugh that trailed away as he met his daughter's accusing gray eyes.

"You trapped me," she cried. "Anyway that's only on the surface. What do you know about Peter's soul?"

"I can make a damn good guess that it's crawling

6

with threadworms. Steer clear, Sarah."

"*Oh,* why even try to talk to you about him!" Sarah gave a furious toss of her head and they were silent for awhile in the gently dipping boat.

Presently, she shivered and folded her bare arms across her breasts. "Much as I love sailing, today I feel edgy as if something out there in the mist was reaching out and . . . touching me!"

Far out on the water, and half hidden by pockets of mist, a freebooter was holding Sarah's image in the center of his telescope. The glass was steady as he balanced on the deck of the *Windshadow* with all the power and grace of a man who made his home on deep water. His feet like those of his crew were bare and hard. His shirt was open to the waist, showing sunbleached hair. Now in his thirty-sixth year, he had the fresh look of an active man full of freeflowing courage.

"What do you see out there, Captain?" asked Symonds, the first mate, a short, red haired man with a high peeling forehead and subtle eyelids.

"Nothing for you, Symonds."

"I hoped you had sighted our victim. We've cut through the wake of a year and a half trying to catch his sloop off this damned New England coast. How much longer?"

Captain Calvin Collier smiled, showing deeply carved dimples and white confident teeth. "How long? Until I can paint our bowsprit with a bucket of his blood."

Half hidden by fog and distance, Captain Collier's scrutiny had an effect on Sarah and Zenas. They both felt uneasy, as if a storm were gathering.

"So it *is* that proud son of a bitch in the fancy

sloop," said Zenas, very glum.

Sarah laughed, a high, sweet cascade of notes that blended with the sound of the gulls. "Since you refer to his mother, she was a fine Boston lady like my own mother."

"Hell's own," said Zenas.

Sarah glanced sideways, baiting him. "She always told me that I'd know a gentleman by his manners. Smooth as driftwood—the exact opposite of your father, she said."

Zenas belched, a retort that he had trained himself to deliver at will ever since the day his wife, her brief passion for him over, began to wrinkle her nose in fastidious recoil at his rough fisherman's ways. Sarah's nature was divided between her mother's elegant manners and a laughing delight in Zenas's earthy self.

"Mother would have admired Peter's cool manner," she said. "He comes from one of those fine houses she used to mention."

"And mention and mention and mention," said Zenas.

"He may not be your kettle of chowder, but I'm sure a very sheltered girl such as my mother was would never have any trouble with *her* father over a man like Peter Garrett."

"Her father, old Bemus!" Zenas gave a disgusted laugh into which he wove the words, "Sheltered" and "God damn." He cocked an hilarious eye at the gulls as if he longed for any creature to share this irony with him.

"After all," Sarah began fiercely, "Mother was a fine lady. She just happened to fall in love with a . . ." Her voice trailed away. She was at heart, very proud of Zenas.

8

"I'll finish it for you—a *man*," Zenas said. "Something new for that crowd on old Bemus' pleasure boat."

"True enough, but you must admit that it was quite a long step for a beautiful Boston lady."

"Long step for me too . . . on a gangplank!" Zenas opened his mouth to say more but shut it again. He would rather speak respectfully of his wife now that she was dead. It would be easier to do that if only his irritation had died with her. She had always put him in mind of a blowfish from the mouth down but if she had claimed that she was once beautiful who could dispute her now? He sighed heavily. Now take the other sister, Hope Bemus—and he wished he had—there was a *real* looker.

Zenas cut off a piece of quahog and baited his hook. "Come on Sarah, let's fish. There's something wrong with every off-Cape furriner, you know that."

"Well . . . yes, and I'll admit there's something just a *little* off about Peter, but it's something you can't see."

"Have to be blind," said Zenas.

"When I'm with Peter, I sometimes feel a chill. It's like swimming over a streak of cold water, then it's gone."

"Throw him back, he's no good." Zenas picked up a small fish he had caught and flung it far out on the water to dramatize his point.

Sarah gave a quick high shrug. "I was trying to really *talk* to you, explain how I . . . but what's the use."

Zenas felt pushed away and the area between generations widened before him like an uncharted sea full of crosscurrents and riptides. He longed for perfect words to navigate it.

9

"Sarah . . ." he began.

She gave him a measured look. "You might as well know it now. I love Peter Garrett."

Zenas sat very still. He stared at his daughter to see if he had missed some change in her, but she looked the same despite this terrible attack on her good sense, her judgement. That she had kept it a secret from him until now was as strange as her choice. She had always told him what was going on in her life. Was the old lady working in her like yeast?

Worried, he tried to find signs of himself in Sarah's face. She had his wife's high forehead salvaged by his own sea-gray eyes, but Sarah's eyes were large with a sun-spangle in them and the pull of an undertow for the young men of Wellfleet. She could have had anyone she wanted. Her nose? By God that was all his, strong prow and clean carving. The old lady missed out on her mouth, so did he, with no more lip than an oyster, while Sarah's lips were full, with a laugh carved into their corners; in the corners of her mind too. Now how could she waste all that on. . . .

"Christ damn, what do you *see* in him?" Zenas asked.

"It's hard to describe, Father."

"Anyone would agree to that," he laughed mournfully.

"From the first, I liked his proud walk."

"Arrogant young bastard!"

"Little things too." She looked into the mist. "His quick, lonely smile—our Cape boys grin. His . . . his elegance, even the clean starched smell of his linen stock is . . ."

Zenas made a sound of acute nausea. "Throw him

10

back for bait," he shouted. "The rotten fellow will draw fish for miles around!"

Sarah flushed. A pulse beat in her high temples as she glared at him, her mouth drawn down. "How can you be so full of prejudice?" she suddenly shouted at him. "Just because he's rich, educated and you're a . . ." She would not say it but stood up and dove into the water to silence herself. She swam and let the pull of the tide and her skirt, heavy with water slow her motions and her temper.

Zenas reached under the prow for his bottle. "Ah, you *friend*," he said as he corked it after a long swig. He pulled in a bass and put it in the prow, then began winding a line around a piece of wood, guiding it through a notch in his toenail which was as thick and ridged as a clamshell.

Sarah, calmed by the water, pulled up into the boat and sat in the stern, wringing out her skirt. They sat in silence except for the spasmodic flapping of the bass under the prow.

Aboard the *Windshadow*, Symonds reached for the telescope. "My turn, Captain. What do you see out there between the pockets of mist—a rich man's sloop?"

Calvin Collier thrust the mate aside.

"With her hold full of wine," Symonds went on, "and a dozen lewd, lovely girls frolicking on deck?"

"You dreamer," said the captain. "Find me such a cargo off these puritan shores, Symonds, and I'll give you the next ship we overtake, line of duty, of course."

"Better take this one before it gets too late."

The captain ignored him. Intent on the glass, his mouth dropped open slightly.

11

Symonds' voice tightened with tension. "You heard me, before it gets *too late* for us all."

"You fool, this is only a small fishing boat. The damned mist keeps floating between us and I can't quite . . . ahh, now I have them again. Old man in the prow, girl in the stern. She has been in the water, her dress is wet, clinging. Her hair shines like wet seaweed."

"A small boat and a fisherman's wench. Is that our only prize for idling off the coast? I tell you the crew is getting ugly." Symonds spoke urgently.

"How can they do that? They are already there." The captain's laugh was a warm, deep-chested bellow. He kept his eye on the glass. "Double everything, Symonds, rations, rum and, if they still grumble, the hell with them!"

"Aye, Captain, but that's what we ask, a fair chance to earn a dock in Hell's harbor."

The captain's bronzed face was dark against the sky. His mouth curved with delight at what he saw in the glass. Below him a fish leaped out of the water and shook its tail with a shower of brilliant drops.

Look at him, thought Symonds. Shoulders like a draft horse, stomach pulled in hard by his strongest muscle, pride, "Captain," he pleaded. "We are already full of rum and vigorous as the Devil yet here we stay, hovering off Cape Cod and for what gain?"

"Revenge, Symonds. Bloody revenge. That should ease their rum-soaked hearts."

"The men want a little booty along with it, to wash it down, so to speak."

"Symonds, you are getting monotonous." Calvin Collier adjusted the glass. "When I can get her

12

features clear, I'll lower away and go after her. Here, take a look, a short one."

Symonds seized the glass. His mouth drew down at the corners. "A clam digger's hag." He spat over the rail.

"Liar," Captain Collier retrieved the glass. "Ahhh, the strands of fog are lifting, she's almost clear."

He gave a quick shudder and the blood seeped from his face leaving it yellow under his tan. "By Christ, for a moment I thought she was a Mist Maiden! I used to hear about them off the coast of Cornwall where I came from. Sea-bitches, formed of spume and foam. The legend goes that, if you saw one, from that moment on she held you fast, entangled in her net woven of time and mist. At the end, in your hour of mortal peril, you would see her again, drawing you up in her net."

Symonds began a laugh that was no more hearty than that of any other rightly superstitious sailor. As it trailed off, he looked out into the floating mist. "Maybe she *is* a Mist Maiden and it's a sign that we should get out of here and forget revenge. It's all over and done with and we're free men now, Captain."

"It's not over until we chop him up for bait."

"And I suppose eat every fish the bait catches. Captain, will you listen to *reason?*"

"I don't speak foreign languages."

"You can think better than we can; you've had an education and that's more than the rest of us have."

"I keep all that in a sling."

"All right, keep it there and listen to rough sailor's sense. We've combed this coast for many long months and can't catch up with the young bastard. He's too proud to hide but he keeps on traveling.

13

This could go on and on. Now every dog on the brig has his point of honor. With it, he can stand up to the Devil; without it he's everybody's man. But we're all sick of sailing on *your* point of honor!"

Captain Collier leaned over the rail and looked at the horizon. Mist descended to windward. Tendrils of it drifted over the brig as if the Mist Maiden had already thrown her net at him. He shook his big shoulders and the muscles rippled like a horse dismissing a fly.

Symonds, trying to get through to him, addressed him by his first name. "Calvin, we've been together a long time." Under his drooping lids, his eyes glowed with exasperated affection.

The captain turned and looked full at him. "All right, what now? Get it said."

"All right, you speak of us being free men now, but this is jail right here, a jail of hot sun, light airs and fog. We could be out on the deep water in a few hours. Calvin, listen to my advice. Sail around your point of honor for now then come back later. Take the bastard by surprise, suddenly, when he thinks the coast is clear."

Captain Collier put down the glass. He shook his head at Symonds. "Why put it off?"

Symonds sensed an aperture in the captain's resistance. He moved into it. "Why? because not only will you ease us all here on the brig but you can torture the young bastard with fear, send him messages. Be like a dog worrying a bone as he gnaws at it. Tickle him with a dagger until he looks over his shoulder in fear wherever he is. We can keep track of him until we're ready to pounce."

The captain threw back his head and gave his warm roar of laughter. "You're a transparent old devil. But . . . the idea itself has merit. I can see him trying to build up his clammy courage while he waits and waits. After all, the anticipation is the worst. Death itself may not be so terrible. We don't know what the arrangements are. Maybe death is a benefit! But the fear of it . . . ah . . ."

"If that's so, then we have been dealing out benefits over the years." Symonds grinned.

Captain Collier drew his sunbleached eyebrows together. "He's going to feel us behind every sail on the horizon and every tree on a dark night. Meanwhile we can go about overhauling some prizes—line of duty, of course—using our Letter of Marque. We'll get the crew back into a good work-a-day mood again."

Symonds nodded. He knew when to stop.

The captain shook drops of mist out of his curly hair. His deep, resonant voice rolled over the brig. "Find the wind and stand by to take her round the Cape, you greedy bastards!"

He turned to Symonds. With the feline intuition that ran parallel with his vigor, he had correctly estimated the mate's feelings for him as a mixture of envy, exasperation and deep affection. Drawing back his fist, he tapped Symonds lightly on the jaw. "That's for giving me advice that I took." He gave a chuckle.

Symonds staggered back against the mast and rubbed his jaw, acting out the role of a man nearly felled by a blow. He grinned at the captain, his subtle eyelids at half mast, to conceal his victory.

Captain Collier kept his back to the fog and to the place where he had seen the Mist Maiden. He bounded over the deck calling to his crew in a voice full of hard cheer. "A little nearer to the wind and

15

take her out to the deep water where she belongs!"

Sarah Mayo spread her long hair out over the edge of the boat to dry. She spoke half to herself. "I've been seeing Peter for quite a while. We walk up Shirt Tail Point and sit under the pines every evening. I know he loves me but somehow . . . he says everything but the words I am longing to hear. Why?"

Zenas compressed his lips against the obscenities that rose naturally to them.

She laughed at his expression. "Don't worry, his passion is at anchor. Peter is always always on guard. He's tense as a sail in a high wind. Now and then he lets drop a hint of some past disaster or a doom hovering over him. It's . . ."

"Romantic gull dung!" Zenas broke in. "He's trying to scare you off, build a case against marriage."

Relaxed by the water, Sarah tried to be reasonable, even mild. "You're only guessing, Father. You don't know him."

"Maybe, but I know a hell of a lot. I know that when I try to help my grown child, it's as if I were dead and trying to get through to the living. You don't hear me."

Zenas pulled in his line and scowled at the empty hook. "Why didn't you bring him home to meet me before you went walking on Shirt Tail Point with the rest of the lovers?"

They avoided each other's eyes and watched a tern scoop something from the water. They both knew that it was out of the question to bring anyone home to meet Zenas, who was always at the taverns. Her silence answered him as she shook out

16

her long wet hair, holding it out to a sudden light breeze.

"Well anyway," Zenas said, "the young fool is as unbalanced as a dory full of monkeys. I was there when he first sailed into the harbor in that proud sloop of his, all gleaming with too many brights. " 'Ahoy there, *Silver Handles!*' I called out."

"Oh Father, you *didn't!* The *Challenger* a coffin!" Her stream of laughter broke off as a shudder raised both her shoulders and stopped her breath for a moment. An elusive something flitted across her mind, a shadow too swift to be recognized, a warning too faint to receive.

"Well, I did," Zenas went on. "He jumped as if I'd shot him. Then he stood still as a gull on a pole, staring at me, waiting as if I had a message for him. I gave him a scare—wonder why? Maybe he's yellow."

"You imagined it, Father. Peter is very brave. He says that courage is all there is and that, at the very end, it all depends on having one grain of courage left over."

"Crazy young bastard, he's in love with himself," Zenas said.

Sarah's voice rose. "I'm *trying* to explain him. Peter feels a kind of dragging anchor of . . . well, fate, that . . ."

"Fate!" Zenas yelled. "Oh Christ damn! Don't go on about his fate any more, you'll make me vomit." He lifted the bottle. "Well, here's to his dragging anchor, here's to love at low tide and here's a gulp for his good-smelling linen and two more for his lonely smile . . . Christ, who isn't lonely." He turned away with a baffled laugh.

Sarah leaned out over the stern and pulled on the

17

rope that trailed a dory with its small sail furled. "I'm going." Her voice shook with frustration. "It's hopeless to even try to talk to you any more, *hopeless.*"

Turned from him, she felt a twitch at her heart as she saw his lost look. His mouth hung open a little with surprise and disappointment. With a little rush of emotion, she leaned forward on her knees and stroked his freckled hands while she searched for some way to tell him how well she remembered her childhood when he had been the swaggering king of the sea around the port of Wellfleet. Now he was as ridged as an old sea turtle, still fiery, but she had put dismay in his eyes. She searched for the right words but, young as she was, she had lived long enough to know that the perfect words would come to her later when the moment had gone.

"I understand," Zenas said. "There is not a Christ damn thing for you to look forward to at home with me." And he too in this moment of closeness, longed to say how full the old days had been and how well he remembered her little girl's face when he had brushed the sand off her closed eyelids on the beach. He looked out over the water, his profound bloodshot grey eyes blinking rapidly. "Hell's tide," he asked, "why choose *him?* He's not at all like me."

Ah, she thought, here we are at the heart of the matter. It's a betrayal. Peter is my mother's kind.

"I didn't really choose him," she said. "I think Peter has always been out there for me, on the incoming tide."

"Like flotsam." Zenas looked up at the sky. "It's getting late. I see you are pulling in the dory, so sail home if that's what you want. I'll stay a while and

18

get one more striper." He sighed, unable to bear any more.

However, when Sarah and the dory slipped into the mist, Zenas suddenly sprang up. "Sarah!" he bellowed. "I forbid you to see him. You hear me? I *forbid* it!"

Sarah's voice was close by in the mist. "Too late," she called. "I can't hear you." Her laugh, merry and intensely feminine, hung on the air.

"Little sea bitch," Zenas shouted. "You hear me loud as a fog horn!"

Sarah leaned back, one arm over the tiller. Soon the melancholy sounds of her father's boat, the bass flopping in the hold and the squeak of the bottle cork were lost.

She found some wind and tacked skillfully around the pockets of mist and into Wellfleet harbor. As she furled sail and rowed in under the bowsprits and the anchor chains of the big ships, she was feeling all the sadness of coming to the end of something she valued. Out on the bay, an aging man was alone among the gulls and would be even more alone, if her plans went well.

# Chapter two

"Character is destiny
and I am the architect
of my fate,"
said the gnat,
as a majestic bull frog
extended his tongue
and ushered
this personage in.

That same evening, Sarah and Peter walked through the town of Wellfleet to their eyrie on Shirt Tail Point. As they passed by the tavern window where high-pitched squawks told of Zenas's presence among the wenches, Sarah increased her pace, raised her voice and in general heightened her charm to distract Peter until they were safely away. As they passed the docks where sailors were always loading and unloading their carts and drawing them over the cobbles, they encountered the usual stares. The carts ceased their rumbling as Peter walked by. He would have caught the eye anywhere but in this whaling port, he was an oddity.

To wear both gun and sword was common in a seaport, but they looked wrong on him as he strode along with his lofty carriage, skintight breeches, snowy neckcloth and a Brutus haircut that brought spiked tendrils of hair down over his forehead. He turned his head slightly to the right and left, glancing over the faces of the people he passed as if he were watching and listening for someone even as he talked to Sarah.

Sarah thought him incredibly handsome and

22

elegant. If at times it occurred to her that some-where in his sensitive face, a piece of jigsaw puzzle had been put in upside down, it only increased the fascination he held for her. His changing moods excited her. Sometimes he looked like a generous, upright boy; then a fear, followed by a touch of ancient cunning, would wash over his features. To Sarah, Peter's challenge was like her beloved sea in doubtful weather. She drew a deep breath. Tonight is the night, she told herself.

When they passed a group of old men who sat on tar barrels gossiping in the evening shadows, Sarah shook out the folds of her best blue dress, deco-rated tonight with shell ornaments she had made. She smoothed it over her small vigorous waist, a distracting gesture designed to take Peter's atten-tion away from the oldsters and dim their twanging voices.

"Well, if it ain't young Sarah Mayo out for another stroll with that proud young fool off the racing sloop." Cackles, then a call. "Hey, what's the matter with our own randy young sailors, girl?"

"Come on, Peter, hurry past them," she said.

"Smart young pup." An old man spit in the direction of Peter's fashionable Hessian boots with their swaying tassels. "He walks like a man carrying a jug of fear, real careful that it don't slop over."

"Yup," agreed his old crony, "he's got a lot more on his mind than walking out with Sarah Mayo. Wish I were in his fancy boots. God damn but I know what I'd be thinking about!"

"And that's all you'd be good for, old man, thinking about it!" His friends cackled like ropes creaking in the rigging.

A small tendril of laughter escaped Sarah as,

keeping step with Peter's stately walk, she began to climb up the hill. Peter glanced at her in surprise. "You found those old men amusing?"

Sarah flushed but said with a note of defiance, "Didn't you?"

"In no way."

Sarah looked into his eyes. He really was displeased, not pompously, rather as if laughter itself had recalled a terrible memory. He squeezed his eyes shut for a moment as if to close out a vision.

Sarah shook her head slightly in annoyance. She must control her laughter. It had been a romance-killer before, with other young men, a kind of enemy in her own throat that made itself known at inappropriate moments.

They climbed the rest of the hill in silence and came out on a ledge where they sat down on a carpet of pine needles. They were well hidden by the surrounding trees but, through an aperture, they could see the crowded harbor below with its forest of masts. Here and there a web of rigging held a sailor working like an insect caught in a web.

Peter put his arms around her and they kissed in silence then caressed, whispering words of love. But Sarah would go no further. She had never allowed a young man so much leeway as this.

They lingered while the lights began to gleam from the helm windows in the older boats and the wind carried the sailors' voices as they called out from boat to boat.

The wind blew salty strands of Sarah's hair across Peter's face. Her agile, healthy swimmer's body was exasperated by these evenings together, so closely entwined, so hungrily kissing—and nothing more allowed.

Peter drew back. He looked at her, his eyes brilliant. He drew a deep breath. Now, she thought, now at last Peter is going to ask me.

"Sarah," he began.

"Yes?"

"This is our last evening together."

She turned away in disappointment, flinging over her shoulder, "Oh Peter, you've said that before, and . . ."

"I know, and I intended to leave but then . . . I begin saying your name over and over, SarahMayo-SarahMayoSarahMayo—repeated over and over it sounds like the surf on a calm day. And . . . I don't leave."

"All right then, Peter, this evening let's not talk about saying goodbye, only about being together."

"But I can't stay here. I can't *stay* anywhere!"

"Everyone stays somewhere." Sarah clasped him in her strong arms. "And since we love, stay with me, here."

"I can't involve you in my fate."

Sarah gave an impatient sigh for his dramatic phrases. "Peter, *tell* me what troubles you and we'll tack and sail around whatever reef is in your way."

Peter was silent. He looked out to sea.

"Peter." She shook his arm gently. "Can your family be of any help? They must be substantial people. Surely you can . . ."

"I have none left," he said. "I lived with an uncle who died and left me his fortune. There are two cousins who are nothings from Norwich. I work in their firm—when I work."

"Nobody is a nothing," she laughed but gave him a critical look. "My family consists of a father who would advise you as he does other young men, to

25

drink, fight and wench but always be exactly honest and keep your heart plumb."

Peter smiled. "Do you want me to take all of that advice?"

Sarah gave her joyous laugh and pulled him down to her lips. "Just the last part!"

"As for a fight," Peter went on after a moment, "there I have no choice. There is only integrity. That path is cleared, the rest is swamp."

Sarah looked out over the harbor lights. High flown talk, she thought. What does it mask? She was saddened to realize that this splendid, dazzling young man, with his fresh stock and fine ways, could be an occasional bore. "I never give much thought to my integrity," she said. "I let it function all by itself."

Peter took out his handkerchief and brushed his nostrils with it, a nervous habit of his. He stood up and pulled her to her feet. She could see that he was gathering himself together to make some kind of depressing farewell speech like the other evenings.

"So you are going to fly away?" she asked.

"This time I must. There is no other way. I have lingered too long. I have no right to draw you into my . . ."

"Then fly light, light as a gull and drop off some of that integrity on the way, why don't you?" She recalled Zenas's favorite comment, "Gull dung!" and her sudden irresistible laughter filled the air. Shocked, she tried to suppress it. Surely this coarse streak came direct from Zenas.

Again, Peter found her laughter offensive. He lit the lantern he had brought along. "We are out later than usual. Your father will be . . ."

"I might as well tell you, Peter. Father is not home

worrying about me. He is in the tavern. He took this habit when my mother was alive and . . ."

"No, stop, don't tell me any more! Don't fill in any background. I already have enough memories of you to torment me for the rest of my life. Let's not make ourselves any more real to each other." Peter's eyes shone in the lantern light. The Yankee squint was gone, opened wide. His eyes were like the eyes of a child who fears to go upstairs in the dark. He made no further move to leave.

Sarah walked to the edge of the small cliff. "We are already so real as to be branded with each other." She stood looking out over the harbor. If Mother were alive, she thought, she would know how to bring Peter to port. How briskly she used to dispose of the young sailors father brought home. "Underlings," she would say beneath her breath to Zenas.

"Luff and away," Zenas would tell them. "The old lady from Boston sends regards but don't come back after Sarah until you captain a whaler of your own. But bear this in mind, boys, my Sarah could round the Cape on a five year voyage and still be fresh as seaweed at high tide."

Sarah gave a little laugh at the memory. Peter came up to her. "What is it? Must you laugh so much? What have I said?"

"Why are you so suspicious of laughter? As if it were always aimed at you? I was thinking of my mother. Like you, she was an off-Cape foreigner from Boston."

"What was her name?"

"Bemus."

"But that's a fine old Boston name!" he exclaimed in surprise.

"Thank you." Sarah's voice was curt. "Bemus is too distinguished a name for me?"

"I mean . . ."

"Never mind. I received your message, sir, but my mother would be furious with you. She used to say, 'My Sarah is the equal of any well-bred Boston miss, I've seen to that'.

"Then Father would say, 'She's *more* equal. I've taught her to swim and sail and to be as honest as a compass'.

"Then Mother; 'She's not for some uneducated lout of a whaling man. Sarah has *my* blood in her veins'.

" 'Moth dust from a Boston attic,' Father would taunt her.

" 'Gentleman's blood,' Mother would say and so they would go on and on, Mother calling him a vulgarian, Father calling her a dried-up Boston cod cake. If only they could have *seen* the loneliness and courage in each other!" Sarah's emotion was vivid on her lovely face as Peter held the lantern up to it.

"There was Mother, holding to a standard of grace and elegance in our little cottage, and Father, staying home with us when he longed for the deep water, and neither of them were able to see that the more they despised each other, the more they had to be the way they were; Father too earthy, Mother too fastidious, and both of them struggling to make me like themselves. And all the time I was Sarah Mayo, a separate planet. Are they both still warring in my blood?"

Peter, very moved, pulled her to him. The tension left his face, she could see the young sincerity in him. She caressed his face with both hands, framing it. "I love you. We can build a life loving the difference in our natures. That's the way it should be." She looked into his face compellingly. "Peter, this is the last time I will lower myself to ask. From now on, if you want me, you will have to find me and beg, looking at me as I now look at you."

His face changed. "Beg!" he muttered as if the word had awakened a bitter memory.

"Peter!" she shook him slightly. "Come back from wherever you are."

His mouth twisted in a half smile. "You recommend a wife for a man who is being hunted? A man with a tireless enemy?"

Anger flared in her, she flung herself away. "Leave me then!"

"Would you marry Death? That's what it could be for us both."

"You're in love, Peter, but with your own fate."

Peter came after her.

"No, don't follow me—follow the man who is hunting and haunting you. Go after *him*, why don't you? Go hunt the hunter. I won't cower with you because there isn't any place on earth where people can cower."

Peter stared at her. "Hunt the hunter," he said slowly.

"Do that, doom-bitten Peter, and take back your love-making that kisses and fondles and says a noble goodbye. Here—this time, I'll say it for you. *Goodbye!*"

Fierce with pride, she started running down the path and was caught in the arms of a group of sailors who came up the winding path with a jug of rum.

The sailors held her, laughing at her struggles,

until Peter, one hand on his sword, retrieved her.

"So this place is took, eh?" A sailor looked around at their pine-carpeted nook. His deeply-pocked face looked like lava in the moonlight.

"It is. Get going," Peter said.

"And the wench too?"

"The *lady*. On your way," Peter said.

The sailor hesitated, glanced at Peter's sword, the pistol in his belt, and with a shrug went on. He continued his conversation as the sailors went back down the path. "So like I was saying, Cold Steel Collier himself come up over the side of our boat grinning—you could see his white teeth and his damned dimples in the lamp light. "Give up, you boatload of minnows!" he roars like a sea lion. "Collier is here!"

"He don't use his nickname?" asked a young sailor with a loud voice. His vulnerable face looked envious. "How'd he get it?"

"Earned it. No one can outfight him but he don't want the name, hates it, says day for that kind of thing is over. You call him that an' you'll get yours quick, Sonny," said a sailor with buckteeth and the shoulders of a walrus. "Come on, come on, let's settle down with the jug, we're all thirsty."

Sarah noted this last speaker's terrible hands as they swung the lantern beside him. Huge and knobby, they were like tree roots. They seemed significant in some way.

Peter went a few paces after the men, his head tipped, listening to their talk. He looked taut and in the gleam of the lantern, his face was grooved with tension.

The men looked back at him curiously, then walked on with a shrug and an exaggerated sailor's swagger. Their voices grew fainter but the loud voice of the young sailor could still be heard. "Look out for the jug," he said, and they were gone.

Two nighthawks wheeled over the point shrieking, then flew away until the sound diminished to a faint echo. Sarah, standing on the edge of the cliff, shivered with a sudden inexplicable emotion. The eerie sound seemed to have a bearing on something, to be an omen of things dying away. "You were brave," she said to Peter. "They could all have attacked you and . . ."

He brushed her words aside. "Where are those sailors from?"

"I'm trying to thank you and . . ."

"Are they local men?"

"Yes, I think so. Peter, you were splendid, and . . ."

"They must have had some encounter with freebooters—pirates . . ."

"Some sailors do. Yes, of course. Why?"

"They look like rough characters and not particular in their choice of jobs."

"Certainly not overly fussy. Why?"

"I've reached a decision, something important to us both in time. Your suggestion has merit."

"Ah," Sarah looked at him gravely. So he realized at last how impossible it was to separate.

"I *will* hunt the hunter!"

Sarah lifted her hands and let them drop. "Still on that," she said in a small voice.

"I'm going to set a trap for a tiger."

"Did I say trap?" Sarah asked.

"I never was cowering in the bushes as you implied. I was ready at all times. As ready as he. I have never retreated, only kept moving."

"It sounds like the same thing to me," Sarah said.

31

But she knew now that there really was some menace and it was not just a queer quirk in his brain. His enemy was real. When Peter drew her back to their old eyrie on the top of the hill, she went willingly. Surely now was the time to find out everything.

"Will you tell me who has placed this terror on you, Peter?" she asked.

"No," he said, "I cannot."

They were silent a moment.

"Well, so be it. But whoever he is," she said, "turn around and attack. It's the only way, Peter. I used to have nightmares in which I ran up a winding stairway with something horrible following me. One night in my dream, I turned and threw myself on my pursuer, hitting and tearing in a fury. I woke up and have had brave, brave dreams ever since."

Peter nodded. "Yes, it is the only possible way and . . . Sarah, it could open out a life for us together. A life free of danger."

He was still a long time frowning, as if charting a course through reefs. A green fly lit on his arm. Sarah watched the fly groom its head with its front legs then twiddle them together as if warming them in the shaft of lantern light. It scraped a hind leg over a wing that was like a flake of mica.

"Fly, it's past your bedtime." Sarah brushed it gently away. She felt a tenderness for all living things. Was that part of being in love? She searched her heart; the romantic and sensual pull toward Peter was as strong as ever. His restraint and secretiveness had aroused her will to win. But now that he included her in his future plans, she felt perversely a fearful drawing back. She had forced him. Inexperienced as she was, it occurred to her

32

now that, in love, to win was perhaps to lose?

Down on the rocks below them, the sailors had settled with their jug. One of them sang in a tender lullaby voice, an old sea chantey of a drowned sailor. As she listened, Sarah felt lost and cold. She shivered.

Peter took off his coat and put it around her as the men joined in the chorus:

> *Deep water*
> *Deep water*
> *Rock me gentle*
> *on the waves.*
>
> *Three sea gulls stand*
> *on my drowned chest.*
>
> *Deep water*
> *Rock me gentle*
>
> *Three gulls fight*
> *for my two blue eyes.*
>
> *Deep water*
> *Deep water*
> *Rock me gentle*
> *on the waves.*

Sarah was overcome with a feeling of pressure, like the silent thunder felt in the nerves before the storm crashes. The song's last notes were like the sound of the diminishing scream of the hawks, all blending to make her feel that she was forcing open the door of her life and it was too late to stop.

She jumped up and screamed over the ledge at the sailors, "Take your jug and your stupid song away from here! I'm Zenas Mayo's daughter and I say get out!"

The startled sailors on the rocks below dropped their jug. It crashed to a chorus of groans. "Stupid bitch," said the young sailor. "Look what she made us do! Who's Zenas Mayo anyway?"

"We'd better pull anchor and dock somewhere else tonight, that's who he is," said the pock-marked sailor.

"Her father that tough, eh?"

The other men answered by getting to their feet.

Sarah looked at Peter with a gleam of laughter in her eyes. "You see? I come from dangerous stock. Think twice before crossing me, Peter."

Peter stared out over the water, something excited and vindictive in his features. The young sailor began to whistle the refrain of the chantey.

"I said, stow it," Sarah called, "Or I *will* sic Zenas on you!"

The whistling stopped abruptly as a sailor clapped a hand over the young sailor's mouth. "Last man we want fixed on us, you fool," he said.

Sarah turned to Peter. "I'm sorry. You had better walk your brawling lady home. The song upset me. It seemed to mean something to me that . . . Oh, I don't know."

Peter's hand tightened on her arm. "It meant this to me. While I'm alive I can still throw the gulls off my chest before they get my eyeballs." He put a foot up on a rock and looked out over the harbor. "We make our own fate,"

Sarah thought of how Zenas would wince at the needlessly exalted expression on Peter's face. "There you go again," she said.

"And from now on, I'm going to carve it myself." The wind came through the pitch pines in a sudden roar that reduced the bold note in Peter's voice to a mumble.

# Chapter three

I am power.
Why struggle?
Lop off my branches,
blast my roots and
I'll spring up again,
nourished
by the bloody loam
of centuries.

A cleaver-thin servant leaned over the railing of the widow's walk. He was watching from the roof of the finest mansion in Wellfleet as the well-dressed young man below stood hesitating at the front door. Why? The rich seldom hesitated at doors.

The servant leaned further over the rail as the young man below turned away, went down the walk, then must have reached a decision, for he turned back, charged up the steps and knocked firmly at the door.

The servant raced down from the roof of the square, white mansion, knowing how his master disliked surprises. Before the knocker sounded again, he had consulted with his master and shortly afterward, the servant, who had a sinuous eel-like way of coming around corners, opened the front door to the young man.

"Good morning," said Peter gravely. "Is this the residence of Deacon Handy, the town Selectman?"

"It might be, why?" The servant wore his usual fixed expression, that of someone who maliciously bides his time.

38

"May I see him?"

"For what purpose, sir?"

"I understand the Deacon owns most of the property on the ocean side."

"He may have some land there."

"I would like to see him about it."

"May I ask why, sir?"

Peter gave him a cold look. "I'll discuss that with your master."

"No use trying to buy any of it," said the servant.

"Please take him my name. Peter Garrett, from Boston."

Peter watched the man eel around a corner in the hall. Somewhere in the depths of the house, he could barely hear a harsh contemptuous voice. The words were lost to him although he strained to hear.

The Deacon was saying, "Stupid Sam! Why didn't you find out why he takes this awkward interest in my land? Now I *have* to see him to find out."

The servant knew it was useless to describe his efforts. Efforts did not interest the Deacon, only results. He returned to Peter, jerked his head at him and led the way though a smell of dust, fine food, old cabinets and wine to where that corpulent and dignified pillar of the church, Deacon Handy, sat in his library. That he was served by such a weasel as Sam, the town attributed to a bachelor's liking for eccentric servants.

Deacon Handy rose. He did not extend his hand but inclined his head, implying reproof for this invasion. Peter bowed. "If I have disturbed you, sir, I apologize."

"Sit down, Mr. Garrett, sir."

Peter sat down and crossed his legs. The tassels on his Hessian boots swayed for a moment, the only motion in the room.

Deacon Handy pursed his small red mouth in a sugary smile and waited. His chair was pushed back from his desk for the greater comfort of his stomach which broke through his coat in a grand and prosperous curve of embroidered waistcoat hung with ball buttons, trinkets and watch chains. "Here I am," it seemed to say, "solid, worthy, just, and full of the finest living." The rest of his person said nothing at all. Eyebrows like gray eaves nearly hid his eyes and his jowls had a mute, wounded look where the high starched points of his shirt collar gouged them.

Peter waited respectfully for the Deacon to begin. The Deacon took his time. He watched the tassels on Peter's boots and, at his leisure, saw the well-cut perfection of his clothes. He noted well a certain vulnerability in his handsome face.

Too well-bred, thought the Deacon. He knew this type of finely drawn, ingrown young man, a type given to complicated fears and compulsions.

The Deacon cleared his throat. "To what circumstances do I owe the pleasure of this visit, Mr. Garrett? Is that the name?"

Peter handed the Deacon his business card. "Retired temporarily for reasons of health," he said.

Must have been in the way, thought the Deacon as he studied the card. "May I ask what position you have in this firm of realtors when you are there? Do they—er—retire you often temporarily?" The Deacon's stomach leaped with a trapped laugh.

Peter gave the Deacon a cold, arrogant look. Did this Cape codfish-ball consider himself Peter's superior? "My finances are in good order, if that is the purpose of your question."

40

"Well, I'm glad to hear that, young man. Now what brought you here to see me?"

"I understand that you own most of the property on the ocean side. As you can see by my card, I am interested in real estate. Would you consider selling some of it to me?" Despite his pride, Peter leaned forward eagerly.

"That is very isolated land," said the Deacon. "Lonely."

"Very good," said Peter. "I want a high bluff over the water and privacy, miles of it."

"Are you retiring so young? You look healthy enough."

"I plan to use it as a . . . a shooting preserve," Peter's lips curved upward, pleased at the special meaning his words held for him.

"Hmmmmmm." The Deacon considered.

"If there is already a house on the property, good. Otherwise I'll build one," Peter said.

"Who said there was any property for sale?" The Deacon asked.

"If it's a question of price . . ." Peter shrugged. "I am prepared to pay handsomely in cash and at once. That is, for the right place."

All the trinkets on the Deacon's waistcoat jingled at the word "cash." Otherwise his composure was granite.

Peter waited and the Deacon watched for signs of the fancy young pup's effrontery crumbling before his own superior poise.

Peter stirred restlessly. "Well, sir, it appears that you have no such land or it is not available for my purpose."

Deacon Handy had been waiting for this. "And what is your real purpose, sir? We both know that

41

there is not much game out there where the wind hurls the sand aloft."

"Naturally I intend to live there. I don't know how long. My health . . . it all depends . . ." He stopped abruptly.

A shaft of sunlight lit up one side of the Deacon's harassed jowls and rested on Peter's long hands. The Deacon watched them for signs of tension and was rewarded. Peter pulled his sword out an inch from its scabbard and rubbed his thumb around and around on the steel as he talked.

"No one lives on the dunes—or the backside, as we call it here," said the Deacon.

"I welcome loneliness," Peter said.

"Loneliness can be expensive on my land. Even a hermit's hut would . . ."

"Hermit's hut?" Peter's face lost its guarded expression. "Far from it. I'll build a fine fortress of a house or add to one already there. Besides a few miles of beach, I'll need space for a lookout and a good stable with fast horses and room for a number of menservants in the stable."

"A lookout?" The Deacon asked with an air of suspicion that astonished Peter.

"I see no reason to outline my plans further, unless you have something for me." Peter bowed his head stiffly and made a gesture to depart.

Deacon Handy picked up a bell on his desk and rang it vigorously. His servant came at once. Too soon, Peter thought; he must have been listening.

"Decant some Madeira, Sam," the Deacon said.

"Which quarterboard, sir?" Sam spoke absently, his eyes on the visitor. "The Queen of Peru?"

Deacon Handy half rose, a scowl weaving his eyebrows together. "You cretin, we have no such

42

wine here!"

Sam cringed, his hands clasped over his chest like a supplicating lizard. The Deacon seemed about to strike him but gathered his fury up into his purple jowls and turned to Peter, forcing a smile and an explanation, neither of which came easily to him.

"Custom here, my dear young man. Wine is stored in the cellar under the quarterboard that shipped it. That is, if one is lucky enough to find such a useful label washed up on the beach."

Peter leaned forward. "Is it true that Nauset Beach is known as the graveyard of the Atlantic?"

The Deacon's smile came naturally now. "If you made a chart of the waters around the outer sandbar and shoals off Nauset Beach and tried to mark down all the names of the ships that had struck and been pounded to bits by breakers, why you would not have room to list them on your chart."

To the Deacon's surprise, the young man was smiling also, as if at some very pleasing thought. The Deacon settled back in his chair to explore this.

"Suppose," Peter said, "that a brig, ignorant of these waters, came in close enough to launch a boat. What then?"

"The brig's quarterboard for some lucky collector and a matching set of skeletons for Davy Jones." But just as it seemed to the Deacon that possibly he and Peter had found a common interest, Peter changed. His smile and his color faded. A look of lofty integrity replaced the hard, eager smile.

"The matched set does not please you?" asked the Deacon softly. "One skeleton only, then?" he asked even more softly.

Peter took out his handkerchief and brushed it against his nostrils. He watched the curtains blowing in the hot summer wind.

"I don't know what you are talking about, Deacon Handy," he said.

Certain subjects bring on a catarrh in the young man, thought the Deacon, to whom all human signals were of value. "Well, well," his voice was genial. "I believe we are going to be friends. We may even find that we have a few little hobbies in common . . . Ah, here is Sam with the wine."

Peter and the Deacon had several glasses together. Deacon Handy steamed with curiosity but the young man gave no more evidence of eccentricity and his eyes maintained their protective Yankee squint. All to the good, thought the Deacon. Nothing like a New England clamshell for secrecy, and that air of integrity was invaluable.

"Sam," the Deacon called. "Bring around the broad-wheeled carriage. Mr. Garrett and I are going to the backside."

Peter looked at him quickly. "So you have . . ?"

"Not another word." The Deacon gave his little sugary V-shaped smile. "I have a surprise for you."

Sam, thin and pliant as beachgrass in the wind, helped the Deacon ease his bulk into the carriage, then hopped up to the driver's seat.

During the slow, winding jog over the sandy road, dwarf oak and scrub pine gradually became a dense forest that separated the town of Wellfleet and its harbor from the ocean. They passed several ponds and the Deacon made small talk about the pleasures of eating freshwater bass as a change. "Have to be a good swimmer to venture out in a boat on one of these ponds," he said. "They are bottom-

44

less." He appeared to find this fact of great importance. "Weight something and God only know when it stops going down or where it finally lands if it does!"

Young Mr. Garrett appeared to find this a chilling piece of information but one that gave him cause for speculation. He narrowed his eyes.

When the carriage left the woods and climbed up to the summit of a bluff, Peter gave a gasp that cost him thousands of dollars. He jumped out with a quick, strong leap and ran to the edge where he stood in silence looking out over the ocean.

"Pleasingly isolated, isn't it, Mr. Garrett?" called the Deacon from the carriage. Hooked, he thought, and already flapping in the hold.

Peter was already on his way up to the cottage high on the cliff to the right of the road. Its shingles were a satiny gray and the long slanting roof faced the ocean as if the house turned its back to the wind and hunched its shoulders. Little windows looked out with random charm from the eaves. On either side of the front door stood scrub pines sculptured by the wind. The door itself was sturdy and handsome. The hinges were dull but the knob shone as if with frequent use. Peter did not notice; he was busy looking up at the roof and gauging the outlook of the house.

Deacon Handy took his own good time easing his stomach out of the carriage. "Bring in the basket of wine," he said to Sam.

Peter, regardless of his nankeen breeches, whipped through the scrubby bayberry until with dramatic suddenness, he stood on the edge of a cliff that rose steeply, holding its sand to a height of one hundred feet above the white and desolate beach with its long scroll of breakers.

"Like it?" Deacon Handy came puffing up to the edge of the cliff.

"It's wonderful!" The young man was almost off guard.

"A mile and a quarter of this beach goes with the house," said the Deacon, "and twenty-five miles of lonely beach stretches out on either side."

"Is there a way up through the bluff?" Peter asked.

"See that crevasse to your right? Slide down it, if you don't mind sand in those fine boots. There's a staunch rope ladder for you to climb back up, or for your guests . . . if you expect any?"

Deacon Handy glanced sideways at the young man and noted a change of expression, almost a flick of fear. "Anything could happen here and no one the wiser," said the Deacon.

Peter blew his nose briefly.

"Weed affect you?" the Deacon asked.

"No." Peter walked away along the bluff muttering a few words that the Deacon strained to hear. Was this indecision or a swarm of qualms? Certainly he was planning something outside the law. Could he be slightly touched in the head? He seemed a man obsessed. Well, well, no matter. The Deacon went over to Peter.

"Now," he said briskly, "let's have a look at your house, shall we?"

He said "your" so lightly that the young man did not protest. Hooked all right, thought the Deacon, right through the gills. On the way in, he pointed out the yard, landscaped by nature with poverty grass, mouse-ear and bearberry. "Never have to do any work here," he said. "But then you are minded

46

to hire some help?" But Peter was looking up at the roof again.

Inside the Deacon handed him a glass of wine, which Peter drank down like water, as he went over the sound and beautiful house. "I'll have a square tower with a walk built atop the roof," Peter said. "With a gun room and a casement window looking out over the water."

The Deacon pursed his lips and became very thoughtful. A long pause ensued. Finally he said, "Build that tower higher than one story and you'll find it blown off in the first storm."

"Then I'll settle for one story," Peter said.

"From there you'll be able to see through that one dip in the cliff. You'll miss the shoals and the sandbar and it's only a slice of ocean you'll be looking at. Will that satisfy your purpose, one little slice of beach and ocean?"

"I'll settle for that. I'll need a spyglass on a revolving stand and a good land crew down on the beach to . . ." his voice trailed away.

The Deacon brightened considerably. "To what? You have a habit of not finishing your sentences, young sir. It leaves one up in the air."

"If any marauder should get by my land crew and climb the rope ladder which I'll have extended to my tower room . . ."

"You'd have an excellent shot as his head came above the sill," finished the Deacon with a laugh. "I'll make sure to call on you through the front door."

Peter's smile disfigured his face, "Yes," he said. "Just as his head comes over the sill."

He slowly tightened his hand around his empty glass until the crystal crushed. He looked down,

47

amazed, and took out his handkerchief to blot the blood on his hand. "I regret the glass," he said in a calmer voice, "and will replace it."

"Mr. Garrett, there must be something you want to do very much. Am I right?" Deacon Handy waited a moment, but this strange young man felt under no compulsion to answer questions. "Well, that's neither here nor there," He gave his cold, jolly smile. "Your tower can be built in a week or two. You know, by a remarkable coincidence, this improvement will suit me very well."

"Why you, since it will be my house?" Peter asked.

Deacon Handy passed him a fresh glass of wine.

"Now for such necessary details as price." Peter's elaborately off-hand tone betrayed his inexperience.

"Why not go back to my library," suggested the Deacon, "and discuss it all there as well as several minor conditions to the sale?"

"Let's go then." Peter walked quickly out the front door. As he went by the nodding pines, the claw-hammer tails of his coat blew forward about his waist and his beaver hat sailed far away over the bearberry. "Quite a wind," he said. "Not that it matters, but does it always blow like this?"

Deacon Handy's eyes met those of his servant who had retrieved Peter's hat. "Like this?" His laugh was a slow grating sound like the limbs of a tree rubbing together, "You call *this* a wind? This little zephyr without one grain of salt in it?"

"Wait until you see a real wreckers' wind," Sam put in.

The Deacon whirled on his servant. "Be quiet, Stupid. Put the basket of wine in back with us and attend to your driving."

Sam's beady eyes burned with his hatred of this name his employer gave him, both in private and public.

On the way back to town, the Deacon clasped his hands over his stomach and smiled. Peter had several more glasses of wine. They chatted pleasantly about various vintages and Peter said, obviously quoting, "Liquor is a charming, intimate friend with designs on your fortune and your life."

The Deacon laughed immoderately at this mild effort of his client. Peter settled back with a flushed face and the Deacon rejoiced to see the young man glowing with wine. He hoped for indiscretions and a general relaxing of his guard.

"May I point out the convenience of those barrack-like buildings in back of your house, near the marshes," he said. "Stables beneath, rooms above, where I sometimes let my sailors live between ships. They are rough but loyal fellows and will be grateful if you give them shelter. You mentioned menservants, I believe?"

"Oh yes," Peter said. "I'll need some strong efficient fellows."

"A sound idea out on those lonely dunes. Why don't you hire some of my men? As a ship owner, I always have a few idling on half pay."

"Thank you," said Peter. "But I have in mind a rough and ready land crew, perhaps not too averse to a little skirmish in case . . . in case of trouble. In an isolated spot, one never knows."

"Ah," said the Deacon. "One never knows. Now the men I have in mind for you are by no means pillars of society. Good sailors and ship builders, you understand, but a little on the rough side. There's Zeke who can cook like a fool—even his face

49

is dish-shaped. Comstock for the horses—his face won't frighten *them*. Wylie is handsome—put him in livery, but don't ask him about his part! Keep George at a distance—his face is so pitted it puts you in mind of a diseased clamshell. Good man in a fight, though. Hilary's fat, but you won't need your telescope with Hilary around the place. If a gull drops a shell on a distant rock, Hilary can tell you whether it's mussel or clam. A mighty useful quality."

Peter could hardly keep the excitement out of his voice. "Is Zeke bucktoothed with huge shoulders and hands like a strangler's? Are George's pocks as big as pennies?"

"You've seen 'em somewhere," said the Deacon.

"Yes, there was a young sailor with them. He had a very loud voice," Peter said.

"Gone," said the Deacon. "Too noisy, too naive."

"Gone where?"

The Deacon changed the subject. "What do you say, sir? Will you sweeten the bargain I am going to make you by hiring these worthy men of mine who are between jobs?"

"Why yes," said Peter. "Yes, that might work out very well for me. I think I can help you out."

"Thank you," said the Deacon. "You won't live to regret it, I promise you." This remark amused him beyond all reason that Peter could see. He repeated it, wheezing with jolly laughter. Peter thought this pillar of the church must be drunk.

"Where can I meet these men?" he asked.

"No need," said the Deacon, "I'll take care of everything. They'll have that new tower room, walk and all, finished for you in a few weeks. They work fast. I presume, of course, you want them to do the work—can't find better builders than ship builders."

"Good enough," said Peter. "But I want to see them right away to explain their other duties."

"I can't put my hands on them at the moment," said the Deacon.

"I insist on interviewing them, or I shall look elsewhere," Peter said.

The Deacon considered. "Well, I suppose it could be managed. Try Wreckers' Tavern." He lifted his upper lip. "*I* never go near the noxious den, but I can send a message to Mrs. Cassidy, the proprietress—whom I know only by name, of course. If the men aren't there, she can find them for you, possibly."

"Wreckers' Tavern," Peter repeated. "Where is it, sir?"

"On Commercial Street. The short-sighted town fathers want to close it up but I have dissuaded them. Why send its foul customers into the taverns we frequent ourselves?"

"I will stop in there this afternoon," said Peter.

"Do that. Describe them and Mrs. Cassidy, who knows everybody, can find your bodyguards for you."

Peter put his glass down on the carriage floor. "Bodyguards? Who says I need bodyguards?"

Deacon Handy enjoyed watching this transparent young man alternate between dark, vicious excitement and watchful poise. "Mr. Garrett, sir," he lifted his glass, "to your health." He gave a wheezing laugh. "And to your plans."

"Thank you, sir." Peter held up his glass to be filled. Then, each busy with his own thoughts, they lapsed into absent-minded small talk, then into silence as they jogged through the pine forest and finally onto the main street of the town.

Deacon Handy cleared his throat. "Going to live out there alone except for your bodyguar . . . excuse me, land crew?"

"I . . . I don't know yet."

"Have to be as quick-footed as a sandpiper to stay single in this town," said the old bachelor with a cold chuckle. "So many men lost at sea."

Peter finished his wine. He leaned toward the Deacon with the first gleam of boyishness the older man had seen on his face. "Do you happen to know the Mayo family?" he asked.

"Lots of Mayos on the Cape," said the Deacon.

"A fisherman and his daughter, Sarah. Sarah Mayo," Peter said her name with a caress in his voice.

The Deacon's eyebrows drew together, his jowls darkened. "As I said, lots of Mayos on the Cape. Here we are. Let's go in." And he hurried to get his stomach out of the carriage.

Peter, still talking, followed him into the library. "Mr. Zenas Mayo seems to be powerful here in some way that I don't understand."

"Time we got down to business," said the Deacon harshly. He spread out a map showing the cottage and its surrounding property. "Now here's your estate." He looked up. The young man had a faraway look in his eyes. Was it the heat, the wine and the motion of the carriage or . . .? "How well do you know Sarah Mayo?" he asked abruptly.

"Quite well," said Peter. "Why?"

The Deacon tingled all over with nerves and envy. That will cost him more, he thought, as he put some rapid figures down on a slip of paper. "There you are," he passed the paper across the desk to Peter. "I'll absorb the material for the new tower room. My ship-building works can supply them. After all, what are a few dollars between friends?"

Peter stared at the paper. "A few dollars!" He blinked to bring it into better focus. "Is this, actually. . .?" His mouth dropped open slightly.

"The price," said the Deacon.

Peter let down his guard for a moment. "But this takes almost all—I mean, a giant bite out of my fortune."

"It is the price," said the Deacon, very cold. "The size of your fortune is not my concern."

"I'll have the additional expense of a crew of servants plus the *Challenger* in harbor." Peter took the Deacon's quill pen out of its shot glass. "May I?" He began to figure on a slip of paper.

I'll make him pay in every sense of the word, thought the Deacon. The young fop, daring to dream of such a beauty as Sarah Mayo! The Deacon had personally seen to it that every one of Sarah's admirers went away, one after another on his whalers. He felt tension now and the pressure of gas within his vast stomach.

"While you are figuring, Mr. Garrett, bear in mind the rising value of your property on a resale."

Peter looked up quickly. "It may be a short term investment. I am not prepared to say now, but," he shrugged. "what's a fortune? I'll make another."

"Hah, hah," said the Deacon. "Of course you will. What could be easier, eh?" He wondered again if the young man was all right in the head.

"Here you are, sir." Peter wrote out a draft on his Boston bank.

The Deacon took it out of his hand so swiftly that

it seemed to jump as to a magnet. As he looked it over, he felt a compulsion to talk about Sarah Mayo. He might as well. The damage had already been done, as far as his nerves were concerned. They were twitching, and gas rumbled all over his vast stomach.

"Now about this interest of yours in the Mayo family," he said. "Sarah is a vivid, charming young girl but for a young Bostonian of your background, well . . . it seems like an odd . . ." He gave a disparaging wave of the hand.

"I don't believe we were discussing my interest in Miss Mayo." Peter's face was expressionless.

The Deacon pursed his lips and shook his jowls in the manner of a worldly-wise elder giving confidential advice. At the same time, dark blood empurpled his neck and he writhed in his chair to ease his stomach.

Peter looked askance at him. "I must take my leave now, sir. I have a number of things to do this afternoon."

"Ever met her old father?" asked the Deacon. "I remember well the day she brought him to my church. The odor of fish and rum that came from him nearly overpowered the congregation. He sat there contradicting the prayer book in a loud voice and arguing with the sermon. At one point he yelled out, 'You are boring the Almighty. He'll move on to another Universe and then where will we be?'

"Of course we rushed him down the aisle and out the door but he resisted us and turned around to shout, 'There's a stink in here, a stink of moldy prayers kept folded till Sunday. Shake 'em out in the air, ha, ha, God damn!' And other oaths. We pushed him out the door in short order but he poked his head back in and cried out in a great voice, 'Phew!'

"I see you wince at my story, young man, as well you may." The Deacon shook his head with an air of piety.

"I wince for Sarah's sake," Peter said. "Otherwise, Zenas Mayo is just another of our famous New England eccentrics. Boston is full of them."

Deacon Handy stifled a hiccup. "Her mother was a batty Boston bluestocking who educated her daughter very well, I'll say that for her. Bemus, her name was. Old man Bemus was a scalawag. A lot of people would like to find *him*. How's that for a family?"

"Very interesting," Peter said.

The Deacon clasped his stomach and stirred restlessly. Some day Sarah would regret so rudely turning down his generous offer of marriage. She had dealt his vanity a punishing blow as he had pointed out the many advantages that she, a mere fisherman's daughter, would gain by marrying the richest, most powerful and respected man on the Cape.

Sarah had replied, "All very true, Deacon, but a curse goes with it . . . *you!*"

Deacon Handy would never forget. A vengeful worm turned in his entrails when her name was spoken and his tongue became agile with spite.

"Miss Sarah Mayo," he went on, "follows the family tradition of eccentricity. She swims and sails for pleasure instead of quilting with the other young girls. In the old days, she'd have been called a witch and chased out of town, forced to wander homeless."

The Deacon had often imagined her in terrible distress, coming to him to plead for help, perhaps

55

in a storm, her clothes wet and clinging to her body, her hair falling down her back, shining like wet brown seaweed. He indulged in this pleasing reverie now but was aroused by the young man's sudden open-throated laugh.

"I'm picturing Sarah as a sea witch," he said. "Brewing gull feathers and sea foam in a bucket."

Deacon Handy looked directly into his eyes and saw his love, the first simple, clear emotion he had seen there.

"You certainly don't mind going below your station, sir." The Deacon almost spat the words.

Peter resented this for Sarah. He stood up and with his next words turned the Deacon from a cold, patient danger, ready to bide his time, into a vicious enemy.

"Deacon, I only draw the line at lingering with vulgar company, so let us press on with the business, sir."

The Deacon held Peter's eyes with his own, which were fixed and hard as a bird's. He tried to oppress the young man by his age, weight and power. "Don't sail too close to the wind, *young* sir, that is for professionals."

"I don't understand you," Peter said.

The Deacon picked up his quill pen and stabbed it into the shot glass. The long curtains puffed out and there was a smell of dust. "That's a pity," he said. "To ignore good advice can be dangerous." He put the bank draft in his desk drawer and slammed it shut with a sound like a shot. He stood up. "Our business is completed. Good day, sir. You can be sure that from now on, I will be looking after your interests. Oh, yes."

Peter, feeling a slight chill between the shoulder

blades, turned abruptly and went out of the big square white house.

The old bachelor swallowed a pill with a glass of wine and belched wrathfully. By now he should know better than to let himself in for it by speaking of Sarah. He felt inordinately hot even for this weather. He loosened his high starched collar and massaged his dented jowls, but nothing eased him.

Sam came in and leaned over the desk. "Sir!" His black eyes were bright with shock. "You can't *do* it."

"Is there anything you don't hear? Money is money," said the Deacon.

They both acknowledged this truth with a moment of silence.

"Now listen carefully, Stupid," said the Deacon. "Go find Zenas Mayo, discuss the day's fishing with him then ask in a gossipy way why his daughter's young man, Peter Garrett, goes into Wreckers' Tavern and hobnobs with the cut-throats there."

"Will he really go there?"

"He will, Sam, he will, and Zenas is not going to like that, not at all. Zenas is a man of action. Now look sharp and follow orders exactly."

It was a source of wonder to the Deacon that Sam, as beady of eye and alert as a weasel, was so easily cowed.

"I'm going." Sam shook his head, "But I still don't see how you can put ordinary people in the house on the dunes."

"I doubt very much if young Garrett's plans are ordinary."

The Deacon picked up his paper knife and pressed the point against the palm of his hand, a small pleasing pain that took his mind off the pressure of gas in his stomach, caused, damn him,

57

by that young fool.

"Sam," he said, "bear in mind that, at our convenience, the house on the dunes can be made vacant again."

# Chapter four

Consider a pitiless woman
whose heart beats
like the grey flutter
of a snake's rattle.
She has the lidless stare
of a crocodile.
Her shadow hovers
like the spell cast over
the place of a bloody crime
and her mouth is a beak
made for holding a human eye.

The Deacon's servant, Sam, was wary. Standing at a cautious distance from Zenas Mayo, he said, "Heard as how you and your boys got a whale off Provincetown last week. Getting scarce, ain't they?"

Zenas paid no attention to him. He was looking down at the fish nets drying on the docks. "God-damn webs!" He kicked them aside. "No sport or dignity in them."

"Ha, ha, that's right," called Sam. "But off-shore whaling is nearly dead. What will you do then, eh, Mr. Mayo?"

Zenas looked at him in surprise. What was this land eel after?

"Catch any striper today?" Sam went on.

"Some." Zenas turned away contemptuously. He noted that Sarah's little boat was dry. She must be up at the house trying on her new things. "Take this," he had said. "Go and spoil your figure with ornaments and ruffles."

When she had snatched the money like a tavern girl, Zenas had felt a pang. She had never been hungry for fripperies before. He sat down on the deck now and patted his empty pockets.

"Oh, there'll be mourning tonight. Zenas won't be laughing it up in the taverns." He gave a howling sigh as he pulled on his boots.

"What did you say?" Sam came closer.

Zenas turned and looked directly at his tormentor. "Get away from me, you weasel, because I don't like you." His deadly level voice sent Sam into a retreat to the nearest tavern for rum and courage.

Zenas looked out over the harbor. Before long, Sarah would leave home and he would be alone again. He'd have sailed the full course charted for him twenty-two years ago by old Bemus. There should have been a warning roll of thunder the day old Bemus and his fancy boat put in to Wellfleet harbor, and more warning thunder the day he hired Zenas to show him and his cursed cargo of blue-stocking daughters where the fish were running.

Hope and Serenity with their high born manners and even higher pitched voices— "Oh, Mr. Mayo, come show me how to hold the line." "Oh, Mr. Mayo, help! I've got a fish!"

Zenas knew full well what ailed the girls but he was not hired, thank Christ, to cure them. He had minded his own business until the day he overheard Serenity talking to her father in her irritating high voice. "Have you really *looked* at our young Cape Cod guide? I'm just *itching* to paint him."

Zenas had given an ironic chuckle at her choice of words. "Paint?" he had whispered.

"He has an innocent, natural beauty," Serenity went on. "How I wish I'd brought my sketching pad. That face against the sky and water. I can see it now."

Zenas, hidden by a mast, went on coiling rope

although his hands shook. He'd show her how innocent he was. Too bad she was so skinny. A man had to have something to hold on to, he could fall off the earth. He glanced around the mast at her, loathing the noble, forthright Boston way she held her chin up in the air.

Shortly after that, old Bemus himself, of all people, arranged things so that his daughter, Serenity, and the young guide put out together in the small boat to get fresh water from a spring. Zenas watched her gloomily as he rowed. Up in the pine grove, she'd soon find out who was naive, whatever the hell that meant. He searched for something attractive about her person to smooth the way. Her mouth did or did not look like a blow-fish. You could argue it both ways. Her eyes were large and, he supposed, pretty, but their deep, thoughtful expression as she looked full at him made him uneasy. She smelled of starched, clean clothes and some kind of foreign flower that never grew near salt water—unwholesome, as was anything far from salt water.

However, when they reached the spring, deep in a pine grove, a miracle took place. She leaned toward him, her deep eyes glowing with surprising fire. For a little while, she was not a stranger but a natural and lovely thing, a young girl who wanted him.

When they rowed back to old Bemus, Serenity, to his shock and surprise, as there had been no mention of it in the pine grove, calmly announced her engagement to him.

Her sister, Hope, whom Zenas had from the first found more to his taste, now held Zenas's eyes for a second with a look that he would always remember. She had turned white with shock but not as white as

Zenas, hooked and thrown in the hold, by God!

Mr. Bemus then rubbed his hands together until his palms were red hot. He made brisk hearty plans; a preacher on board, wine, delicacies.

Zenas decided to slip into the water and swim for shore, but as he moved toward the rail, he looked into the large glowing eyes of his bride to be.

"Remember the pine grove," she whispered, one hand on his arm, and he knew that he would stay. How could he smash a fist into those luminous eyes? But he thought of all the living creatures he had ever drawn in, struggling from the water, and identified himself with them until his heart was heavy with all their lively despairs joined to his own. From that day on, he never used a net.

Serenity had been right in only one respect. Zenas was in fact an innocent but only in money matters. He gave no thought to the fact that Serenity's father was obviously a rich man, but presumed that he and his bride would live as most people did in his world, on the bounty of the sea. Offshore whaling was not what it used to be but he had better try it rather than leave this fine lady to fend for herself while he shipped on a three-year whaling voyage.

While they waited for the preacher, Zenas imagined his bride sitting on the front porch of his little gray cottage, mending fishlines. He stripped her down to a linen shift, bronzed her and bared her narrow feet, then broadened them a little as a bonus. This strained his mind's eye. He shook his head and put shoes back on her.

Serenity, meanwhile, was picturing Zenas in a frock coat and frilled jabot with tight breeches ending in bunches of ribbons. She amputated his short, curly beard, combed his sideburns forward and took him to a long season of literary teas in Boston. "Here comes Serenity with her romantic-looking Cape Cod sailor," they would say. "She always *was* an original!"

After the simple ceremony on shipboard, which Hope, really sticken, did not attend, old Bemus suddenly announced that his daughter's marriage displeased him, so that he had decided to cut her off without a penny.

This news surprised Serenity. Her father had seemed to be encouraging the marriage. However, she was hardly dismayed. There had always been money and the down-to-earth daily life in a sailor's cottage didn't come clear to her. . . yet.

"Who wants money?" Zenas said. "I'll take care of my wife, you take care of your boat. Next time try being displeased earlier, let's say around the time you send your daughter off in a small boat with a man."

This advice did not appear to sink in. Shortly afterward his other daughter, Hope, still thinking of Zenas, joylessly accepted a young man of good family whom she had disdained from childhood. Mr. Bemus, all for it, only waited a few minutes after the nuptials before expressing displeasure with her choice and cut her off without a penny. His disinheritance of both his daughters, however, turned out to be an academic gesture. Old Bemus, his daughters off his hands, disappeared at once leaving behind him a maze of mismanaged funds with a pack of creditors baying through it.

His daughters now found it easy to understand the old man's haste to marry them off to anything that breathed, but both girls felt sure that so resourceful a man was prospering somewhere although they never heard from him as long as they lived nor did they care to.

Zenas shrugged off his memories. He got up and stamped his boots on. Then, feeling an uneasy, crowded sensation, he looked behind him. Sam was standing so close that Zenas could smell the rum on his quick, shallow breath. He was struggling to speak despite his fear of Zenas.

"Look there!" he pointed down the street. "Isn't that your daughter's fine-feathered friend, young Garrett, off the racing sloop, *Challenger?* Walked right by you without saying good day. That's funny—he says good day to some mighty rough men in Wreckers' Tavern. He's going there now, I see."

Zenas made a grab for him but Sam, with a squeak of fear, eeled around a tar barrel and away.

Zenas looked over at the taverns. By Christ, the young man *was* stopping under the swinging sign of a gull on a skull. Didn't the crazy young bastard know he could get his fancy clothes torn off his back? The place swarmed with Mooncussers, God-damn Mooncussers. He'd like to weight them all and sink them in one of those bottomless ponds in the woods. But only a Mooncusser would have the stomach for such a job.

The young man hesitated at the door, glanced up at the swinging sign, then went in with the air of a mariner charting a course through dangerous waters.

"I'll be damned," Zenas said to the gulls. Uneasy as a riptide, he left the dock and followed the fool into the dark, low-beamed room. He took a seat just near enough to get a good long, hard stare at him. He was fascinated by every shade of expression and

65

detail of his features. What in hell did Sarah see in him?

Now he was loosening his neckcloth with a forefinger as he glanced about. Little too rough for our Boston dandy, thought Zenas. He'll be out of here in no time. Air's too thick for that aristocratic nose of his.

Zenas watched him signal to Thankful Cassidy, the proprietress, who was standing by the casks. Thankful shook out a dirty rag and wiped the planked table in front of her with a slow, greasy figure-eight motion while she looked the stranger over.

Thankful's face, larger than that of a big man, was the cadaver white of those whose only climate is night. Her coarse hair hung in a braid as big around as a black snake and her eyebrows met across her fleshy nose. Hairs grew on her chin like patches of beach grass on a dune and her eyes never blinked.

Thankful could stand astraddle the surf like a man while she used a grapple to her own profit. If a sailor survived the wreck of his ship and rode in on the waves, when he saw Thankful standing over him, he surely believed himself among the demons of Hell.

Zenas loathed her, not only because she was hideous but because a pitiless woman is a fearsome thing. He believed that Thankful was born without a conscience as some are born without hearing or sight.

Now she was going over to young Garrett. He watched him shrink back a little at the sight of her—but no, they were exchanging smiles, a quick flitting one from the young man that was like a wince. Thankful bared large gray teeth that reminded Zenas of old tombstones.

"Well, sir, what can I do for you?" Thankful's deep voice was tuned to carry across the booming surf. But the young man began an inaudible conversation. Zenas tried to move in closer to this mystery but Abraham Cassidy, Thankful's bandylegged husband, jostled him back.

"Excuse me, kinda crowded here. Better not change your seat," said Abraham who had the cold jollity of an innkeeper and the shoulders of a gorilla.

Zenas, rather than be thrown out, stayed in his place, surrounded by sailors from all over the world who came to Wreckers' Tavern for its good liquor, the Portuguese girls upstairs, and above all the cozy criminal undertow that ran through the tavern encouraging plans and the forming of partnerships.

The Cassidys, man and wife, had such a compelling air of criminality about them that the most nervous malefactor was soothed by it. Furthermore, no one in Wreckers' Tavern ran the danger of being drugged and thrown aboard a whaler to complete her crew. The Cassidys protected their own. And, thought Zenas, someone powerful in Wellfleet protected the Cassidys. He'd find out sooner or later and have him by the throat.

Both Cassidys bent over young Garrett who straightened up with a look of cool poise that Zenas recognized as applied courage. Thankful studied him somberly. She looked at Abraham and shook her head. From then on, it seemed to Zenas, she was trying to hold Abraham back. She tapped his shoulder with a forefinger the color and almost the size of a peeled banana, but Abraham shrugged her away and went on talking to Peter.

Zenas watched Garrett's intent profile. Handsome? Maybe so, but too sensitive for Zenas's taste. Not plumb somewhere!

While her husband was occupied with Garrett, Thankful Cassidy looked across the room and was thrilled to encounter the contemptuous gray eyes of Zenas Mayo. She had always admired his strong face and the whole of his lanky independent person. Herself as merciless as a tiger, she liked strength in others. The customers of her tavern, being for the most part criminal, depended upon and feared each other. But Zenas Mayo was a free man and without fear. He curried no favor and went his way as self-contained as a sea clam.

Half a lifetime in the tavern had made Thankful an expert in the secret coils of a man's nature. Her instinct was developed to a high degree. Behind this young Garrett's upright air, she sensed a bundle of fear tied together by his will.

She turned away and looked at Zenas Mayo again to refresh herself. Now there was a *man*. Even his angry honesty was all male and forgivable. She burned for him with the ardor of a collector as well as that of a woman. It was a sorrow to her that Zenas so seldom visited her tavern. With her eyes fixed on him, she hunched up her shoulders and dropped her eyelids in an effort to diminish her size as she wiggled her fingers at him in a playful wave.

Zenas got up and left the tavern. On the street, he took a deep grateful breath.

"Christ damn," he said, "but the air is good outside!"

# Chapter
# five

Be provident here
inside the shark's mouth.
Plan for the future,
taking the long view
between rows
of jagged teeth.

Thankful Cassidy went about her business at the bar. Now and then as she swept away the foam from a mug of ale, she looked sourly at her husband who stood talking to the young stranger. Thankful recognized the gestures that decorated his favorite tale. Her scalp prickled with boredom. To Thankful, the fancier of the caliber of a man, Abraham, with all his brute strength and scowling, heavy face, was a very small boat with a top-heavy cargo of nothing.

She clumped up to him in her man-sized boots. "Garrulous fellow," she boomed, "you'll drive the young gentleman away with that old chestnut about your ear."

Peter's intensity belied his easy tone. "It's a *new* chestnut to me, madam. We were speaking of freebooters. Do they ever put into port around here?"

"Freebooters, pirates, privateers, it's all the same. With Letters of Marque or without, they all ply the same trade, don't they? Just some are fancier than others. Anyway we serve 'em all. We're not the militia," said Mrs. Cassidy.

"How do you recognize one from the other?"

70

Peter looked around the tavern.

"A privateer has more swagger. He's not running before the law. They catch him, he's got papers from some country or other, but who knows what he's really up to out there on the deep water?"

"Very interesting," said Peter. "Can you tell these legitimate pirates from the others who come in here?"

Thankful pursed her lips. "Why, it's a feel you get about them. A pirate has the look of a sea thing, not quite human, adrift as he is with no moorings and the water for a home. You can't mistake him. He smells of seaweed and his face has a cleaner kind of wickedness than most, sir."

"What do you mean?" Peter took full advantage of this woman's expertise.

"To my way of thinking, sir, a pirate is more appetizing than a land criminal. Look at it this way; in the deep, under a pirate brig are miles of monsters, sharks and such, tearing and killing. The pirate is only the top layer of it all, a natural part of the sea."

"You seem to be an authority. I presume the same can't go for killers on land. They lack the endorsement of all those creatures in the water below."

"Well," said Thankful modestly. "I've always been a bit of a philosopher. I'd say any killer is a natural part of nature. Take a look. Animals, birds, insects, all tearing each up to feed. Your land killer generally is feeding on money or revenge. Well, as I said, it takes all kinds to fill our tavern."

"Stow it, or I'll pin your big ears back!" Her husband spoke directly into one of them.

"Better than having one sliced off," said Thankful. "If I was you, I wouldn't be so quick to mention ears!"

Peter glanced up at the side of Abraham's head which was as smooth as a pancake except for a hole where the ear had been. "You were telling me that a privateer did that," he said. "Do you happen to know his name?"

"Cold Steel Collier they call him, although the day for that kind o' thing is over and done with. He'll run you through for calling him that. Calvin Collier his name is, and one of these dark stormy nights I'll be waiting for him on shore and I'll slice off both his hairy ears and run 'em up on his own masthead if there's anything left of his brig—the *Windshadow*, he calls her."

His wife gave him a smart kick on his ankle. "What are you talking about dark stormy nights for? You mean some nice sunny morning, don't you?" Another kick.

"Tell me more about Captain Collier." Peter felt an inner tremor blended of excitement and fear.

"Know him?" Abraham asked.

"I've seen him," said Peter. "Go on with your story."

"Sliced it off clean, he did, with a little flick of his sword. 'I'll fry it for my breakfast,' he says, holding my ear on the end of his sword. 'Save the other one for me, when I have an appetite for it. I'll be back.' I can hear him laughing now."

"So can I," said Peter.

"Let him come," Abraham went on. "I'm ready. I'll carve Abraham on one rump, Cassidy on the other. Then I'll take out his eyes and pickle 'em in a bottle right up over my bar where I can wink at them."

Peter was interested in only one part of Abraham's story. "So . . . he got away?" He gave a bitter grimace.

A man at the end of the tavern laughed aloud as in reply. The smell of stale beer, stale clothes and stale evil made Peter dizzy. He put his head in his hands for a moment.

"It was this way." Abraham Cassidy launched into his favorite recital. "I was boarding his brig . . ."

"Boarding her?" Peter asked.

"Hand over hand as fast as we could."

"Why? What was the occasion?"

Abraham pursed his lips.

"You fool!" Thankful hissed into the hole that had been his ear. "He's just here as a tourist." She turned to Peter, saying with an ingratiating smile, "Boarding her, sir, for the noble purpose of saving lives. The brig foundered off Nauset Beach. Stuck on the outer bar, she was."

"Yes," said Abraham, "that's the right of it. I was on an errand of mercy." He brayed with laughter, slapping his meaty thigh.

"Stop laughing like a jackass," said his wife.

"Well, to go on with my story." It took Abraham a few moments to follow her advice. He wheezed away a few last gasps. "Well, as I said, to go on with my story, the brig was stuck fast on the bar. The surf pounded her and in a few minutes her rich cargo would . . ."

"You mean her *crew*," Mrs. Cassidy corrected him. "And you see, sir, they gave battle, not knowing the humane purpose of my husband's visit."

"That's how it was, sir." said Abraham. "Six of us in the whaleboat and they drove us off with their swords and pistols. Killed one of us, too."

"A hero he died," Thankful sighed.

"But some dark night, we'll lead him onto our reef

73

and . . ."

Thankful raised her huge foot and aimed another kick at her man. He evaded her, causing her to nearly lose her balance. "Oh, excuse me, sir—I stumbled. Abraham means to say if the Good Lord causes a wreck . . . Oh what a fool, he can't say anything right!"

"So if the Good Lord . . ." Abraham rolled his bloodshot eyes upward . . . "should wreck his brig, I have five men that would swim out through any kind of surf after Captain Collier."

"Ah *hah!*" said Peter. "Very interesting. But if Collier ran up on a bar in heavy surf, he should have broken up. Are you sure he didn't, after you left, perhaps?" A flicker of hope crossed his face.

Abraham spoke grudgingly. "No, it was seamanship. He comes by his fame there honest enough. The brig stuck and the sails come down on the run. We waited near as we could, risking our lives in the surf, sure she'd break up any minute."

Thankful appeared to stumble against him again. "*Afraid* she'd break up, sir," she put in.

"Then I heard Captain Collier yell, 'Get that jib on her, men!' " Abraham paused, as if seeing it now. "They thought he was crazy. So did I, but they got the jib up and the wind filled her. The bow swung off with the pressure but the brig rose on a breaker and came down with a blow that shocked her. The men were hanging on to whatever they could, but Calvin Collier was riding easy out by the foremast. 'Give her the other jib,' he yelled. They stood still and looked at him. He pulled out his short sword and they gave her the other jib. The wind hit it and swung her bow around almost clear but a breaker lifted her and she struck hard. Her masts swayed like pendulums, then all of a sudden, she slid off into the deep water."

Peter raised his hands and let them drop to the table.

"We could hear the damned crew cheering for Collier as we started our long pull back to the beach. He stood on the bowsprit waving goodbye with his sword and laughing."

"Yes," said Peter. "And you could hear his cursed laugh over the breakers."

"Hold!" Abraham looked at him curiously. "How do you know that?"

They both stared at him. Peter shook his head as if to free it of the image of the captain. Then straightening up, he became all business. "Those five men who were with you in the boat, the ones who would be willing to even swim out to take Captain Collier. By any chance, are some of those sailors in the employ of Deacon Handy?"

Thankful put a restraining hand on her husband as she stared at the young man, inhaling his qualifications as a whale inhales small fish. She had received a message to be on the lookout and cooperate with a young off-Cape furriner, but this one was out of his depth, a baby swimming with sharks. She drew back. Whatever his purpose was, she did not like the smell of it.

"I had sort of expected that the Deacon would get word to the men that I . . ." Peter began. He looked from one to the other. "Perhaps cleared the way . . ."

Mrs. Cassidy could sense his queasy aversion to them both. She exchanged a long look with her husband.

"And why should that holy and respectable man be sending messages to this tavern?" Mrs. Cassidy asked.

"Only because he said you might know of the men for me to hire. I'm looking for a land crew to protect some property of mine." Peter described the men as well as he could remember the ones he had seen by lantern light last night.

"I don't even know Deacon Handy except by sight," Thankful said.

"Where was I?" said Abraham. "Did I give you the part where Collier leaned over the rail and sliced off my ear like he was serving a portion of white meat?"

*"Yes!"* his wife yelled. "Over and over!" She folded her huge hands on her stomach and waited.

Peter looked from one hard face to the other. He showed his disappointment by his shrug and spreading out his empty hands. "Well, that's that. Perhaps you can sell me some good wine for my boat which is in harbor here. I want to lay in a good supply in case of a celebration." A young, hopeful expression came over his face as he took out his money case.

"Why not?" said Mrs. Cassidy. "Good wine is a celebration in itself."

Peter put all the money he had with him on the table, a large amount. Abraham lunged at it but Thankful held him back. So much cash had to be a bribe. Her black eyes were hard as a horsehair sofa. "What kind of wine and how much of it? That's a powerful lot of money there on the table."

"What do you recommend?" Peter felt that he was getting somewhere now. Should have thought of this before? "Deacon Handy served me some excellent wine from . . ." What was the name of that quarterboard? "The *Queen of Peru.*"

He looked up in surprise at the reaction to his

casual remark, inspired only by a desire to show them that he had visited the Deacon and that he knew good wine.

Mrs. Cassidy's hand dropped away from her husband's arm. They nodded at each other. Abraham stepped up close and leaned over Peter. "You have a taste for *that* wine," he said, as his hands closed on the money. "Why didn't you say so in the first place? What's the name of your boat?"

"The *Challenger,* racing sloop."

Peter wondered at the power of this particular quarterboard, Sam had received a harsh reprimand from his master by mentioning it; here it served as a magic password.

"I'll send the wine along with a land crew of five tough but reliable men you will find to your liking. Expect them after dark tonight."

"Why so late?"

"What's late about it?"

A shadow passed over Peter's face. "I'm sailing at flood tide but I can delay a few hours." He stood up, started to extend his hand to Abraham but put it in his pocket and said with a hitch of awkwardness in his manner, "Tonight, then." He gave an unnatural laugh. "Goodbye." He strolled, then hurried as he neared the door of the tavern.

Thankful Cassidy looked after Peter. She was unable to assess him despite her talent in this field. "God help us," she whispered in her husband's ear hole. She often called on the Deity for his assistance. "Does the young fool's right hand know what his left is doing? He wants to find Captain Collier, that's clear, but he hopes he's dead. He's celebrating something—probably a woman from the look on his face but, at the same time, he's sailing away at flood tide! Doesn't make sense, does he? The jackass is proud, nervous and probably crazy. If he worked for us, we'd sink him in the bottomless pond. If you want my opinion of the Deacon's folly . . ."

"I don't." Abraham counted his fistful of notes. "And you steer clear, or I'll pin your big ears back."

"I've got two more ears than *you'll* have if you go after Captain Collier again. He'll see that you match up on both sides of your silly head."

Abraham Cassidy grasped her iron arm. "You'd like that, eh? You'd like to see the other ear sliced off?"

"Maybe I would at that," Thankful said. "There would be less of you."

# Chapter
## six

*The boat may age*
*but her swift, clean lines*
*will remain a credit*
*to her designer.*
*The draftsman of*
*her time-twisted crew*
*has not come forward!*

Zenas Mayo stood by the wharf as a connoiseur stands before a beloved painting; missing no detail yet inhaling the whole. It was late afternoon and the tide was rising fast. Beneath him the piers were studded with parched mussels waiting for water to freshen and spread their long green beards. Zenas could feel their mute longing in his own person.

"I am connected with the whole Goddamn sea world." he said to several gulls who exchanged glances with him. A boat full of lobster pots rubbed against one of the piles with a two-toned mumble. Zenas leaned over to look. Each pot wore a wig of collapsed seaweed and shell. Within, the tenants crawled over and over each other, staring up at Zenas with their stalked eyes. "You gluttonous cannibals!" When alone, Zenas often talked aloud to the sea creatures around him. "Someone better boil you up before you devour each other."

His mouth began to water. He had a few lobster traps of his own. Hunger urged him into his dory but once out in the harbor he forgot the lobsters as he shipped oar to look at Peter Garrett's beautiful sloop. She lay at anchor beside the whalers like a race horse among drays.

Zenas's eyes caressed her well-turned prow and the curve of her cutwater. A man could love a boat like that, he thought. When she gets old, scrape her hull, paint her up and she looks fine. Who could say the same for a woman?

It was high time, however, that he pay a visit to the owner. Zenas's face hardened.

While waiting for the young man's return from Wreckers' Tavern, Zenas dropped a hand line over the side of the dory. A striper or two might be following the early alewives bound for Herring River. Time passed or rather lapped gently around Zenas as it always did when he was fishing.

He jumped with surprise when Peter Garrett hailed him from the deck of his sloop. "Good evening, Mr. Mayo."

The young man's voice came across the water so distinct and polite that it scraped along Zenas's nerves. He itched to take offense anyway. "What makes you think my name's Mayo?" he asked.

"You are fishing and you take a keen interest in my boat. You *are* Zenas Mayo, aren't you? I'm Peter Garrett."

Zenas began winding up his hand line. He had not seen Peter's friendly smile. A cold young bastard, he thought. See how he makes use of every small advantage, even to finding a man staring at his boat.

"Yep," said Zenas. "You guessed right. And since the owner of this boat won't call on me, I came to see for myself what kind of a sieve he sails."

Peter laughed at this pleasantry but Zenas's eyes were cold as the November sea.

"Well then, come aboard," Peter called, heartily for him.

Zenas rowed around the sloop, tied his boat to the mooring and swung himself up the ladder. Peter held out his hand. Zenas ignored it.

"Glad to have you aboard, sir," Peter said. "I have been meaning to call on *you*."

"A damn sight too busy for that, aren't you? Hanging around the folk in Wreckers' Tavern." Zenas gave him a piercing look.

"I was getting some rare wine sent aboard. Until its arrival, can I offer you some West Indian rum?" Peter put a hand on the older man's shoulder. Zenas jerked away from his touch. He put his hands in his pockets and sauntered about the deck looking up at the foremast and around at the brass fittings with admiration, then at Peter with loathing.

At last, Peter was forced to accept the fact that the man was hostile to him. A still, proud look came over him.

Zenas's nerves buzzed with hatred. "Shipping wine to celebrate *what*?" he asked. Peter followed Zenas to the wheel where he watched him turn it and run his hand over the sextant. "If it's to drink a toast to an engagement," Zenas continued, "you can drink up all the wine by yourself."

Zenas swaggered as he peeled words off his outrage and flung them at this elegant, poised young fop. He slapped the mast and caressed it with a hand as dark and lined as an old plank. His veined nose sniffed the clean tarry fragrance of the boat like an epicure.

"At least you like my boat," Peter said.

"Maybe," said Zenas.

Peter looked into his face and, with an ease of

manner that infuriated Zenas the more, said, "Come, let's be friends."

Here was the moment and the doorway to understanding, but Zenas's craggy face was closed. He wanted no intimacy, he hated any expression young Garrett could wear. If anyone was going to offer friendship, it should be Zenas.

"My Sarah will never strike a false lure with fine clothes and tasseled boots," Zenas said. "She's a fine girl, got the best damn education on all the lower Cape, her mother saw to it. And she learned to handle a boat from *me*. Hell with you, hell with your sloop! I withhold my consent, now and forever. Try and change me. You can both dash your wills over me like surf but I'll stand firm."

He looked Peter up and down. His eyes brimmed with contempt. "It's the clean-lined sloop that has caught my Sarah's eye—what else? It couldn't be the owner. I could blow you away like a piece of sea foam."

Peter turned white at this insult. He put his clenched fists in his pockets. "You are Sarah's father," he said.

"You're Goddamned right I am!"

"I'll have to keep reminding myself," Peter said.

The sunset filled half the sky with red and the gulls screamed overhead while Zenas searched for the ultimate insult. Loss and loneliness were written clearly now on his seamed face.

Peter's voice was under good control. "May I know more about this interesting consent you are withholding?"

Zenas stepped up to him. "I'll tell you why, among other things, the Cassidys don't sell a case of their Mooncusser wine to strangers. How did you rate wine from a Mooncusser's quarterboard?"

Peter drew a deep breath. It was important to mollify this fiery man. "Surely a case of wine, even from a doubtful source, can do no harm. I fail to see why you busy yourself with this."

"I make it my business. What are you up to, Garrett?"

For a moment it seemed that the force of Zenas's will might compel Peter to save himself by taking Zenas into his confidence. He hesitated, started to speak but, looking into Zenas's eyes, they seemed to him as stern as those of a bird. He hesitated, started to speak, then waved his hand and turned away.

Zenas's harsh voice followed him. "If you so much as bring my Sarah near the outer edge of your new friends, I'll cut your wrists and troll you in back of my boat until every shark in the bay has a mouthful!"

Peter gave a wincing smile. "We are all at the edge of evil, but I'll keep my footing and you look after *your* footing, Mr. Mayo."

"Your good friends, the Cassidys, slipped on blood and fell over the edge long ago, Mr. Garrett. Whatever your business, I warn you again, leave Sarah out of it. Set sail while you can."

Peter looked directly into the wrathful eyes of the fisherman. He could see Sarah in their sea gray depths and this calmed him. "Sir, I will not quarrel with you. My business is my own and I intend to complete it before I come to see Sarah again."

Peter's self-contained, gentlemanly manner repelled Zenas. "Finish it and don't come back to Wellfleet, or by God I'll . . ."

Peter brushed this aside. "I said with the flood tide. My affairs should take a week or possibly two, then I'll be back for Sarah. Meanwhile will you please take her this letter."

Zenas took the letter but when Peter held out his hand and their eyes met. Zenas gave an abrupt, harsh laugh. "You still can't believe that I don't like you."

"I am trying not to believe it."

"The hell with turning the other cheek! Be a man. Hate me! A man would have thrown me off his boat long ago. Now pull in your hand before I bite it off."

Zenas went down the ladder and jumped into his boat. "Come back for Sarah and I'll cut out your heart with a clam knife and chop it up for bait," he called.

Peter made an uncertain gesture, half resentment, half regret at this unfortunate meeting.

Zenas rowed with violent strokes of the oars. Even at a distance, his suffering was clearly outlined. "And no self-respecting fish would take the bait," Zenas howled over the water.

Zenas, who had been a promising scholar until he shipped aboard a whaler at an early age, took a look at the envelope Peter had handed him. His handwriting had a tendency to dwindle and die away at the end of each word. If the young fool would only do the same. Now for the letter.

Trying to ease himself past the reef of his honesty, he sat with his hands ready to rip open the envelope but somehow it seemed such a sly dishonor, he could not. He suddenly threw the letter into the water. At the time the gesture seemed to end his temptation and be protective of Sarah. If she didn't know Peter was coming back, she might hate him for leaving without a word, and end it. Then it came over him that he had done something vile. He spent

85

several agonizing moments trying to retrieve the letter with oar and boat hook, only making it so waterlogged that it sank.

Out under the grape arbor beside their little cottage, Zenas's supper was waiting. A mug of beer from which all foam had departed, a clam pie with a flaky brown crust and a score of attentive flies. Sarah usually put supper on the table at an agreed-upon hour, if he didn't arrive, she served herself. When his food congealed, she cleared it all away. Zenas was profoundly unpunctual and this was the only way to keep their tempers smooth.

Tonight, however, she waited, although it was dusk when Zenas came up the hill. He stopped short at the sight of her dress. "What's that?" he asked.

"What's the matter? Don't you like it, Father?"

Zenas gave a stricken yell. *More* changes that he could neither bear nor prevent! "Where is your hair, your long shiny hair?"

"Up on top, see? I just had it cut around the face. It's called the Titus haircut. Peter has one. Like it?" She touched the little tendrils around her face.

Zenas's face filled with dismay. "You look like a Goddamned sea urchin!" He stamped with distress. "You've been to Chatham to get French clothes off the wrecked brig *Napoleon*. Wish the silly fashions had all gone down with the ship!"

"This is what women are wearing off Cape, out in the great world." She revolved slowly.

Zenas stamped again with outrage. "You're *naked!*"

"Not really, but you can't wear petticoats under these new muslin dresses. They are supposed to cling." Sarah was serene, well aware of her beauty.

"Christ damn, you can see right through it! Are

86

women going around the street like *that*?"

"Of course."

"Sarah Mayo, you are not going to wear a nightgown on the streets of Wellfleet! No whaler would ever leave port."

Sarah gave her joyful hearty laugh. She put fresh beer on the table and preened a little.

Zenas sat down on the bench. He pushed his pie away and looked down over the harbor. She had wrought this change for Peter, that mound of gull dung—top grade and fancy, but gull dung. "You might as well know, I have been to see him," he said.

Sarah leaned toward him. "What! You talked with Peter?"

Zenas nodded mutely and turned his face away. She was too radiant, he was unwilling to spoil it.

"What did he say?" She caught her breath, remembering last night's dubious victory.

Zenas remained silent. Her voice sharpened. "Father, you are hiding something."

"Let me eat," Zenas reached for the clam pie. But his stomach twisted as he remembered the letter at the bottom of the harbor.

Sarah pulled the pie out of his reach. "No, not until you tell me!"

"First I'll have my little appetizer." Zenas went in the house and poured some water in the kitchen basin. He washed and tossed down enough rum to pickle his conscience, he hoped. But he foundered under a heavy cargo of doubt. Was Peter that bad? Was it fair to moor Sarah here? She was not his, only lent to him. Nothing was his, not even his own body, rented for a lifetime by—what, an aspiring hermit crab?

"I know that expression of yours. It's a weather breeder. Get it *said*," Sarah urged.

"I'll try . . . time goes by so Christ damn fast, the tow rope slips through my hands. Once I planned to get some book learning but, while your mother was alive, I had to maintain my position as a rough sailor—point of honor. Ah, Hell! Maybe I resent your young gentleman because of what I am!"

"And what is wrong with what you are?" Sarah asked with sudden ferocity.

Zenas opened then closed his mouth. Could he explain a sadness like an undertow that ran parallel with a lifetime? He was a rough sailor who could navigate the ocean but he had no compass for the great world outside the Cape where human knowledge was building up every year without him, beyond him. He had run down his sails and anchored his mind!

Sarah understood some of his distress, at least the outer edges of it. She took his hands in hers. Her luminous gray eyes looked full at him. "I will always be proud of you and all the things you taught me. No one else could ever, *ever* have shown me how to be strong and live with the sea, and how not to drown on land in a sea of trouble but to float above it as if I were on the water. No one else on earth could have taught me that. I won't ever be far away. I'll always want to go for a sail with you in our old boat."

Zenas knew that this was the reaction of a fine lady, and suddenly he realized that this had nothing to do with education, fine clothes, or her Boston blood. It was a certain tide in the heart, that made a fine lady or gentleman. Why, hell, it might have come from him!

They sat down in the arbor overlooking the boats. Sarah's appetite had always risen above illness or sorrow, but now Zenas noticed that she gazed at her supper in the irritating, remote way her mother had, and, like her, gardened the food on her plate, making it neater as she ate a minnow's portion.

Zenas was not hungry either. He swallowed a few mouthfuls with the help of beer and stared fixedly at the grape leaves overhead. The sensitive, unsure look on his face depressed Sarah. She valued the old, ranting Zenas.

"Father," her voice was coaxing, reasonable, "you must have seen *some*thing in Peter."

"Why?"

"Because I do and you and I are so much alike."

"Well . . . let's see. One thing, he did stand up to my anger very well. The young bastard was cool, I'll say that."

"You were angry?" She was aghast. "I somehow pictured it as a cautious, getting-acquainted meeting."

"I was mad as hell but he stood there all frank and friendly in his fancy boots with the tassels and his white neckpiece. No other man is that calm when I'm out to get him. Maybe the young fop is afraid of something so big no other fear matters to him."

Sarah stood up. She took a long trembling breath. "So you were savage with him. Oh *couldn't* you have behaved just this once and given him a chance? Of course he wouldn't bend!"

Zenas pushed his plate away. "Nobody asked him to bend. I refused my Goddamned consent."

"You *what?*" Sarah seized his shoulders. "Consent to *what?* Father . . . he has never offered!"

Zenas jumped up. "Then he's worse than I

89

thought!"

Sarah turned white with humiliation. "What did he say when you . . . when you refused your consent?"

"Why, the bastard said, 'tell me about this interesting consent.'"

"How *could* you? How *could* you do such a terrible thing to me?"

Zenas felt a shock as he realized that there had been no occasion to refuse his consent. He tried to recover with the comment; "Well anyway . . . it will be a long voyage before he invites me aboard again—or you, with any luck."

Sarah's eyes were wide with fury. A flash storm raced through her. She tried to control it but it was like thunder in the brain, lightning in the nerves. She shuddered all over with a craving for violent words.

"Offer or not, what right have you to refuse?" She screamed her mother's words at him. "What is there at home for me with a profane old drunkard!"

Zenas stood up unsteadily. He held out a hand as if to ward off a mortal blow. For some reason, he tried to smile.

These gestures of his struck her to the heart and the storm, already grounded by her tongue, died away. "Father . . . You know I didn't mean that, not in my heart."

Zenas nodded, speechless. He felt hollow, scooped out, and as if the word "drunkard," were a talisman, thirst began twisting his vitals.

Sarah looked out over the harbor for a few minutes. Then she turned and said in a quiet voice, "Putting aside the horrible embarrassment of my father refusing an offer that was never made, give me one good reason, if it *is* made, for refusing it."

Zenas's voice was flat and tired now. "He's been hanging around Wreckers' Tavern."

"Is *that* all! He doesn't know its reputation."

"One look inside at the company is all anyone needs."

"I said one good reason."

"He is doing business with the Cassidys."

"Impossible!" said Sarah.

"Call it a taste for low company then. Some mighty fine looking sons-of-bitches have it like a blight."

"Peter is an off-islander. He doesn't know about Mooncussers."

"You can see evil on a face when it's burned in like a brand."

"It's just . . . foolish of Peter, that's all. He doesn't know."

"The kind of foolish who thinks everyone is pleased that Peter is rich, and wants to help him get more so. Lots of young fools like that in the world."

"Peter is no fool!" She tried hard to hold in her temper, remembering her father's blasted face, his effort to smile, his upheld hand. "Father, you still haven't given me one good reason."

"If keeping company with Mooncussers isn't enough for you, it is for me. I told him to sail clear of Wellfleet and Sarah Mayo."

Sarah smiled. She lifted her chin. "I don't need to ask you what he said to that."

Zenas opened his mouth to tell her about the letter sunk in the harbor but her proud smile stopped him. What faith she had in those shiny tasseled boots! The young bastard had his beautiful sloop that was enough for him. Let him leave the real prizes, girls like Sarah Mayo, to the real men, the whaling men of Wellfleet.

"You see!" Sarah's eyes flared with pride. "I know how he would respond to an order like that. Just as I would, he'd sweep it away like that." And she swept his beer mug off the table.

Zenas looked away from her and down at the broken mug. Above the pool of liquid, mosquitoes began dancing like dots of smoke in the dusk. Zenas watched them fixedly. "Look out," he said. "Your new slippers . . . in the puddle of beer."

"Father," her voice gave a lurch. "I *am* right, am I not?"

Zenas's dry throat was stubborn. Go on, he urged it, tell her that the bastard is coming back for her. He gave an involuntary yawn. A fresh breeze came with the evening and he could see the tavern lights. They pulled. He began to move away from her.

"Father!" Her voice was ragged, "Tell me!"

Overwhelming thirst clutched Zenas. Profane old drunkard, he thought, and he tried to pull out the words that were fastened like so many leeches on his heart.

"Tell me what he said," she cried.

Yes, tell her, why don't you, he commanded himself. Tell her about the letter. Stay, he begged himself even as his legs began carrying him over the familiar path down the hill to the taverns.

"Come back!" she screamed.

Zenas turned. His face was white and glaring with the knowledge that he was going to betray her. He pointed down to the harbor where some of the ships were making ready to go out on the flood tide. Lanterns were dipping on masts and the *Challenger* had already run up some sail.

Zenas gave a mute despairing wave of his hand and went on down the hill.

# Chapter
## seven

*When the night
and flood tide
come in together,
we must embark!*

ut in the harbor, the *Challenger* leaped and bucked against her anchor like a young horse. Night and the flood tide came together in a rush as Sarah ran along the dock, her eyes and thoughts intent on the sloop.

She brushed past the sailors loading boats by lantern light and dodged the ones who caught at her. Their hearty obscenities were as familiar to her as the cry of gulls.

When she came to her dory, she hitched up her delicate skirt and climbed in. Salty seepage washed over her gold sandals but the familiar smell was pleasing.

As she rowed steadily toward the sloop, she felt a clouding of her bright, hard impulse. It seemed to her that she was rowing out to meet something threatening and disastrous that was already in place, waiting to unfold, and that she could not pull back if she tried.

In and out she went among the creaking, bowing ships until the *Challenger* loomed over her. There was no life aboard her. Part of her sail was up but no crew. Why would Peter send them ashore when he was preparing to sail out on the tide?

Sarah rowed slowly around the *Challenger*'s stern then drew in her breath sharply. She almost cried out but quickly reversed her oars and remained half hidden around the stern. From there she watched the whale boat full of rough men from Wreckers' Tavern. They must be from there—she recognized some of the dirty types she had seen going in and out of the Mooncussers' den.

The men made fast to the *Challenger*'s ladder. When that was done, they lit a lantern, half covered it with a piece of sail, then sat quietly looking up at the sloop. The half light of the lantern revealed portions of their faces; a cheek that was deeply pocked, a forehead with a carved frown, evil looking men like so many moray eels. Some of them were the same men who were singing on Shirt Tail Point last night.

Sarah was about to call out and warn Peter of his gruesome callers when he hailed them quietly. They were expected! Peter leaned over the rail of his sloop, holding his lantern so that its beam fell on each face in turn. No wonder he had sent his crew ashore.

The men, relaxed and brutal, stared up unblinking. They had no deference for authority, knowing how easily the frail thread of life behind it ran out along the length of their knives.

Dismay flashed across Peter's face—or was it only a flicker of light from his lantern? "Come aboard." His voice was firm. "I have been waiting for you."

Peter's lantern lit up their faces one by one as three of them climbed the rope ladder. The last man up was a newcomer to Wellfleet. His vacant, handsome features with their imprint of peaceful evil were unfamiliar. Sarah could imagine him cutting open a clam or a throat with equal emotion.

Peter greeted this terrible crew with civility but was careful not to turn his back to them as he ushered them below. At once the sloop seemed less buoyant, as if the visitors weighed her down.

So, Sarah thought, her father had been right. Peter was charting a dark course. Shocked, she looked back at the lights of the harbor. Her old simple life pulled at her, those great moments out on the water when fish leaped iridescent in the sunset and when she dipped her hands in the sun's radiant path on the water, she felt mysteriously at one with the bay and all its creatures. She let the boat drift away from the *Challenger* with an eerie sensation of lightness as if she drifted between the mooring lines of her life, between time itself.

A muffled yell came from the starboard side of the sloop. "Staaaaaaand by to bring up the wine!"

Sarah gave a deep sigh. It was only wine. Forbidden Mooncusser's wine that was like blood from a ship they had wrecked. Well, it was something that Peter should not have done, but lots of off-Cape people did buy wine from Mooncussers thinking that it was only scavenged. She would have to educate Peter, that was all.

She drew near in her little boat, watching until Peter completed his business and the men pulled away. When he finally stood alone in the prow, looking up toward Shirt Tail Point as if he longed to be there, she felt a strong pull toward him, a blend of something sensual, and a feeling that her destiny was here. Peter was a strongly romantic figure, standing alone on the prow of his ship staring at the place where they had vowed love, kissed and came near to the natural and inevitable finish. There is no turning back now against this tide, she thought. *Something has charted my course.*

She took off both sandals and threw them. One missed, the other hit him on the shoulder. He whirled about and held the lantern out over the rail.

"Sarah!" His voice was hoarse with shock. "What are you doing here?"

"What are *you* doing with sail up, getting ready to meet the tide?"

They stared mutely at each other. Then Sarah sculled around the prow and standing up straight and proud in the boat, she made the dory fast to the rope ladder and held up her arms to him.

Peter leaned far over and caught her hands. Her bare feet walked up the side of the sloop like cat's paws. One shell earring fell off and she imagined it sinking slowly to the bottom to become a rented house for a hermit crab. It was like her old life dropping away.

On deck, Peter gave a sharp gasp at the sight of her clinging dress. Sarah had forgotten her new clothes, but reminded now, by Peter's flushed face, she moved close to him with a magnetic, seductive look that made the corners of her mouth twitch with suppressed laughter as if she watched herself in a mirror.

Peter kissed her. He shuddered as the tension of his will gave way.

"Are you still going to sail without me?" Her wide sea-gray eyes held his.

"But you can't—just row out to a man's boat . . ."

"But I have."

"Sarah . . . you can't *be* here like this!"

The masts creaked as the *Challenger* rocked in

the flood tide. A cool west wind flapped the sail and lifted Sarah's light skirt. Her bare toes were like a child's, brown and even.

"But you see . . . I *am* here," she said.

# Chapter eight

My cold, unpleasant love,
you knot the tourniquet
too tight around your heart.
There are definite signs
of gangrene!

The crew of the *Challenger* tiptoed past the cabin in leering consideration for its occupants. "The sun will be a whole lot higher before you see those two on deck," they told one another with a wink and a thumb jerked aft.

The crew itself rose late. They were sloppy and somewhat demoralized. For the last month, young Mr. Garrett and his bride had been sailing up and down the New England coast on a long bacchanal of pleasure. After the wedding, which had been attended only by the crew, and the preacher from Barnstable had been put back ashore, the young couple had kidnapped the fiddler, an eccentric young man given to the bottle and strands of beautiful and slightly dissonant melodies of his own composing. They paid him well and, fully in the spirit of their wild gaiety, he played for them all night and slept all day. Wine flowed freely for everyone.

When the sloop put in to various ports for water and provisions, the young couple, drugged with wine, music and love, bought anything that pleased or amused them. Sometimes the crew wondered if their captain, rich as he seemed to be, would have anything left.

After a visit to his Boston bank, the captain had apparently wound up his affairs and was now spending as if his fortune was as bottomless as the famous ponds in Wellfleet woods.

The hold was heavy with furniture for that new house of his on the dunes. And his wife had a taste for fashion and rich baubles. Did he know what he was doing? Was he bewitched? If his wife kept on at this rate, would he have to sell the *Challenger*? The crew worried and the festivities went on.

The fears of the crew were allayed when Peter announced that the *Challenger* was a wedding present to his wife and would be anchored in Wellfleet harbor with full crew, to be taken on cruises from time to time.

"A cruise *from time to time*? Where is that located? Please chart me that course." Mrs. Garrett had given her lovely laugh that was deeper and richer now.

Sarah could have sailed on like this forever. Her romance was with love as well as Peter and her happy, free sensuality made this the first perfect time in her life. She sensed, however, something awry in the past and in the future and instinctively avoided both. So did Peter. They lived for the moment, loved to exhaustion, and lolled on deck in the moonlight, listening to the fiddle. They also drank quite a lot of the wine from the ill-fated *Queen of Peru*.

Sarah had written Zenas begging for his love and blessing. At one of the ports—she had given him as an address—she received a typical message:

"It's too late now for anything *but* my Goddamned blessing. Here it is. Zenas."

This had amused and satisfied her. She knew her own good intentions on his behalf. Meanwhile she gave herself up to the delights of love and to the hot relish of extravagant buying.

The night of their disaster started off like all the other nights of this wedding cruise except for one thing. They were sailing aimlessly off the coast of Maine. Otis, the cook's dog, was tied to the foremast as usual. The fat cur's belly was swollen with tidbits from the galley but, regardless of this, his master had come up with a handful of delicacies for him. He treated the dog with reverence, bringing offerings as he would to a powerful prophet, for he sincerely believed in the dog's power to warn of foul events to come, ending in death for someone.

"Hear that," he said as Otis split the night with a long wavering howl. "That's the death howl. Somebody here is going to die. The dog knows all right, but he don't know *when*." His round, greasy credulous face looked around at the nearby members of the crew. "Someone's time is running out for sure. Otis knows." He patted the dog's obscenely fat yellow rump.

The youngest member of the crew, a thin youth with legs and arms like twigs, said, "If he's got no sense of timing, what's to stop him from howling on and on? We're all going to die some day, so make him stop!"

"Drown the mutt," said the fiddler. "He's making hair grow right out of my spine!"

Sarah and Peter came strolling by. They had drunk a goodly amount, to use one of Zenas's favorite phrases. This goodly amount of wine caused Sarah to laugh a bit more than the occasion called for. "Sir," she called to the fiddler. "May we see your amazing spine?"

Peter, suddenly out of sympathy with her laughter, drew her away from Otis who was looking directly at him as he gave vent to his prolonged howl.

The men were silent. They looked at Peter, watching him, as he and his bride walked away to the stern and sat down on a pile of rope.

An east wind scudded clouds across the moon tonight and salt spray slapped against the sloop, sprinkling their faces. When the boat dipped, they rolled into each other's arms.

Sarah sang him a foolish little Cape Cod song:

> *Oh the Cape Cod girls*
> *they have no combs.*
> *They comb their hair*
> *with codfish bones.*

She was overcome by helpless, fresh young laughter. Talking through it, she said, "Now I know why you married me. Own up, it was for my dowry. You shrewd Yankee, you counted all the codfish combs and lobster pots!"

Peter gave a difficult smile. "I may shoot that dog," he said.

"You are always closing the shutters of your mind against my laughter. Why? No, really, Peter . . . tell me why?"

Zenas could have told her from his own experience that, when you start saying, "You are *always*," or "You *never*," it is a danger signal.

Peter made no answer.

A brig luffed and dropped anchor near by. But the

*Challenger* was on such a relaxed pleasure cruise that no one aboard was sufficiently alert to give warning of company.

The fiddler went on playing despite the wind. The dog howled along with the music.

"Hey there, fiddler," Sarah called out. "Play something the dog doesn't know!"

Her voice was slurred at the edges and her laughter rang out over the water as she looked at Peter with merry eyes, a lovely, sensual, slightly drunken lady.

The crew went below and soon they were alone, except for the fiddler who fell into a doze with his fiddle still tucked under his chin.

Sarah leaned over Peter, caressing him, looking full into his eyes. "Tell me something. Let the past be vague and the future shrouded, but this I *must* know. Your pupils wince and contract when I laugh. Why? Is my laugh ugly?"

"No, it's full and musical but sometimes you laugh at . . . at odd moments," Peter said.

"I'll tell you why I laugh so much if you tell me why you recoil from the sound of it."

"I haven't asked you to tell me anything," Peter said.

Sarah hugged him. She put her mouth near his ear and said, "I insist on telling you! Picture a great tapestry, such as the women made for the museum in Chatham. A huge scene, full of events, battles with Indians, storms, disasters, great whales in their death throes, funerals, marriages, stately historical meetings, sunsets, graveyards and love scenes. Now picture running through it all a bright comic thread in a garish color. The thread stands out for me, and I laugh. I can't help it. Maybe it's

106

an affliction!"

"Love scenes!" Peter was uneasy. *"Everything?"*

"Everything. But I didn't put the thread of comedy there, Peter. I *see* it, that's all. It will be noticed. It peeps out at me and . . . I laugh."

"I dare you to laugh now," Peter said.

They were silent with lovemaking. Later Sarah leaned back in his arms and watched the clouds scudding before the moon. She held out her glass. "More wine for the drunken lovers! Sea drunkards are better than land sots. I wonder if I am more Zenas after all instead of Mother. They always fought together and now they are fighting in me!"

When Peter had poured the wine, she said, "Now tell me why my laugh makes you wince as if your soul contracted?" She leaned close to him. "Tell me, Peter, keep your part of the bargain."

"Why talk when we can love?" Wine had unraveled him and was fraying his syllables.

Sarah felt the east wind pluck at her nerves. "Peter, be fair. I told *you* things." She looked at him compellingly.

"A special kind of hearty laughter reminds me of . . ."

"Of what—who? Who laughs like me?"

"No one laughs like you. What I seemed to hear is an echo."

"An echo of what?" If she could find out this one thing, the rest might follow.

The brig lowered a few men in a whale boat. They wound the oarlock with cloth and began rowing silently toward the sloop. The fiddler who was supposed to be on watch had sunk into a still deeper sleep. His bow dropped from his hand. Otis alone, with a deep warning growl, watched the approaching boat. The oarsmen were making slow progress against the wind.

Sarah said impatiently, "Peter, don't go to sleep, tell me, an echo of *what?*"

Peter's voice was drowsy. "Of someone who laughs and laughs as he insults, inflicts indignity, an animal . . ."

"My feminine laugh actually reminds you of some crass sailor?"

He shook his head and closed his eyes.

"Go *on,* Peter, tell me more about those echoes!"

"The eyes of the giant sea turtles in the hold where I slept," he said in a dreamy voice. "Profound, pitiless eyes like the eye of someone looking through a peephole. I had no hope."

"Go on."

"It was a relief to get out on deck. The men threw me food—maggoty bread, turtle meat. I caught it. I was half starved. But I always waited for a full minute before I ate it, a point I was proving. I forget why."

"But Peter, why were you a prisoner in that hold?"

"I found out. I knew what they were doing. They came for me with their swords, but the captain held them back. He saved me. Why? I never knew."

"Then what happened?"

"From then on I lived as a prisoner in the hold."

"I can't piece it together, Peter."

"I knew that at any moment I could be killed. I was ready. I dreamed of the hollow-eyed skull behind my face. Courage was all there was left, the final residue of a man."

Sarah, in the midst of her horrified sympathy, found something conceited and self-loving in this last. "Oh, don't talk like that," she murmured. "Just be matter of fact, that's more—manly somehow."

"Matter of fact? All right, the business the ship was on stank worse than all the turtles in the hold. I was ready to yell a warning to any ship we overtook. They knew this, those devils. They tried to harass me to death."

"But the captain intervened," she said.

"Well . . . not altogether."

"Obviously, Peter, since here you are."

"Not out of kindness. I don't know why he kept me alive. It's strange—I have almost forgotten his men but I remember everything about him. He hated me as I hated him. We were extreme opposites. I felt he kept me alive as a sort of—curiosity. He spoke like an educated man but he seemed to detest in me the very things he had perverted in himself. He sort of gloated over me as if to remind himself of what he might have become had he not chosen his course."

"And you hate him for the same reason, perhaps?" Sarah handed him more wine. "Who is this man?"

Peter was entirely in the grip of the past. "That cursed voice, I can hear it now. Educated yet cruel. 'Dear boy, don't be so stiff-necked with my crew. I'm having a hard time keeping their knives out of your vitals. Watch that fastidious recoil or I can't answer for your life.' His laughter crashes through time and reaches me anywhere." Peter held his head to one side. "I can almost hear it now." He jumped up. "I *do* hear it now!"

Sarah, caught into his mood, listened intently and it did seem that somewhere in the night, a throaty, big man's laugh was echoing on the east wind.

"It can't be, of course. Our imaginations are

playing tricks. Peter," she urged, "tell me about this from the beginning, not in bits and pieces."

Peter was tense and silent, listening. Suddenly Otis shattered the air with a loud warning bark.

"Otis hears it too," Sarah cried. "Someone out there is laughing as if at a huge joke." She ran after Peter to starboard and there, anchored broadside to them, was the brig, her sails gleaming in the moonlight, her guns rolled out in full view and trained on the defenseless *Challenger*.

A whaleboat touched against the sloop just below them and a man stood up, holding a package high in his hand. Peter shouted for his crew. "Get below," he told Sarah.

"No," she said.

"We come on a peaceable errand, sir," said the spokesman, a small man with a wise face and red hair. The lamp in the whaleboat showed him and his companions dressed as only privateers dress, in oddment of old navy uniforms, an international assortment, with here and there a touch of battered civilian finery.

"You don't look peaceable," Peter gestured toward the brig.

"Usual precautions, sir, that's all. I came only to deliver a present."

Peter made no move to take the present. "Get the crew," he said to Sarah, "and stay below yourself."

"I will not!" she said. "My place is here with you." She turned and gave a shout that awakened the fiddler whom she sent below to collect the crew.

"I'm first mate, given this package to deliver. As soon as it's in your hands, we'll sail away," said the red-haired man.

Peter looked at the row of guns facing him.

110

"It's only a harmless little present, Captain's honor." The first mate gave a subtle smile.

"Who guarantees your captain's honor?" He did not ask the captain's identity, and the pallor of Peter's face was visible even by moonlight.

"I can guarantee his guns," said the first mate.

Peter thought a moment. His crew began to gather at the rail, disheveled and unready. They stared at the brig in terror.

"Your delivery service is forceful," Sarah called down. "We'll send a thank-you message the same way, some day."

The mate gave a short laugh. "I'll relay your message. The captain likes a witty woman. Now how shall I deliver your wedding present, my dear? Will you lower the ladder?"

"A wedding present for me? Will I be shot if I don't like it?" she cried.

A few scattered guffaws of appreciation came from the crew in the whaleboat.

"We accept nothing until we know the contents," said Peter.

"But we know the contents of the guns on the brig, don't we?" Sarah said.

"The captain of the brig sends his congratulations to the bride," said the first mate. "And if he could see you, he'd walk right up the side of the sloop!" The men in the boat laughed heartily in agreement.

"Who is this acrobat?" Sarah asked.

"He said to tell you and your husband that the present is from a dear friend."

Sarah cupped her hands and shouted. "I accept my present. Pull in your guns, Captain Dear Friend."

A shout of laughter came from the brig.

111

"Sarah, *no!*" Peter pulled her back but she shook him off and reached far down over the side. "Why not? I'll take my present and that's the end of it. We can't stand here all night, arguing with guns."

The red-haired first mate stood on the edge of the boat and managed to place the package in Sarah's hands. The men set their oars against the sloop's side and pushed away. The mate gave a shrill whistle and the brig began to roll her guns back into place.

Sarah ran to the cabin with her package, while Peter turned to his slovenly crew. Pale and shaken with anger, he told them that the pleasure cruise was over. From now on they must be at their posts, clean and alert. No more wine, no more music, nothing but crisp orders crisply followed.

The crew was chastened, "Yes sir'd," and took several lookout posts. At that moment, Sarah screamed. The crew hesitated.

"To your duties," Peter shouted over his shoulder as he ran to the cabin.

Sarah was standing in their cabin, shocked and wide-eyed. She pointed, speechless. He saw a piece of paper on the table with a huge scrawl: "Congratulations, dear boy. May I call as soon as you are settled?"

Peter reached out and took up a perfect string of pearls that lay beside the note.

Sarah recovered her voice. "No . . . look *there!*" she pointed to the floor where a glass jar, tightly corked, rolled a little with the motion of the sloop, as did the white occupant of the jar with its neat lobe and its winding tunnel.

"What . . ." Peter began.

"A human ear pickled in alcohol needs no label,"

Sarah said.

The brig was at some distance now so it couldn't have been a laugh that the east wind carried over the waves, and yet . . .

They stood watching the jar roll and its occupant turn over. Sarah shuddered but in a moment, her vigor, strong stomach and curiosity revived her. "Well!" She gave a breathless little laugh. "Did he shop for it, or was it something he had around the house? And why not give us a matched pair?"

"He sent this as a warning for me. Sarah, your jokes are in poor taste at this time."

"Taste . . . don't mention taste with this jar of pickled ear rolling about. Besides, we might as well joke a little. It's here and it's ours. We can't turn it in for something else. Shall we hang it out to dry and use it as a bookmark?"

"You are unbelievable," he said slowly.

"It's the Zenas in me. Stop staring like that. Let's move on to the rest of his offering, the pearls."

"Leave them alone!" His voice was sharp, quick.

"Heavens, what beautiful pearls!"

"Sarah, give them to me."

"No—why? They are mine, from Captain Dear Friend." She slipped them over her head and around her neck where they hung in a radiance that almost melted her bones. "They are true sea things, grown for me."

"They are priceless pearls," said Peter. "*His* ego would allow nothing less. The poor owner must be at the bottom of the ocean."

She glanced down at the jar. "The ear must have been even more priceless to someone."

"I think it must have been Abraham Cassidy's," Peter said. "Take off the pearls."

"No, why should I? You mean Cassidy of Wreckers' Tavern? I used to think his head looked like a cooky with a hole in it. But . . . I am not flattered. Captain Dear Friend should have sent me a nobler ear."

"You horrify me," Peter said. "Your misplaced gaiety." He seized the pearls, yanked them, breaking the string, and picked up the jar. He ran for the cabin door.

*"No!"* Sarah realized his intent. "Keep the pearls, the beautiful pearls." She ran after him to the deck shouting, "Give them to me! They are mine."

Peter threw the jar as well as the pearls far out into the water in the direction of the departing brig.

Sarah cried with rage. "How stupid of you! Who cares who sent them? Pearls are pearls."

She stormed back to the cabin and threw herself on the bed. Peter followed and stood in the doorway looking in at her.

"Sometimes I think you are a whole series of strangers," he said. "This lust for ornament, the lover of the simple sailing life, the earthy wit, the . . ."

"And right now you are making yourself unpopular with every one of us," Sarah laughed. But seeing the misery on his face, she was contrite. "I'm sorry," she said lightly, sincerely. "Pay no attention to me. It was a seizure, an attack of hot greed which I should censure. After all, I didn't have the pearls an hour ago . . . I haven't got them now."

Reaching for higher elements in her nature eased her. She gave him a radiant smile. "So put your arms around me."

But Peter's arms were too tense for caresses. Cords of tension stood out on his neck.

"This could be a very good time to tell me about

114

*everything,*" she whispered in his ear.

"And let you share it all? Drag you into this mess?" He gave a short laugh. "I think not."

"But I am sharing it anyway. Don't you see that?" She hugged him warmly but the climate of her love was too hot and bright for Peter now. He pulled away, drew out his handkerchief and rubbed the edge of it back and forth against his nostrils. What was it about the nearness of this enemy of his that made his nose weep and a few wheezes come into his chest?

"Well then, to hell with the past! Peter, you have a wife now." She clasped her long, tanned hands together and her whole person looked vivid and wild with the drama of the evening.

Peter, loving his sensual, merry wife, longed to respond appropriately but he remained tight and silent in his cage of nerves.

Later that night, clasped in Sarah's arms, he failed them both, again and again.

Sarah, unable to sleep, looked out of the porthole. She knew exactly whom to blame. Was that the brig, shadowy in the moonlit mist? She imagined a distant shout of laughter at her dilemma.

Why should Captain Dear Friend, whoever he was, pirate, freebooter, privateer or eccentric rich man, have so much power over her husband?

"Damn you," she whispered into the night. "Damn you for ruining a whole night of love."

# Chapter nine

*Words fly in and out*
*like bees*
*from that hive of mystery*
*the human skull.*

hen morning came and Sarah looked down at Peter's sleeping face, he seemed to her young and vulnerable, but his high forehead, glistening in the hot still air, was a hive of secrecy. She wanted to beat at it, shouting, Let me in, let me *in!*

The silence was disturbed now and then by Otis's yawping bark and an occasional slosh of water as the crew cleaned up the deck for the new regime of discipline.

Sarah felt depressed by the night before. She put her arms around Peter, but even in his sleep he was tense and resisted her.

She got up full of frustration, threw something on and ran up on deck. The sun was already hot and the wake a lazy ripple. Light airs and breezes barely dented the sails. For Sarah, the expert sailor, this presaged a stagnant day.

The dog's seal-like bark sawed at her nerves. She hunched her shoulders and closed her eyes, wincing.

"Yawp," cried Otis.

Sarah raced over to the animal, shouting, "Stop it, stop it!" He flung his howl up to the mizzentop.

118

Sarah took off her slipper and gave the astounded dog a few sharp raps on the rump. "There, you stop that disagreeable sound," she cried. "People are not going to like you."

Otis gave a whimper. He cringed and Sarah dropped the slipper as they looked at each other in surprise. "How could I?" she asked him. She reached out gently and touched his head, feeling a rush of affection for this fat, pampered beast.

Sarah put on her slipper and rushed to get some crackers from the cabin. Otis took one with suspicion and dropped it on the deck. Sarah kneeled down beside him and put an arm around his thick yellow body.

Otis, quiet for the first time, pressed against her. He had not been offered affection before, only food. They stared at each other with questioning eyes.

Sarah felt a strong responsibility for the dog's welfare. Why was this? she wondered. Because she had injured him? Ah, there were too many mysterious layers in the soul. Were people everywhere weaving ropes between themselves and the people and creatures they injured, fettering themselves? Was that the explanation of Captain Dear Friend?

She went to find Peter but he was avoiding her. Busy most of the day, dressed formally in his captain's coat, he was a different person from her happy, relaxed bridegroom. He strode about the deck now, occupied only with the affairs of the crew and the defence of the sloop if the brig should approach them again. He would not meet her eyes.

How childish of him to be embarrassed, thought Sarah. That evening, she clung to him, begging him to come below and talk everything over.

Peter shook his head. "Things to be done. We'll

119

put in at Salem and leave a message if we have to blow the sloop in ourselves. He always visits Salem when he is on these waters."

"He? You mean Captain Dear Friend. Are we going to deliver a thank-you note?" She smiled. "A present would be even better. I would suggest Otis and his prophet's howl, except that I have adopted the dog."

Peter, unsmiling, made an angular, nervous gesture and walked away.

"Peter!" She ran after him, took his hand and looked full at him. "I love you, remember that every minute."

"We'll be in Salem soon," he said. "Go shopping there, buy anything you want, then we'll be off for home and . . ."

She gave a half smile. "You want me to make do with shopping?"

"Give me time," he said. "I have a lot to do before . . ." He gave a despairing shrug and walked away from her.

"How can you?" she said. "I am the person you love. It must be like walking away from yourself."

He made another abrupt gesture, muttering, "I must write something. Excuse me." He went below and closed the door of the chart room behind him.

Left alone on deck, Sarah watched the moon come up and the ocean rise toward it as if drawing deep breaths of moonlight. A breeze came and the sails flapped gratefully. The fragrance of heather and pine suggested the nearness of land.

Sarah's chest swelled. All this beauty, this stabbing loveliness! She longed for Peter and ran impulsively down to the chart room. She could see the light of his lamp under the door. Her heart seemed to swell with love and longing. After this quarrel, they would love gravely and with drama. It would be like a meeting after a journey. She tapped on the door.

Within, Peter sat as still as a grouse.

"Peter!" she called gently. "Let me in. *Please* let me in."

Peter made an unfortunate choice. He finished the note that he was writing. He had intended to make it curt and deadly, but he added flourishes and then, carried away with what he was writing, made a fresh copy. Time went by.

"Oh, *Peter!*" Sarah, standing waiting outside the door was shocked by his silence, shocked for both of them. She caught her breath in a gasp and ran away.

Peter heard the little gasp. He retained it somewhere even as he read the final draft of his letter.

*Captain Calvin Collier*
*Aboard the brig* Windshadow.

*Sir:*

*We must put an end to this pursuit and an end to your stupid jokes such as your present to my wife. The pearls lie on the floor of the sea, the atrocity in the bottle floats above them.*

*I wait impatiently for our next meeting. You will generally find me at home. My address will be Dune House, Oceanside, Wellfleet, Mass.*

*I shall be there until we have completed the matter between us.*

*Peter Garrett*

He addressed the letter care of a notorious tavern

in Salem where pirates, privateers and their fellow businessmen visited whenever they had a hold full of booty to dispose of.

The letter would be received almost at once by someone who would carry it to the brig which was no doubt still in these waters, hovering. Peter had felt him hovering over his life for a long time.

Sarah's little gasp now came to the forefront of his memory. He put the note in his pocket and ran to the chart room door. Good God, how much time had gone by? He found only a crumpled bow from Sarah's dress in front of the door. He picked it up carefully and went up on deck to give the note to one of his crew with instructions to deliver it as soon as they anchored in Salem harbor.

By the time Peter came down to the cabin, Sarah was in bed. Her dress lay in a heap on the floor. She held the covers up to her chin. Her wide open, luminous eyes sparkled with fury. She had waited too long in the dark corridor and pleaded too tenderly.

Peter stared at her. "I've hurt you." His voice expressed his misery.

Ah, thought Sarah, this is like the episode with the dog. Peter feels as I did then . . . the bond between!

Peter went over to her. He caressed her face, his hand tentative, unsure. "Forgive . . ."

"Good night," she said coldly. "I plan to sleep."

"Sarah, I . . . something I *had* to finish in there. I couldn't . . ."

Her laugh was a musical trill full of feminine menace.

"So now at last, you have time for lesser things?" she asked.

122

He smiled wryly, pleadingly, to let her know that he shared everything and understood that she must be this way . . . now. The door to his secretive nature was ajar and his love illumined his face.

"I love you," he said simply. "There is nothing that you can say or be that I will not love."

"Get away from me." Sarah turned cold at her own words. "Because I don't even like you."

Peter hesitated with the puzzled expression of a man who realizes that he has just been shot. He turned away without a word but, for some inexplicable reason, he began gathering up his night clothes and cap. He looked as stately as possible during the performance of this homely duty but his face was blurred with misery and he seemed to be amazed that he was doing this of all things, *now*.

His back looked self-conscious as he walked away. The tassel ornament from the top of his nightcap came off and fell to the floor.

"Oh Peter," Sarah called in a sweet, clear voice. "You have left me your tassel to make a night of it. Thank you, oh *thank* you."

Her laugh rang out with hysterical hilarity. "There it is," she cried. "That thread of comedy in the tapestry I told you about. Only this time it is your tassel, in memoriam."

Peter turned and stared at the tassel as if he could find an answer in it to the general perversity of things. He threw his night clothes into the corner of the room and went out.

Meanwhile his wife pounded her pillow and looked up to the ceiling as if to implore the powers that be to take some of the burden of this joke away from her.

At last, still gasping with laughter, Sarah pulled the sheet up over her rosy face and to her surprise discovered that she was crying.

# Chapter ten

*The earth gave a tremor
of defeat,
as the hairy talons
hooked over the threshold
of the Universe
and the fearsome face
looked in.*

The gulf between Sarah and Peter widened since neither of them would reach across it. In their hearts they called out to each other but in fact they were silent.

During the next few days, Peter became even more fastidious than usual. His handsome narrow face seemed glossy with cleanliness. He shaved twice a day.

Peter is determined not to offend even by some trifle in his appearance, thought Sarah with tigerish satisfaction, although she too reached for perfection in her manner and appearance.

One hot afternoon, still moored in Salem harbor, Peter sat alone on deck. Gulls wheeled around him and floated serene and arrogant on the water. The sordid flotsam of the harbor was more agreeable than water lilies to them.

The crew had gone ashore, as had Sarah to whom Peter had given an unusually large sum of money. "Get anything you want for yourself or for our house," he had said, proudly offhand.

"Thank you," she had replied with a formal nod.

Two of the crew had gone with her to protect her

and to carry packages. The young sailor with twig legs had been dispatched two days ago to that certain tavern in Salem. He had delivered Peter's letter there and checked in the next day to find out if it had been delivered. It had.

As the day wore on, purchases of every size and shape began to arrive aboard the *Challenger*. Peter put his chin in his hand and sat listening to the shouts of the sailors and to the carts rumbling over the cobblestones of the port. The heat of the afternoon became heavier and more oppressive; still the packages arrived, piling up now on the dock below.

Peter got up and walked the deck. Once he pressed his hand against his money case as if he felt a twinge there. He gave a loud, lonely yawn and kicked at one of the boxes curiously.

"The lady is extravagant, isn't she? Your bank account must be throbbing like living flesh," said a deep flexible voice.

Even as Peter whirled about, he knew that Captain Collier would be sitting on the boom, his head against the mast, in his favorite position, and he was.

His open shirt revealed his big torso and his stomach held in hard by muscle and vanity. He gave the impression of having been there for some time, watching Peter and smiling his joyful, feral smile.

"Shut your mouth, dear boy," he said. "You will look less stupid." Captain Collier shook his vigorous brown hair which was burned with sun and rimed with salt. "As you see, I pay you the compliment of coming in person to accept your kind invitation to your country estate." He threw back his head to give his laughter full throat.

"So you threw the pearls away? Too bad. They came off one of Napoleon's ships which I overtook in the line of duty. Very fine quality like all my gifts—particularly the ear, once a prized possession of its previous owner who was forced to part with it due to circumstances beyond his control. Oh well . . . it was only a token, a reminder among your joys not to forget absent friends."

The captain gave a relaxed chuckle. Like most talented talkers, he enjoyed the sound of his own voice and its amazing range.

"Tell your hirelings to look sharp, I may drop in and pay a visit to your country estate unannounced." He shook with laughter. "I hope you haven't thrown away your fortune to buy a place in which to entertain me. That *would* be too bad. I can always adapt myself to simple surroundings. However, dear boy, there *is* something very appropriate about you spending your bounty money, your informer's money, on me!"

Peter ran over to his coat but he had for the first time neglected to bring his gun on deck.

"I see that your disillusioned bride," the captain gave a broad grin, "has gone shopping. As a substitute, I presume." He waved a hand at the boxes, leaned down, ripped one of them open with the end of his sword and lifted a dress high on its point.

"*Very* nice. A charming outline," said the captain.

However long anticipated, his sudden presence affected Peter like the paralyzing tonic with which a spider injects its victims. He pulled himself together with a visible effort of will and drew his sword.

"Get it over with," he cried. "After all, this place is

as good as any other for what must be." His face filled with sunset courage. "You damned pirate, hiding behind Letters of Marque! I'll rob the gallows of you."

A puff of wind ruffled Captain Collier's wiry hair as he and three gulls who were perched on the stern of the sloop regarded Peter with interest. The captain waited until Peter's sword arm, too long taut, began a tremor like that of a sentry holding a salute past bearing.

Suddenly, the captain jumped down from the boom, his knees like springs. He dipped in under Peter's guard quick as a darting lizard, seized his wrist and forced it to ram his sword into the mainmast. Then with his dagger, he made a light surface cut on Peter's throat. The struggle, however, had taken more strength than the captain cared to show. His white teeth gleamed in a smile as he controlled his panting breath.

Peter, now freed, picked up a wooden case and hurled it at the captain who leaped lightly onto the rail of the sloop where he balanced with ease.

"I misread your invitation," said Captain Collier. "Was it for your funeral?"

"We'll see who dies." Peter looked up with widening eyes as Captain Collier removed a wooden pin from the rigging and hurled it to catch Peter as he ducked. Peter reeled back and fell.

He was out for a few minutes while Captain Collier jumped down and sat on one of the packing boxes, whistling a tune. When Peter opened his eyes, the captain said, "Shall we talk now and exercise later?"

Peter got to his knees, wrenched his sword from the mast and hurled it. The captain dodged behind the mast but the sword knicked his ear. As he wiped away the blood with the back of his hand, he said, "Congratulations. A little more practice is needed. Pity there won't be time. You lack a fierce quality, dear boy, something to strike terror into your opponent. That desperate look of yours just will not do. Try a snarling yell as you charge."

Peter rushed him, but the captain knocked him down and stood on his back. Two of Peter's ribs cracked under his weight. Stooping so that he could see Peter's profile, the captain said, "I hope my little gift did not upset your bride on her wedding trip." He laughed. "Or much worse, *you*, dear boy. What a disaster, becalmed in the marriage bed!"

The captain's accurate guess infuriated Peter to the extent of giving him a surge of strength. He turned over, knocking the man off his back.

The captain's mood changed. Before Peter could get up, he held his dagger an inch from Peter's eye. His handsome face with its deep dimples and its vigor that so often drained others of initiative, now paled with the force of his anger.

"I may do it, and you know that." He flipped Peter over and clamped a hand on his neck, keeping his dagger near the eye.

Peter, thinking himself at the end, had a quietness in his face; no pleading, just a disconcerting, patient waiting.

"But I won't." The captain shuddered. He let Peter up. then gave him a blow on the head that sent him reeling against the mast. Looking down at his hand bloody from the slight cut he had given Peter's neck, the captain yelled in mock surprise, "Why, it's red! I thought of course it would be pale pink." He wiped his hand on the furled mainsail.

Peter, taking shallow breaths because of the pain

in his broken ribs, went over to retrieve his sword.

As he turned, he found the captain's dagger poised over his heart. It pricked him here and there as he spoke. "Always dressed in the latest fashion, eh, Garrett? And inside this lean skull is a brain as hard as a brain coral, hardened to all gratitude or pricks of conscience—like *this*." He gave him a nudge with his dagger. "But that brain holds a pearl of integrity, a black pearl. The kind of integrity that always rewards a good turn, like the rescue of a poor officer marooned by his men, who rightly loathed him."

Peter shook his head in an effort to clear it. Memory flung him back to join present and past horrors.

"I saved your life one too many times from my murderous crew who at first sight knew you for what you are, you high minded barracuda. Well, let's have at it. I'm ready to hack out that pearl of integrity and wear it on a chain—or shall I spare your life yet again?"

He raised his sword above Peter's head, his teeth bared in a grin.

"I've always been squeamish about killing except in a fight but this is a justified execution. Get down on your knees." He kicked him. "There—that's becoming to you."

He put a foot up on a box and felt the edge of his sword with his thumb. "Suppose I slice you three ways. Will each portion wiggle up wormlike and inform on its savior as it wipes a nasty snuffle with the edge of a handkerchief?"

Captain Collier gave a shudder of hatred that came from deep in the loam where the roots of memory mingle.

Peter, looking up, saw his certain death. His face changed and took on a hapless, surprised, half-relieved look. Captain Collier had seen it before on the faces of dying men. Not by nature a killer except in legitimate battle, the captain stayed his hand.

"No," he said. "After all, an execution, however just, is not to my liking. I'll let you go for now. You don't understand this, of course. If you had me at such a disadvantage, you would follow through. Well, I don't understand it either, except that I have never had a taste for killing except in self-defense. Now, should I accept your kind invitation to visit and find you surrounded by your hired ruffians—oh yes, I have ways of finding things out about you—then, oh *then* I would give you a battle to the death and of course win. Get up."

Peter stood up, measuring the distance to his sword.

"By the way," the captain went on, "this murderous invitation of yours is a change of moral climate for you, isn't it? No more shifting your location every night on your fast sloop or slipping into one harbor after another. Now you ring yourself all around with assassins and sing a siren song to me. In other words, foul means to a desired end. This lowers you far beneath a privateer who, after all, has his Letters of Marque from the King's Navy, along with several other Navies." He gave a warm roar of laughter and pricked Peter several times with his sword point.

"Let's think this through, dear boy. You have become a classic case of a man who hates the man he has injured."

"What about you?" Peter asked.

"My red-blooded actions are inspired by revenge,

132

which has been called by Montaigne a kind of wild justice."

While the captain was talking, Peter, having located his sword, gathered himself together and suddenly sprang for it. He gripped the handle until his knuckles were white and slowly advanced while the captain laughingly watched him.

"Expediency is something you never stooped to aboard my brig," said the captain.

"I do now!" Peter rushed at him.

"Then I win in every sense of the word." The captain eluded Peter's charge with easy grace. He clashed his sword against Peter's sword but, in the short struggle that followed, Peter's nervous strength was undermined by the captain's easy laughter as he backed Peter against the hatch and, seizing his sword, threw it overboard.

"That will be all the sport for now." Captain Collier sheathed his sword. "The only excuse you ever had for your terrible action was compelling honesty. You have killed that and are now a moral suicide. The rest, the carcass, can follow at my leisure."

He drew himself up on the rail and stood there balancing easily above his small boat.

"Speaking of carcasses, you are already putrefying, dear boy. The sea change is visible. It takes a strong man to hate without internal damage. The secret lies in making sure of an equal amount of loving something—life, for instance."

Peter slowly eased toward the rail to push him over, hoping he would hit his head on his small boat and drown.

The captain stood outlined against the hot, clear sky. His clothes, threadbare with age and weather, seemed to have grown onto his muscular torso. An effluvium of male energy and salty sweat enhanced the racy lines of the *Challenger* like the last dab of perfume a beauty gives to her person.

"Nice boat," said the captain, looking around. "One of these days, I'll take it over. Well, goodbye, dear boy. At my convenience, I'll drop in to call on you alone and finish our business, having first skewered your men as an appetizer."

As Peter leaped for the rail, the captain dropped lightly into his boat. His laughter mingled with the splash of his rowing.

The three gulls that had been sitting on the stern flew away at the same time, flapping close to Peter with derisive screams.

# *Chapter eleven*

*We do not truly see each other*
*due to low visibility*
*of the heart.*
*A heavy fog hangs low*
*hiding the full landscape*
*from the light.*

The trip home differed in every way from the saturnalia of the wedding trip. The crew was in good order, the brights shone, the wine was securely corked and there was no music and no amorous young couple to listen to it. The moon shone on a bare deck.

Sarah and Peter had let their quarrel ossify too long. When she had come back to the ship from her shopping expedition, flushed and a little drunk with buying, exhilarated with the novelty of being able to purchase whatever she wanted, she was more than ready to call a truce.

But Peter, stiff with the crunching pain in his ribs and with his mind entirely on Captain Collier and his own humiliation, had been cold and distant with her. The mess on deck, he explained, as well as the damage to himself, was the work of vandals from port, whom he had fought off.

Later that night, Sarah came to the chart room, full of proud words designed to hurt him and relieve her, but when she saw him lying on the bunk, staring somberly at the ceiling, he seemed so forlorn and alone that she ran to him.

136

"Oh, Peter, what's the matter?" she asked softly.

Peter sat up. He looked into her eyes and started to take her in his arms but a stabbing pain in his ribs made him wince and turn his head.

Sarah gave a little cry of outrage. "If that's the way you feel about me . . ." Proud, angry words poured out before he could explain. "So," she finished, "I will leave you and go home." She paused in her tirade, to look at him in dismay as if begging him to stop her.

"Yes, yes, you must do that," he said earnestly. "I've been lying here thinking the same thing. Go back to Zenas for a little while. To stay with me in the dune house now is . . . is unthinkable."

She looked at him incredulously. "Suppose I say no?"

"But you just finished saying that you wanted to."

"That was before I knew that *you* wanted me to!" She ran from the room, realizing that she had put on a thoroughly feminine and unreasonable performance and even relishing it.

By the time they reached Wellfleet, Peter's ribs were nearly healed but his marriage was badly damaged. He had tried to leave Sarah off at her father's house until, he said, the new house on the dunes was ready for her—until, he told himself, Captain Collier had paid his promised visit.

Sarah refused indignantly. "What? Unloaded at harbor after the voyage with the whole town gossiping? Never!"

They stopped off at several taverns to leave messages for Zenas, inviting him for supper, and finally they started across Cape for their new home.

Peter had purchased the dog, Otis, from the cook on the *Challenger* at Sarah's request. He now filled

137

the back of the carriage with his big tan body and with sound as he sat up barking at everything.

Up front, however, all was silent although Sarah's warm and exuberant nature would have broken though their quarrel long ago if Peter's pride had allowed the slightest gesture of affection.

When they came out of the woods and turned up the sandy road to the house on the dunes, Sarah leaped out of the carriage, crying, "Oh how lovely!"

She raced through the beach grass to the edge of the cliff where she drew a deep breath and looked down over the perfect white curve of the sand bank twenty feet below to the sonorous beach.

A growing northeast wind whipped the breakers until they shook their crests and charged down on the sand. Sarah let the dash and roar fill her. She used to come here as a child and the ecstasy she had felt then had left its mark like a streak of lightning etched on her memory.

She slipped off her shoes and stockings and dug her toes into the sandy cliff. Peter came up to her and together they went into the house. It seemed immense compared to her father's tiny cottage or the confines of the *Challenger*. The thunder of surf followed her through every room.

"It is like living in the heart of a giant shell!" she cried.

Sarah loved all of the fine, soundly built house but she cried out with pleasure when she went up to the new tower room high on one side of the roof with a casement window overlooking a slice of ocean through the dip in the cliff. A ladder made of rope led all the way from the beach up through the break in the cliff and over the roof to the tower window.

"Why?" Sarah asked. "Why bring the ladder up here?"

Peter was scowling out through the window. "The fools have built my tower so that it only looks out over a small section of water. I wanted a wide view."

"A spyglass on a stand!" she cried. "I can see a ship through it, far away on the horizon. It seems to float in air. And over there—see it?—closer to shore, a phalarope on the crest of a wave, smug as an old lady in an armchair. Now he's changed from the crest of one wave to another. We're in for a storm, he's telling us that. And listen, we can hear the northeast wind hurling sand on the house!"

Sarah caught her breath. "Oh Peter, we have both forgotten our fight. We are talking as if everything was all right between us."

She laughed, clasping her hands. "I forgive you for being such a cold, secretive codfish. And do you forgive my horrid flash temper?"

Peter nodded. He put his arms around her.

"And we're together again." She kissed him.

"How soon will Zenas be here, do you think?" Moving away from her, Peter looked through the telescope at the distant ship.

"Who knows? He must have been out in the bay after stripers but he'll be along as soon as he gets our message. I hope it's tonight. I'd better go take a look at the kitchen and supplies, and the stable."

It's *essential* that Zenas visit and leave early, Peter thought as he tried to recognize the boat. It was a brig and could be the *Windshadow,* but she was too far out to determine.

Crouching intently behind the telescope, Peter was not aware of his wife's return until something ominous about her silence and stillness made him turn around.

"Peter, who is that man out in the stables? I love my gray gelding, thank you, although I don't know how to ride unless a bridle is like a rudder. But Peter, that *man*—why is he here?"

"Who, Comstock?" Peter paled, but said evenly, "He's here to take care of the horses and carriage. Why?"

"He's horrible. The horses don't mind him but I do."

Peter's face was defensive.

"And who is that creature in the kitchen? I went in to find the makings for a clam pie or a chowder." Sarah gave a gesture of disgust.

"That must be Zeke. I don't want my wife to cook. So just bear with him a little while and then, since you don't like him, we'll find someone else."

"*Like* him! I doubt if his *mother* does! I tried not to look at his horrible buck teeth so I looked down at his huge hands. 'Never have to worry about my hands preparing your food, Mam,' he said. 'They're clean as sand.' And he held them out to me. Terrible hands, thick nails, swollen lined knuckles with black hair on them like tufts of beach grass. A vulture's claws.

"Oh Peter, get rid of these frightening servants. I'll cook and you take care of the horses. We don't need anyone. What else have we got to do?"

"Later, I promise I'll get the cook from the *Challenger* up here and some of her crew."

"Why later? Do it now."

"If you want me to, I'll send Zeke out of the house to stay with the others."

"Send him. But *what* others, Peter?"

"Just the men who were building this tower room

140

for me. A . . . call it a land crew."

"But why do we need them now, and where are they all?"

"Further down the dunes, out of sight. They've built themselves some huts in a sheltered spot."

"Why?"

"They like it there."

"Peter, get them out! They are dangerous men to have hanging around us."

"I promise they will be gone in a little while."

"Why even a little while?"

"They'll *go*. I give you my word."

"When?"

"Soon."

"Peter, tell me what this trouble is and I'll help you with it. If it's got to be a secret, I'll close over it like a sea clam."

She leaned toward him, her luminous eyes full upon him. "Why won't you trust me? Don't you *see* how wild it makes me to be shut out?"

Peter reached out and held her with frantic tenderness. The rising wind threw a swirl of sand against the window. He jumped convulsively and Sarah gave a little scream. "What is it? What are you afraid of? You're as tense as a line playing a ten-pound bass."

Peter dropped his arms. "Afraid? Never! Would I be summoning what I fear?"

"What *are* you summoning, Peter?"

He made an angular, nervous gesture. "I can't tell you, not now."

"Is it someone from the sea? Is that why you had the men build this tower room with its rope ladder hanging down to the beach? I don't like it." She shuddered. "Cut it away, Peter. When the moon is

141

full, I may dream of ghosts coming up the rope ladder—the ghosts of dead sailors come to haunt the Mooncussers who killed them."

Peter's obsession extended the image. "I may dream too—that *he* is at the bottom of the sea and still coming up the rope ladder, laughing and holding in his drowned, bloated stomach with his damned ego."

"He sounds like a marvel. Who is it? Captain Dear Friend? I feel sorry for the poor, hearty laugher, climbing into this trap. Is it sporting of you, Peter?"

Peter gave her a cold, withdrawn look. "Sarah, it is useless to pry. I can't tell you," he said. He turned back to the telescope.

Sarah hit it a blow that sent it spinning on its stand. "All *right*, Peter! It's no use trying to get back where we were." Deprive him, she thought. He deprives me and fills our place with horrible servants, refuses to explain, refuses to confide, *refuses*. "From now on," she shouted, "no love, nothing. Zero!" The corners of her mouth turned up. "That applies to you *only!*"

Peter had to restrain the childish gesture of putting his hands over his ears, to insulate himself from hearing her words. Instead, he adjusted the telescope.

"At least your spyglass is at attention." Sarah tried to hurt. "Ever since that night the ear came, lovemaking has been at low, low tide." Her carillion of laughter filled the room. "Being a bitch can be strong, heady drink," she laughed.

Peter was silent.

"Talk!" she cried. "Say something, fight with me! Do you want me to leave you alone here in this stormy house with those ruffians you've hired? Just say the word."

"Yes." Peter's lips were white.

"You *do?*" She was shocked "Then, damn you, I'll stay!" Her laughter echoed as she ran down the steep, winding stairs to her bedroom where she tore open boxes until she came to her new riding habit. Zenas would be on his way before long. She would get on her horse and ride to meet him. Why not? Surely a horse was no harder to handle than a sailboat. She could hardly wait to see a sensible human being. Her father had no secret to erode him, only alcohol.

The riding habit was a puzzle, she had not tried it on in the shop. Furthermore, she was shaking and stupid with anger. But riding to meet her father and wearing her new plumed hat was a picture she had formed on the voyage—his dismay at seeing her all fancied up and how she would laugh and put the hat on the horse's head and get off to walk with Zenas.

The groom, Comstock, saddled and bridled the gelding for her and offered to help her mount. Sarah waved him away. She could smell Mooncusser all over him. His small commonplace features were creased in vicious lines that would have suited more brutal features and all the more unsavory on his neat small face. His skin was as pocked as the moon.

Otis, who had been following Sarah, took a dislike to Comstock and started a deep rumbling in his throat. Comstock kept his distance.

After several clumsy tries, Sarah mounted and jogged along, hitting the horse's back in countless different positions. When at last she whipped through the scrub blueberry bushes and out onto the sandy road, she saw a tall, distant figure walking with familiar vigor.

Sarah was not disturbed by the fact that she had flouted her father, run away with someone he despised and was now married to him. What of it? A seafaring man should understand such crosscurrents in the water and the same in human nature. She eagerly rode to meet him and, giving a joyful shout, slid off her horse and went toward him with the swift resolute pace of a woman who has walked over sand all her life.

She tore off her plumed hat and hurled it on to a bush where it swayed in the wind. Next, her boots were left by the wayside. She ran barefoot down the sandy road and jumped into his arms.

They said nothing but each held the other as a drowning person holds a floating spar.

"Well, by Christ," Zenas said at last. "What do you think you're wearing?" He turned away to hide the moisture in his eyes.

"Nothing that looks right here on the dunes," she said.

"Never mind. Look here." He pulled a neat package out from under his arm. Sarah imagined his dextrous fingers knotting, splicing the string together just as he repaired his fishing lines. "You've brought my old blue linen dress!" she cried.

"Yes, thought you'd be needing it."

"I do. Oh, I do!" She stroked the soft, worn material and thought of all those new dresses from Salem that had never felt the touch of sun or salt. "I need it very much," she said.

"That waddling mutt your dog?" Zenas asked.

"He's a friend of mine. Be polite to him or I'll sic him on you," Sarah said.

They walked back to where she had left the gelding, munching what grass he could find.

"This yours too?" Zenas asked.

"Yes, but I can hardly stay on. If I don't slip off to starboard, then I drag on the port side." She retrieved her plumed hat and put it on the gelding. Her laugh rang out but Zenas's creaky laughter sounded as if it had been in dry dock lately and this saddened her.

"I have lots of other things I don't need," she said. "He sent me into Salem alone and I bought everything in sight. I wonder why."

"Could be revenge." Zenas knew women. "You were stabbing him in the pocket again and again. Or sometimes it's dissipation. Women go through a store buying right and left, roaring drunk without a drop of liquor in them."

"I was both," Sarah said.

Zenas picked up the gelding's reins and hurled Sarah's hat up in a tree where it remained like a tropical bird with its plumes nodding in the wind. They left the gelding at the stable and Sarah led Zenas over the little islands of poverty grass to the house.

"Where is he?" Somehow Zenas balked at calling him "Peter."

"Out looking for me, I suppose," Sarah said casually. "I didn't tell him where I was going." Zenas looked at her intently. "Come on, Father, let's go on a tour of the house." She avoided his eyes and took his hand.

"Well, it's a Goddamn sound house," said Zenas as he sat down in the tower room beside the open casement window. The north wind blew over his old clean fisherman's clothes and all of Zenas seemed to sparkle in the fading light.

Sarah looked at him fondly. He smells as salty as a cod barrel, she thought, and he's carved by the wind and seasoned with weather. A good Cape man. She had missed him.

Zenas put his chin on his hand and looked her over. "Christ, but that's a horrible thing you're wearing."

"I know it is," she laughed. "It's too elegant for this place."

"Like it here?" Zenas ached with loneliness behind these few wary words. Why couldn't they have settled in Wellfleet instead of out here on this desolate cliff?

"Like it? I've only been here a few hours. I don't know—the surf's pounding at me, the wind's shaking the house. I think . . . . you don't just *like* a place like this, you either cannot stand it, or it becomes a part of you."

She stood looking down into his face and Zenas noticed new lines of discontent by her mouth and the nervous brilliance of her eyes. He felt a wince of the heart. She was not the old joyful Sarah.

"Well," he said. "Now you have your fine gentleman, God rest your mother's busy old bones. Are you content?"

Sarah looked at him in surprise. Lately her mother had been as hard to recall as a sail after it drops over the horizon. "Sometimes I'm happy. Let's say yes and no," she replied.

"Who said anything about happy? Women! Sitting around asking their little selves if they are happy. Christ, what's happy? We're not charted for perfect weather. Why, damn it, you should all have a whack on the rump and be put to work at the shipyards!"

146

"A lot of us would like nothing better," Sarah said. "That's the same tonic you were always recommending for Mother."

"Your mother," he said darkly, "was a Boston Bluestocking who spent too much time probing into our marriage. Be warned."

"Against probing? I defy anyone to understand the surface of things here, let alone pry underneath them."

"Oho," Zenas looked thoughtful. "Ever find out about his dealings at Wreckers' Tavern?"

"Oh, that." Sarah waved it away. "It was only wine. But strangely enough, some of the same men who . . ."

She almost told him everything but held back, a habit of restraint with him about some things due to a fear of his furious action. Anyway it took a very warm tide to open the tight valves of confidence between parent and child.

She looked at him, admiring the proud set of his head and the easy way he sat in his chair as if he were quietly riding out a high wind. That would be a good way to go through life. She gave a sharp sigh and the moment for sharing her foreboding with him passed by.

"This is going to be a Christ damn interesting meeting," Zenas said. "I wasn't overly polite to your husband when I last saw him. Can't remember just what I said." He laughed, remembering perfectly.

"He must have forgiven you, Father. He tried to send you a big present—me. So, of course, I am going to stay right here."

"Bitches, all of you," Zenas said. "But it is a *little* too damn soon to send you back. It was a good two months and a half to the day before I was ready to

147

jettison your mother."

Between breakers they could hear the thud of galloping hoofs. "Here he comes now," Sarah said. "He's been out looking for me, worried no doubt." She gave a shrug but her lips twitched with a pleased smile.

"Sarah! Sarah, are you home?" Peter called by the front door.

Sarah waited a few moments, then called calmly, "Yes, I'm up in the tower."

"Hell's tide, what a welcome!" Zenas eyed his daughter in surprise.

Peter bounded up the stairs. His face lighted up when he saw Sarah. "I was looking all over for you. It's not wise for you to go out alone here. It'll be different when we get the crew from the *Challenger* up here. Then you . . . Oh—excuse me, sir." He saw Zenas, turned to him, and held out his hand. "I'm glad to see you."

Zenas nodded as they shook hands. His sharp gray eyes appraised the young man. That cocky look was gone, that air of a young hero leading a regiment to certain death, so irritating to Zenas, was washed away. His face seemed hollowed and shadowy under its tan. Married! Zenas's sympathies shifted a little. Here was another male creature with wife trouble. That could account for most of the change in him. The Yankee squint had given way to a wide open look of melancholy and despair. Zenas had seen the same look on the faces of men who set sail under a crazy captain and knew that they would never return. There was more here than the simple catastrophe of marriage!

Dinner was served crudely in the low-beamed dining room. When the cook came in to remove the plates and bring the wild blueberry pudding, Sarah looked away from his hands, but Zenas watched him curiously until he went back into the kitchen.

"That's an unusual kind of man to have inside the house," Zenas said.

Peter's face grew secretive and stubborn. He made no reply.

Zenas said nothing more but Sarah could see the old suspicions crease his face. However, he sat easily in his clean, faded clothes, eating without grace but in a forthright way, his own man in all circumstances.

After supper, they sat out by the dunes where the rising wind stung them with sand. "Storm coming," said Zenas. "Don't know if we'll be comfortable out here for long."

The wind and the rolling roar of the breakers suited Sarah's mood. "Good, I long for a storm," she said with such emphasis that the two men were surprised and felt uneasy.

Zenas wondered how satisfying their lovemaking was. Discreetly he spoke of something else. "A good night for Mooncussers," he said.

"What exactly are Mooncussers?" Peter asked. "Both you and Sarah have used that word several times."

"You off-Cape furriner," said Zenas. "You had them breathing down your neck there in your favorite tavern."

"Wreckers' Tavern? Are the men there wreckers?"

"Far from it," said Zenas. "What we call wrecking is a legitimate, everyday business on the Cape. The collecting of salvage is an important occupation here."

"Legitimate? I thought it was all against the law,"

149

Peter said. "Salvage should belong to the owners of the wrecked ship."

"What! Here on the wood-starved lower Cape? Why, every Goddamned spar that comes up on the beach is put to use. My own roof is shaped from the hull that fathered it."

"There *is* a kind of law," Sarah said. "A wreck must be reported at once to the town clerk. That's all."

"And the place to find *him*," said Zenas, "is on the beach loading up his dray. A few Sundays ago, a minister in Truro got word that a wreck had come ashore on a nearby beach. He told his congregation to bow their heads for five minutes in silent prayer for the shipwrecked sailors. Damned if he didn't tiptoe out of the church while they were praying and get his cart and drive across Cape to the beach well ahead of his flock!" Zenas howled with laughter. Otis lying near them sat up and looked at him with the air of a connoisseur.

"I can't believe it," Peter said. "The whole of Cape Cod condoning, even joining in . . ?"

"Why, God damn it, do you take us for Mooncussers?" Zenas broke in.

"Is there some fine distinction between Mooncussers and wreckers?"

Peter's air of rectitude was beginning to get under Zenas's skin. He gave him a level stare. "For a man who keeps such dainty company as the folk in Wreckers' Tavern, you ask a lot of fool questions. Wrecking is a windfall. If a branch fell off your neighbor's apple tree into your yard, you'd eat the damn apples. That's wrecking. But if you sawed off the limb of the apple tree with your neighbor sitting on it and killed him to get the apples, that would be mooncussing."

"The way I see it," Peter said, "the apples belong to the neighbor no matter how they got into someone else's yard and the wreckage of any ship belongs to its owner. I may have a narrow Boston mind, but I'd call it all Mooncussing."

"The hell you say!" Zenas sprang up from the dune where they were sitting. "Be careful how you go throwing that name around."

"Peter," Sarah intervened, "you don't understand. The men we call Mooncussers go down to the beach on a stormy dark night like this one and swing a lantern on a pole until some poor storm-tossed captain far out on the water takes the light for another ship. He sets his course to follow and breaks up on the shoals unless the moon comes out in time to light the beach and save him."

"That's when the men on the beach cuss hell out of the moon," said Zenas. "Almost drive her back behind a cloud."

Peter sprang up and looked out over the water. "There is a sail out there," Something ravenous twisted his face. They looked at him curiously.

"You seem excited at the prospect of a ship foundering." Zenas spoke harshly.

"No, no. I just wondered in the case of Mooncussers, what becomes of the survivors. Surely they can't afford to have their deed reported."

"If any get off the wreck," Zenas said, "and through the surf and pass by the men with the grappling hooks alive, then they will meet the Mooncussers' women standing in the foam, skirts hiked up, swinging a brick in a stocking."

Peter went over to the edge of the cliff and looked down at the towering surf. "So no one gets through," he said. He turned back to the others,

151

adjusting his white stock. "I am shocked that all this murderous business you call Mooncussing has not been called to the attention of the Commonwealth," he said to Zenas. "As soon as I get squared away here, I intend to do something about it. I have always tried, as an honest citizen, to do my duty however difficult."

"You Goddamned prig! Mind your own business," Zenas shouted. "You make a public outcry and all legitimate wrecking will be banned. We are taking care of it in our own way, with muffled oar-locks. We have a private citizens' court trial and sentence. There are two bottomless ponds between here and the town that have seen a lot of Mooncussers go down. But someone is protecting our Wellfleet Mooncussers. Sooner or later, we'll get him."

"That's not the right way to take care of it," Peter said. "The authorities should be . . ."

Zenas was enraged. "It's *our* way of taking care of it, you fishy-eyed hypocrite! I don't know what you're up to out here, but it smells like a hold full of fish becalmed in hot sun. And I don't give a single small slice of Goddamn for your opinion!"

Zenas turned away. "Goodbye," he barked over his shoulder as he began striding over the beach grass which was now whipped flat by the rising wind.

"Wait," Peter called after him. "I have something to ask you. Take Sarah with you. I need time to . . . to change my land crew. It's far better for her to be away."

Sarah caught Peter by the arm and looked up at him. Her eyes were fierce as a sea hawk's. "I'll go, but only as far as the road." And she was gone, flinging off her shoes as she ran.

"Sarah, go with him. I'll come for you later. Sarah, *go*." He ran after them but Sarah turned and drew herself up with so furious a look that he stopped short. The wind tore her name from his mouth as Zenas and his daughter disappeared in the shadows.

"Loving bastard, isn't he?" Zenas said. "Are you going back there?"

"Of course," Sarah said. "How can I leave him alone with his wild plan and what it may bring him?"

The crash and roar of the breakers grew fainter as they walked over the islands of poverty grass and beach pea. A kildeer plover, disturbed from its nest, soared up and filled the air with its protest.

"It didn't help matters to call Peter a fishy eyed hypocrite," she added.

"Earned it," said Zenas. "Your husband's a mixed up fool. Is he hiding from someone here on the dunes with those ugly bodyguards of his?"

"No, I think he must be waiting for someone."

"Who?"

Sarah shrugged and pulled her long hair out of her face as the wind whipped around her. "I can't get him to tell me."

"There must be some knife that will pry open that clam you've married. He's always at low tide so it should be easy. Clam might be empty, though." Zenas broke off his laugh. He was in no mood for his usual ironic howl.

They walked on in silence for a few minutes. Then Sarah burst out. "I want the real thing, not half a love. I don't know how to give half a love!"

"The real thing keeps changing its shape like mist before the wind," Zenas said. "I'll be God-

153

damned if I know what the real thing is, or if anyone knows." He ached with longing to help her.

"I'll know when I find it . . . Oh, I'll know then."

"Maybe," said Zenas.

When they came to the main road across Cape, he said, "If you need me, get on your fancy gray horse and cross to the harbor. You can always come home, you know."

"No. I can't ever go home again, not all the way, you know that. Will you come here, often, *please?*"

"I might," said Zenas. He turned to wave at her before the bend in the road hid him from sight.

Sarah turned toward the dunes where the sand was softer beneath her bare feet. Heavy clouds hid the rising moon. It was dusk, the hour when shadows and people look alike. Down below the cliff, the wind lifted the ocean high and hurled it down on the beach.

Sarah, standing at the edge of the cliff, watched the white crested breakers floating like gulls far out on the darkening water. In the sucking hush before a wave broke, she heard a deep voice behind her say,

"Tonight . . . if the cussed moon stays dark."

# Chapter twelve

*Who hears*
*the sandpiper's*
*final peep*
*as he misjudges*
*the might*
*of a towering wave!*

arah gave a faint cry as she turned. Shadows began to move, join together and come toward her. One of them outstripped the rest with great clumping strides.

At first she felt no fear, having no previous grooves of fear for this one to run along. But, as she strained to see in the fading light, fear came in a rush. A huge woman suddenly loomed over her, a woman with a pale, wide face and thick brows that met across her nose.

Sarah, terrified, stumbled back to the edge of the cliff and fell over, clutching at anything. Her fingers dug into the beach grass turf as she hung suspended.

The big woman kneeled to look at her, not extending her hand. Sarah had seen her before at a distance, going in and out of Wreckers' Tavern. Now the details of this face so close to hers were etched forever on Sarah's brain. The forehead ridged as a tide line and marked with a love of evil. Eroded teeth like old tombstones leaning and, atop it all, the ribboned cap secured with her shawl, to ornament the pitiless face.

"What scared you?" the woman asked. "The sound of my voice?"

Sarah saw the look in her eyes, they seemed to flare in the half light. If she said she had heard anything, she was finished. "No," Sarah whispered. "I heard nothing, nothing. Help me up."

She gave a despairing groan at the stupidity of this request. Help, from this woman?

"You must have heard something. What made you cry out?"

"I was startled. Give me a hand, I'll make it worth your while."

"All looks and no nerve." The big woman laughed into the wind as if exulting over her own ugliness.

Suddenly businesslike, she reached under her skirt and drew out a stocking with a brick in the toe.

A smell of unwashed linen blew at Sarah. This and the white, brutal face formed an impression of evil that held her spellbound as if the woman had extended invisible tentacles like gnarled roots.

"Lying won't help you now," The woman swung the stocking back over her shoulder.

Sarah forced her hands to let go and she slid down the almost perpendicular face of the sandy cliff. The brick pounded into the ledge where her face had been only seconds before and started an avalanche above her. She went down fast and at the bottom was half buried in sand. The weight of her body as it landed and the sand coming down from above her made her almost immobile.

Sarah was dazed for a moment but swiftly recovered, realizing how vulnerable she was with her legs sunk above the knee in sand. Staring up at the cliff, she could make out several shadows slightly darker than the evening sky. She watched

157

them as she tried to free her legs. Now and then her frantic hands scraped a shell against her flesh which hurt beyond belief, as though every nerve in her body was racing just beneath her skin.

Between the intervals of surf, the big woman's voice was powerful enough to reach her. "I tried to," she was saying. "But she fell."

The shadows gesticulated and the big woman leaned over as if to come down the bluff. Sarah kicked her legs free at last and ran down to the wet sand at the water's edge where she could be swift. She raced in scallops between the towering waves, skillful as a sandpiper. But up on the cliff, a huge figure ran along parallel with her—or was it a shadow? She slowed down to see. Did the shadow on the cliff slow down too?

A faint glow came from the crevice in the cliff where the tower loomed with its rope ladder. Sarah ran toward it. Yes, the shadow was moving with her. She could hear Otis now, barking frantically. He was closed in the house just when she needed him.

It was much darker down here and the sand delayed each step as she ran across the beach in the direction of the rope ladder. The surrounding cliffs hid the direct light of the tower. Well planned, thought Sarah. If the tower has been built by Mooncussers, it will give them no interfering stationary light to warn the ships.

Something swung out of the night and hit her in the face. She prepared to fight for her life, dodging and circling in the dark. But when she paused to listen, she had a sensation of emptiness ahead of her. Nothing was here, no presence in the night. She groped ahead and when the rope ladder hit her again as it swung in the wind, she cried out with thankfulness and climbed all the way up to the tower with frantic speed.

Sarah fell in through the open tower window and lay on the floor catching her breath, her eyes on the window. In a few minutes, rage began to pound her. She jumped up, took one of the guns from the wall and raised it toward the window. Furious at the creature who had caused her so much agony, she would certainly have shot her if she had appeared at that moment. Nausea came over her at the memory of the woman's bestial odor. She wanted to crush her, eliminate her.

I could actually do murder, she thought. Right now, at this moment. I could murder. A chill paralyzed her hands so that the gun seemed to hold itself.

The rope ladder groaned against the window sill and Sarah fired a warning shot high into the night. "Go away," she cried. "If your terrible face comes over this sill, I'll fire into it!"

Peter ran in. He took the gun from her and leaned far out over the ladder, holding a lantern in one hand. "There's no one out there," he said. "For a moment I thought . . ."

Sarah screamed into the wind, "If she comes after me, shoot her!"

"Sarah, what *are* you talking about, and what are you doing here? I thought you had gone home with Zenas."

The sandy wind stung them and the roar of the surf filled the room. Peter forced the window shut against the wind. The sudden quiet calmed them.

"What frightened you?" he asked. "Shadows? The storm?" He reached for the telescope.

"God in Heaven!" screamed Sarah. "Frightened of

159

storms that I've known all my life? Shadows? I'm lucky to be *alive!* Someone tried to murder me!"

"Who?" he asked quickly.

"A huge woman who stank like a wolf."

He relaxed visibly, exhaled and murmured, "That is very unlikely."

"What are you saying?"

"That it's very unlikely, that's all."

"I'll tell you what's unlikely! *You.* A huge woman with a dead white face and eyebrows like dune grass nearly kills me and . . ."

"Mrs. Cassidy!" he said.

"Ah . . . you know her?"

"What would Mrs. Cassidy be doing away from her tavern and out on a stormy night like this?" he asked incredulously. "And why would she try to harm you? It all seems very unlikely."

"If you say unlikely once more, just once more, I'll shoot you, too!"

A gust of wind blew the window open with a crash and Sarah screamed like a gull. Peter leaned out of the black windy square. He could see a portion of the ladder writhing in the wind. The whole house seemed to shudder with the force of the breakers. Out on the water, a light dipped and swayed and was almost extinguished in the water.

"A ship!" Excitement mounted in Peter's voice. "Look out through the dip in the cliff, far out . . . a ship in trouble. See how low its light is, almost dipping in the waves?" He reached for the telescope. "No way to see what she is, brig or barquentine."

"Close that window!" Sarah flew to close it. "Listen to me, Peter, please *listen,* a hideous murderer is out there on the dunes waiting."

Peter's face was filled with the dismay of a man confronted with an hysterical woman. "Come away from the window," he said soothingly. "Sit down and rest."

"Don't you dare humor me," Sarah cried. "All I ask is your attention, your full attention." She stood facing him and told him, very carefully and in detail, the events of the night. When she had finished, his hands no longer strayed toward the telescope and the color had drained from his face.

"They are Mooncussers, here to swing their foul lantern if the night is dark enough," she said.

A chorus of yells rose from the beach.

"What's that?" Sarah tensed.

"It must be my men."

"Why would they be down there on a night like this, unless . . ." Sarah looked full at him. At that moment a discreet knocking sounded on the front door. Otis leaped at it with a roar. The knock increased in volume until it rose above his furious barking.

Peter's face was grave and white as he prepared himself for a deadly appointment. He straightened up, felt his sword, adjusted his gun and went toward the stairway door. "It's just as well that my men were of no use," he said. "It's better this way. It was meant to be."

Sarah could smell the fear that came from him like a sharp chemical on the air. But Peter stood calmly enough and with a curious elation on his face. "I tried to take a detour around this moment but you see, it leads me direct to it." He gave a hollow laugh. Halfway down the stairs, he shouted, "Lock the door after me. Don't come out."

Sarah stood looking after him. He had left with

the sort of wrench of the shoulders of a man about to die heroically. Not sure what to do, she decided to follow him. She looked around for a weapon and found a pistol and some bullets. As she loaded it, she blessed Zenas for teaching her how to shoot. She was on her way when Peter came back into the room.

He flung his sword on the table and said, "That was only Mrs. Cassidy." He looked like a man who has had a reprieve but feels cheated somehow.

"She explained everything," he said.

"How could she?"

"She came here on a kindly impulse, thinking you were unwell, even hysterical out there on the dunes. She came to apologize if in her efforts to follow and help, she frightened you."

Sarah's brows drew together, a look of disgust on her full expressive lips. "You believe *her*? You trust that criminal face?"

"How does her ugliness make her an assassin?"

"What was she doing on the dunes, this hag from Wreckers' Tavern, nest of Mooncussers?"

"She came to bring a message to one of the men who works for me. His wife has just had a baby. You must have been mistaken in what you heard her say."

"I was *not* mistaken."

"The wind was howling."

"You believe her and not me!"

"She even showed me several stockings hanging just under her skirt filled with bottles of rum for the men. She said she could carry more that way."

"It had the outlines of a brick when *I* saw it."

"She asked my permission for the men to cele-brate down on the beach and said to sleep sound

162

and not be alarmed if they fight. They celebrate hard. What could I say? A birth is something I presume they make much of in these parts."

"They are here to celebrate death."

"Sarah, be reasonable."

"Be a reasonable liar?"

"I didn't call you that."

"Then what are you telling me?"

"Just that you perhaps imagined . . ."

"In other words, you trust that evil face."

"Her face is nightmarish, I'll admit that."

"But no more." She gave a bitter laugh.

"If I saw it suddenly at dusk out on the dunes, I might jump back too," he said.

"Right over the cliff?"

"But she reached out to help you."

"What about my mortal terror? What caused that if it was all so benign?"

"I should not have brought you to this lonely place."

"Is that your way of saying that I am a fool who jumps at shadows and imagines them chasing me? No, Peter. I trust myself. I must, for there is no one else."

Peter winced. He took her in his arms but she wrenched away.

He pleaded for her agreement. "Her story *is* plausible, you must admit."

"It is not! Why did she try to bash my head in with what she called a bottle of rum hanging in a stocking? Wasteful of her, wasn't it, since the bottle would have broken over my head? Why didn't it break on the dune instead of starting an avalanche?"

"She explained that, too. She said that in her

efforts to help you she leaned too far over and broke off some of the ledge. It hit you on the head and followed you down. Sarah, why isn't this an acceptable explanation? Why are you so stubbornly determined that . . ."

"Why are you so bullheaded? Explain why your men are carousing down on the beach in the dark in a storm with no fire, nothing that would make a celebration—until a ship breaks apart on the shoals or sand bar. Then they'll do some celebrating."

"Sarah . . ." he sighed. "I didn't plan to have you and the men here at the same time. I thought I could persuade you to visit your father until . . ."

"And have the whole town gossiping about why I've gone home?"

"You must have guessed," he hesitated, "that I hired them as bodyguards."

"Why should I have to guess anything? Why don't you *tell* me?"

"I can't. Not yet."

"Why? Because you would come off badly?"

"Thank you for your confidence."

"Thank you for yours."

"Sarah, be sensible. Bear with me for just a little while until . . ."

*"Sensible!"* Her voice rose. She picked up a compass box and hurled it to the floor. "Oh yes, indeed, we are both so very sensible! I board your boat at dusk to go away with a man I love but hardly know. We sail on and on, drunk with love and illegal wine from a murdered ship. You are corroded with secrets which you hint at but refuse to share. Our only wedding present is an ear in a bottle and some priceless pearls to decorate it. You throw them all overboard, *sensibly,* losing the pearls forever but

somehow the ear stays in our minds while Otis gives the death howl. How very *sensible* it all is, oh yes!"

She picked up a glass on the table and dashed it against the wall. "We come here to the lonely dunes where no one lives and our servants are, quite sensibly, villains. You quarrel with my father and tell me to go, but you say you love me. I am nearly murdered by what you say is a benign woman come to this stormy beach on a motherly errand, so that our villainous servants can rejoice down on the beach in a howling storm. We love each other but a shadow stands between us. Is it Captain Dear Friend? Are we waiting for him to bring us another ear or perhaps collect ours?

"Peter, it is all so very sensible that I am going home to my father who is a fine, proud man, riding as easily on all life's breakers as a phalarope— something you should learn to do! So go down now and join the revels on the beach with that fine trustworthy woman, Mrs. Cassidy. I will not be back. Goodbye, Peter."

Peter stood quietly, enduring this low-pitched but violent tirade. Now and then his eyes deepened or he gave a vulnerable wince. But Sarah could almost see him thrusting aside her words before the terrible urgency of his project. This enraged her the more.

She ran to the door and turning, looked him up and down. An angry gleam came into her eyes; at this moment she looked like Zenas. "Take good care of your—telescope!"

With a furious laugh, she wrenched open the door. Leave, she thought. Take Otis along for protection. Run, run along the cross Cape road through the dark to the other side, to the lights and

165

safety of town.

"Wait . . . *wait*." Peter ran after her, took her arm, held her. "I can't do anything about all this, not now. It's best you go stay with your father." He spoke rapidly. "I'll drive you there. Afterward, if I'm still here, I'll come for you and we can start all over again. Everything will be different. No servants to frighten you. We'll sell this isolated lonely house for whatever we can get and live aboard the *Challenger* for awhile. We may have to cut down on crew but we can both help sail. I will, of course, make another fortune in time but . . ."

Sarah made no attempt to pull away from him. She gave him a long, grave look. "Peter, are you telling me that your money is gone?"

He drew out his handkerchief and brushed the edge of his nose with it. "Some unusual expenses and . . ."

"Is it *gone*, that's all I want to know."

"Nothing that can't be recovered in time."

"Don't be so damnably proud. Peter, is your money all gone *now*?"

"Yes." Peter's face was as white as his handkerchief. He turned away and opened the window. The wind leaped in like a ravening lion and mauled them. She saw a tear on his cheek.

Sarah felt full of grace and power. "I am staying here," she said. "I could only leave you if you were rich and strong."

# Chapter thirteen

The air rumbles and grows dark
in a flash storm of misfortune
gathering over
swaggering,
confident,
YOU!

Sarah went down to her bedroom and stood by the window a long time watching the storm. Thoughts of the man who was hunting Peter rubbed at her mind like a boat against the dock. Captain Dear Friend, of course, and all she knew of him was his booming laughter that seemed full of a life-loving sound, not sinister as Peter found it. His brig she had seen, and also his wedding present, briefly. Soon he would be destroyed, in Peter's unmanly trap baited with himself, surrounded with his ruffians. Clearly, that was the plan.

An impression of bounding life came to her when she thought of Captain Dear Friend. It seemed impossible that he could be extinguished. She would warn him if she could. Would that destroy Peter? The captain could have boarded the *Challenger* and killed Peter that night when he sent over the present. Perhaps his purpose was only to terrify, in revenge—for what?

Sarah shivered slightly and tried to think of something simple and light. She watched a plover thunder up from the dunes in the shaft of light from her window. Where was she now, dipping and whirling, the wind's captive, when she should be huddled with her breast feathers fanned out over her bald-bodied young?

Leaning out to try and trace the plover, Sarah saw a ship's light swaying on the water. It was too close, much too close to hold its own against the heavy seas and strong lee tide. Pray God it would come in no further. The reefs out there were close to the surface, the seas high.

She turned up the whale oil lamp in her bedroom but it was a useless gesture because the house lights like those in the tower could only be seen for one brief instant through the cut in the bluff. Sarah held her breath as the ship passed beyond the aperture and out of her range of vision.

A light suddenly gleamed down on the beach at the bottom of the crevice. Sarah leaned far out. So Peter's horrible men were decent enough to warn the ship. But the lantern rose in the air until mast high, it began to revolve, dip and turn as if with the rhythm of the waves. It was hard to believe that there was nothing but beach below.

Sarah's hand clutched the window sill to steady herself. The actual performance of evil came like a hard shock and left her trembling. However often she had heard of this act, this raising the light of a phantom ship to lure another to its destruction, she was seeing it done now, here, before her eyes.

The wicked light revolved in the wind, cued by the brawny arms that held the spar. "Come on," it seemed to say, "follow me. Where one ship has gone another can pass."

"Tonight," Mrs Cassidy had said. "If the moon is dark." These words had been latent in Sarah's consciousness and now surfaced with bloody

169

meaning.

"Peter, *Peter!*" she screamed as she struggled into her clothes.

Peter came bounding down the stairs from the tower room. He shouted with surprise at her wild expression. "What . . where?"

She made him lean far out of the window. "Out there, look!"

"Nothing there," he said.

"The light, down on the beach. It's on a mast, swaying."

"What light? I don't see any light."

She brushed past him to look. There was nothing. "They took it down for oil or they've walked on past the break in the cliff so we can't see them," she said.

"Sarah, your kind of lantern needs no fuel. It was a dream." He drew her away from the stinging wind.

"I know what I saw. You can't make me doubt myself."

He shrugged and gave a skeptical smile that she found detestable.

She shook him. "Your men are Mooncussers, murderers! I saw them swinging a light from a mast to wreck that ship. Go down, stop them! Wait—no, they will kill you along with all the other witnesses aboard that ship."

"*Will* you be quiet and listen to me, Sarah. These men were selected for me by Deacon Handy, a solid citizen, a pillar of the Church. Would *he* recommend Mooncussers? My men are some of the shipbuilders that work for him."

Sarah was silenced for a moment. "The Deacon *is* a solid citizen. I have my own personal reasons for disliking him but he's highly regarded in town. Well, either he doesn't know what his men are up to or he is getting old and careless." She paced up and down the room. "Here we stand arguing while that poor ship comes in closer and closer to the shoals. We'll have to act, Peter, now, without delay."

A muffled, splintering crash echoed through the room.

"He's here!" Peter shouted. "He came through the storm and broke into the house. I might have known he would." He ran for his sword. "He bypassed my men. It was meant to be this way!"

Beside himself, he thrust his sword at the air and for some reason tore his shirt front open as he stood on the landing "In a few minutes I'll be free of it all, one way or another."

Sarah gave a yell of impatience. "Oh, stow your ranting, Peter! No one's here, Otis would be barking."

Peter started down the stairs, his chest held far out, his legs stiff. Loud cheers came from the beach along with another splintering, cracking sound. "Peter!" Sarah shouted. She ran after him. "That noise was the ship breaking up on the reefs!"

Peter's exalted face changed, came back into focus as he followed Sarah out the door and up to the edge of the cliff.

Down below, flaming torches lighted the beach. The men seemed to be prancing as Mrs. Cassidy herded them with a large grapple in her hand. "To work," she bellowed.

Peter shook his head as if to see more clearly, make sense out of the wild scene.

The wrecked ship's light was level with the water. It waved crazily and, as another crash sounded over the water, it went out.

A chorus of yells came from the beach as the men

went into the towering foam of the breakers, holding their grapples.

"Stop them," Sarah screamed. "Stop them!"

"I'm going to help them," Peter said. "They are risking their lives to pull in survivors."

As he went down the rope ladder to the beach, Sarah followed, running after him to the water's edge. Otis sat down on the edge of the bluff and lifting his head to the hidden moon, gave vent to long drawn-out howls.

"What ship is it?" Peter yelled to his men. "A brig? Is it a brig?"

"You are *obsessed!*" Sarah screamed. "What does it matter? People are drowning! Control your men!"

Peter shook her away and ran toward the fat man who staggered through the surf dragging a body on the end of his hook. "Hilary," Peter yelled. "You have a sharp eye for distance. Is it a privateer's brig? Are they pirates dressed in old navy uniforms? Has her captain come in? Can you see the quarterboard?"

Hilary was a mass of blubber with piercing eyes and features that gathered together in the middle of his broad face like cattle bunched on a plain. He looked behind him at the sailor boiling about in the sandy wash of the surf and then at Peter. He gave a shrill whistle. "Here's reinforcements we didn't count on," he yelled furiously.

Despite the wind, his whistle and words were heard. Men began to gather around, their grappling hooks in their hands. The groom came running out of the surf, the torches lighting up his brutal pocked face.

Mrs. Cassidy, her dress stained by a darker fluid than water, stepped in front of Hilary, knocking aside his hook. She gave the men a warning look.

"Glad you came down, Mr. Garrett, sir," she bellowed. Her voice came through the roar of the surf, a well drilled storm yell. "Terrible tragedy here, all the poor sailors coming in dead like him." She pointed her grapple to the body, half-covered with foam. "We'll be a-piling 'em up there by the bluff where the water can't do no more to them."

A shout came from the men as the torches showed an arm revolving, gesturing to them in the center of a breaker. When the wave crashed down on the beach, Zeke the cook went in after it, his huge hands extended.

Sarah was sure the arm was alive and would not be alive long. Zeke disappeared in the waves.

"Careful," Peter shouted, taken aback by the man's savage expression.

"Pay it no mind, sir," said Thankful Cassidy. "The poor sailor is most thoroughly drowned. Poor Zeke won't be able to save him no matter how hard he tries."

"Are there none living?"

"Not a lucky one, sir, more's the pity."

Sarah glanced behind her where the wreckage was already being sorted and piled in a heap with a lighted torch stuck in the sand at either end. Most wreckers, jealous of their loot, guarded separate piles, but these men collected in one mound—for whom?

Sarah pulled at Peter. "Look! Blood on her dress!" The wind tore the words from her mouth.

"I hear her," Mrs. Cassidy said. "And well there might be blood on my dress. Some of their heads are stove in by the rocks and wreckage, poor things. Excuse me, sir. You had better take your lady back to the house and stay there with her until she

173

quietens. Poor fanciful dear. I will stay on here with these brave men of yours, although I'm nearly fainting with the horror of it. I thank God I happened to be here and they happened to be here on this dreadful night."

"I'll help you," Peter said.

Thankful's immense legs were astride in the surf. She swung her grapple as if it were light as a parasol and her eyes flickered in the torchlight. Sarah had not the slightest doubt that, given the chance, this woman would kill her as easily as she sank her grapple into a piece of wreckage or the skull of a drowning sailor.

"We'll go for help. We'll bring Wellfleet back with us. *Peter!*" Sarah called, wild with urgency. "Come sound the cry in Wellfleet!" She ran out of the circle of light. "*Peter*, come with me!"

Still, Sarah hesitated, fearful for Peter. Then she heard Thankful Cassidy roar, "Keep him safe, boys. Keep him out of the water. He's our best witness. Go far out in the surf to do your duty."

Thankful turned then, and with a look of animal ferocity came running toward Sarah. For one moment, Sarah froze with horror. The woman looked demonic. The sudden scream of a dying sailor released her and she ran straight for the cliff where she climbed up zig-zag taking one stride up and sliding back a half stride. Surely that monster's weight would keep her from following up the cliff! As for Peter, his obsession made him safe. He would not see what was clearly before his eyes—"Their best witness," the murderous creature had called him.

Heart pounding, Sarah reached the top of the cliff and pulled herself over, clutching bunches of dune

174

grass in both hands. Looking back, she could see Mrs. Cassidy clearly in the torchlight, looking up to mark the place and gesturing to one of the men who came for the bluff at a dead run.

Sarah raced for the stable's dim light. She found and bridled the gelding. No time for a saddle—it was enough to have achieved the bridle. Without taking time to look over her shoulder, she could tell by the pricking of her skin that someone was out there in the dark waiting for her. Where was Otis when she needed him? She could hear him back at the cliff, performing his death howl duties, an eerie accompaniment to the cries of the men.

She mounted bareback and askew, but she was on. She urged the horse out into the night in a burst of speed to rush past whoever was waiting.

It was harder for her than climbing the cliff, but being a sailor she was able to steer the horse, as she called it, in the dark. She steered better than she rode and had no trouble getting him to the road through the woods. For a few moments she heard sounds of pursuit but, at a fast gallop, she soon left the sound behind.

The scrub pines twisted and thrashed in what seemed a black, sinister cave of wind ahead. Sarah buried her face in the gelding's mane. His warm animal smell gave her comfort. And the memory of the sailor's arm, alive and gesturing in the wave, somehow gave her courage to stay on. She clasped her legs on the horse's rippling sides and by lying almost flat, rode without slipping all the way to Wellfleet town.

When she came to the square where the lights of tavern windows still shone, she drew the gelding to a stop and with a volume that made him rear up,

175

she gave the drawn out, spine-tingling call of the lower Cape:

*"Ship asho . . . oo . . . ore and all hands perishing!"*

# Chapter
# fourteen

*He knows what is right
from what is wrong,
and he does both
just as you do.*

Flames rose in hundreds of lamps and soon there was a sound of people running in the dark streets. Stable doors groaned. Men pounded out of nearby taverns, their lanterns swaying drunkenly.

Sarah launched another cry. Others took it up: "Ship ashoo . . . oo . . . ore and all hands perishing!"

The streets were filled with lanterns now. "Where? Where?" people shouted, not wasting time on words.

"Straight across on the backside," Sarah screamed over the clamor.

"I'll be damned, it's Sarah Mayo," someone said as he ran by.

Women poured out of their houses, half-dressed, some carrying or yanking their children. Soon the first drays began rumbling along over the cobble-stones to the road across the Cape, their owners running alongside to finish tightening the harness-ing.

In a few minutes the road was clogged by a stream of people carrying sheets, huge baskets, and every receptacle they could quickly lay hands on. Women, driving big empty drays, clogged the road and screamed for the crowd to make way as they snapped their whips at those who would climb aboard and slow the dray with their weight.

All this frenzy swirled around the gelding until Sarah had trouble holding him. At times she hid her face in his mane rather than see the faces around her, puffy with sleep and vivid with greed. Many of them were kindly people whom she knew and liked, but they hurried now as if their lives depended on it. Lives *did* depend on it, she thought, but that was not what made them run.

The few men who were free of this looting passion left their wives at home and, carrying nothing but good will, galloped as fast as the sandy road and the mob with its baskets and handcarts would permit. These men took pleasure in crowding the drays and panicking the horses that drew them. They rejoiced as the hooves of their horses threw sand at the hustling, swearing crowd.

The scavengers looked after these fast riders with a hatred equal to their own loss of self-respect. But a number of the men got off their slow-moving carts and led them into the woods, then, their hands free of bags and baskets, began running along the side of the road with a fleetness of foot and spirit they had not felt when both were weighted down with greed.

Sarah saw Zenas. She got down from her horse, which was stolen at once, and ran to him. He was frenziedly busy with a group of young boys, the only volunteers he could find to put a whaleboat on a cart to drag it to the backside for rescue work.

Zenas showed no surprise at seeing his daughter but gave her orders as if this was her natural place. "Good work on sounding the alarm. Now get up to the sail loft there with the boys and make sure they throw down a big enough coil of rope."

"Father, I've got to talk to you! That wreck was . . ."

"Get the thickest Goddamn rope in the place!" He hurried elsewhere.

Sarah tucked up her dress and went up the ladder to select the rope. In a few seconds they threw the rope out of the lift window and stowed it in the whaleboat.

Then Zenas and the boys began pulling the heavy cart themselves for all the horses were already on the road ahead of them.

"I have something very important to tell you," Sarah screamed.

"Steady the boat," said Zenas as he ran to the front where he could take the heaviest burden. As he led the whaleboat over the narrow winding forest road that crossed the Cape, he cursed at every obstruction with such intensity that people gave way to him and when he could not force a dray to give them room, he circled it, somehow pulling the cart with the boat around through the bearberries, scrub oak and pine.

Sometimes he held a lantern in front of his face and roared like a lion at those who were in his way. His grooved face seemed full of heat lightning. It was the face of a man using to the full all the resources of the human will and, as such, it filled some people with a supernatural fear and they gave way.

"Move over, you greedy ghouls!" he roared. "One side, you damned coffin worms or, by God, I'll cut you down!" He seized an oar and threatened them out of the way. "Off the road, you creeping looters!

180

Let these brave boys through."

A wide wagon holding the entire family of a prosperous farmer, all of whom had turned up noses like pigs, including a suckling baby, stared at Zenas, stolid and unmoving. He seized their horse by the bridle and wrenched the wagon off the road.

"Get over to starboard there! Make room for these boys who hold their own lives too high to let others drown."

Old Mrs. Curtis, a rich woman in a red satin dress, looked out at Zenas from her carriage, her little mouth drawn together like a dot in the center of rays of wrinkles.

"Go take your basket and sit on a tombstone where you belong, old crone!" Zenas pulled her basket over her head and whacked her horse out of the way with the flat of his oar on the animal's rump.

"Father, look out!" Sarah cried. "You'll hurt her. Now you *must* listen to me. Mooncussers did it . . . I can witness . . ." Her voice was lost in the noise.

"One side!" Zenas was already raging at the next obstruction. "Let these tired boys and an old man through with the boat. There are lives to be saved!"

Zenas panted and pulled in silence for a while. The boys were white with strain. They were all slowing down and Sarah had no breath left to implore her father to listen.

"You, Jeremiah, up there on that pile of empty bags!" Zenas shouted to a tall old man with a red beard that matched his veined eyes. He was one of Zenas's favorite drinking companions.

"You up there, riding high and comfortable when there are lives to be saved! Get down here, you cozy bastard, and lend us some muscle."

"Not me, ho, ho! There's a case of wine drifting my way, always is, and I'll be there to haul it in. Ho, ho!" he gave a silly smile and waved his hand with a flapping motion like that of a fish half dead in the hold. "You get away from me, Boy."

Zenas reached up and pulled him out of the cart, his eyes stern as a gull's. "By God, Jeremiah, you stand up and pull with the rest of us or you'll never drink again!"

Jeremiah looked around in surprise. He saw the boys' faces gleaming white in the lanterns and heard their heavy breathing. He swayed a little, but seized hold of the wagon shafts and began pulling steady and hard. Soon he echoed Zenas's insulting shouts with his bass, "Ho, ho!" His veined eyes gleamed and he put his red beard in his mouth clenching his teeth on it for the harder pulls.

A covey of young married women rolled along comfortably in their carriages. They would wait at a little distance from shore, standing guard over whatever their men found for them—rolls of material, a quarterboard to hang over the barn door, perhaps a box of fashionable clothes that would hold their high style despite a soaking in salt water. They twittered in speculation over the cargo, calling from carriage to carriage in high, excited voices.

"Goddamn it," Zenas yelled at them. "Sailors like your husbands are drowning while your forked tongues discuss the loot! Over to the side of the road, bitches, let the whale boat through!"

Sarah passed by them with her wild hair and bare feet, both hands steadying the whale boat. Shrieks of recognition greeted her. "Why, if it isn't Mrs. Garrett! What are the fine ladies wearing in Boston,

182

Sarah? A faded blue dress and bare toes, is that the fashion?"

Sarah looked at them unsmiling. She shook out the folds of her old blue dress, glad she had worn it rather than her new finery. "It's always in fashion to save a life," she said. "So kick off your fancy shoes and help me steady this boat, why don't you?"

They waved and laughed at her, not unkind but merry beyond all bounds over this outing.

"Goddamned young biddies, one side!" Zenas roared in a voice like the surf.

"Ho, ho," said Jeremiah. He ground his teeth on his beard and his muscles stood out as he slowly tilted the carriage until its elegant occupants fell out in a flurry of shrieks and petticoats.

Jeremiah pulled a bottle out of his pocket, lifted it to his lips, finished it and wiped his forearm over his beard. Then he ran after the boat and put all his strength to it.

Sarah ran around the boat, steadying it first on one side, then on the other. Sometimes she screamed out her information on the cause of the wreck at the throng on the road, but no one would listen. It was like uttering the soundless shrieks of a nightmare. But the blazing torches and lanterns, the hundreds of voices, the wind tearing at her and roaring through the pines and, above all, the fierce struggle to get through exalted her until, like Zenas and the boys, she felt incapable of failure and as light in spirit as sea foam.

Slowly the wind died down and the tips of the scrub pines began to look darker than the sky. Here and there a bird sang beside the road. Zenas had bellowed and fought his way well up to the front of the line. His dripping shirt clung to his old sinews

183

like sculpture.

The work had sobered Jeremiah and his fine blue mariner's eyes lost the outraged glare they had when liquor made certain things about life clear to him. He no longer shook with delight over Zenas's insulting remarks but bent his head like an ox and pulled the wagon in order to spare the boys who had become too tired for speech but whose faces glowed with the sweet, pure thrill of the crusader.

In a few minutes, the wagon and the heavy whaleboat drawn by the two town reprobates and the pale, excited boys, burst through at the head of the line and led the whole procession down through a sandy crevasse, up the beach a ways, then along the wet hard packed sand to where a circle of torches lighted the wreckage.

# Chapter fifteen

*Fear runs easily
along grooves
etched by old terrors.
It is the secret
and indelible
tattoo.*

By the time Zenas got his whaleboat down to the shore, the moon shone pale against a light morning sky and the wind had gone elsewhere. Offshore, the wreck of a good-sized ship tilting on the reefs was clearly outlined against the sky.

Zenas shouted down the crowded beach for volunteers and winced with a stab of pain when he had to refuse his exhausted boys who came forward first.

"I need experience at the oars," he said gently. "And a little more strength than you . . . men can give me after the long haul you've had."

Sarah ran everywhere telling people why the wreck had happened and who had caused it. But it was as if she were uttering some commonplace remark. No one listened, they were too busy. As the body of the ship broke up in the pounding waves, usable and valuable items washed ashore.

Finally Sarah stood still, baffled and bitter, watching Peter argue with his men, urging them toward the whaleboat. Finally giving up, he left them behind still combing the waves for more loot and went to volunteer himself.

Here and there a few able seafaring men, shamed at seeing this dandy ahead of them, went forward and offered their services, some in gallantry, others because so much of the wreckage, a giant's share, was already piled up and claimed by Peter's rough men.

The whaleboat soon filled up with brawny men but Peter had been passed over. "Why?" thought Sarah. He was the first to come forward. Father doesn't even trust him at the oars! Or was it that the breakers were still too high for a safe launching or return and Zenas wanted to safeguard Peter for her sake? Peter, however, stood disappointed on the shore. Did he want to die gloriously and have done with it all?

A cheer from the beach broke into her thoughts. Zenas who had been waiting for the right wave, drove his boat through the breakers like a striking fish. The crowd shouted as if each had a part in this act of bravery. When most of the loot was gathered, decency and humanity revived as self-interest faded. After all, there might still be a survivor clinging to the wrecked hull to windward.

Some people, chilled and tired, started for home with their loaded drays. Some waited for the hull to break up, hoping that more treasure would drift in. Many of them gathered near the water to applaud Zenas when he returned. His moral and physical authority was now established; his forceful journey through the crowded road would remain a town legend.

Sarah stood down by the breakers watching the bobbing whaleboat. Foam swirled around her legs then retreated, carrying away sand until her feet were all but buried. The sky turned red. Gulls shrieked and sandpipers capered on the ribbed sand. Everywhere things came to life and the rhythm of the ocean was the same as it had always been. The tragedy had not changed one grain of sand.

In front of the dip in the cliff, seven drowned sailors including the captain and his wife lay in a straight line. The dash and roar of the waves sounded hollow and solemn around them. Up above the cliff, a single lark rose, caroling.

Sarah turned back to the water. Out beside the remains of the wreck, Zenas was throwing a line over the hull. One of the young sailors in the whaleboat pulled himself up the side of the crumbling wreck, his sailor's cap still on his head although the waves washed over him twice before he crawled across the deck. The crowd recognized him, remembering the man's foolhardy face and his broken front tooth. They were quiet with apprehension—although the cap staying on was a good omen, they told each other.

A sigh of relief went up and down the beach when the young man stood up and signaled to the boat. And these were the same people, Sarah thought, whose faces had filled her with aversion as they hustled along the road with their receptacles, eager for the booty they might find!

Zenas got his boat alongside and sprang onto the hull. They could see the young sailor hand him a limp body. The trip back was hazardous. The whaleboat hovered just beyond the breakers while conflicting shouts of advice came from the beach. "Now . . . take this one." "No . . . wait for the third wave!" "Come in after a big roller."

Zenas bided his time, selected his own wave and

brought the boat in far up on the shore. The men leaped out, Zenas reached down into the boat and held up a small, frail man, fainting with weakness. That he should be alive at all while the bodies of his brawny shipmates were stretched in a line on the sand seemed wonderfully strange. He was like a little toy paper ship, fragile, non-resistant, riding out a storm. There were some, however, who did not rejoice at this live survivor.

Zenas carried the rescued man up to the dry sand.

"Bring warm coats and brandy for my little sand flea here! We found him clinging to windward. Another half hour and he'd have joined the rest."

The crowd cheered wildly. Peter came over to Sarah and she noted his shiver, his blue lips and his look of inner confusion.

"Peter," she said. "Are you still convinced that your men are innocent?"

"I . . . don't know. I actually *saw* nothing but men going out into heavy surf to find survivors."

"And they came back with dead men every time," she said.

"Yes."

"And still you . . ."

"I don't know. There is something that doesn't feel right."

"But you put it aside because you have this other pressing matter?" She gave him a look of such contempt that he put up a hand as if to ward it off. Sarah felt a compunction she did not want to feel and turned away quickly.

Going up to the rescued man, who was now covered with warm coats and attention, she kneeled beside him.

189

He lay quietly with his eyes closed and soon the crowd had satisfied their curiosity and dispersed, leaving Sarah in sole charge of him. "Come back to life quickly," Sarah whispered. "Come back, stand beside me, testify, bear witness to murder and save others!"

In a few minutes, the survivor opened pleasant, wise, protruding eyes and raised his head a little. Sarah gave him a sip of brandy. He lay back again, closing his eyes against the red glare of the dawn.

Sarah never took her eyes off his face. Soon it seemed as familiar to her as that of a close friend. His receding chin and large adam's apple bobbed as he carefully swallowed the sea water that came up into his mouth, in order, she gathered, not to offend her. He was clean shaven except for a small island of hair on one cheek where he had skirted a pimple. She could almost see him doing it. She seemed to know him so well.

He was not dressed in sailor clothes but in a fine but ruined suit. He must have been a well-groomed dandy, taking passage on the ship. At the corners of his mouth were two deep wrinkles. Altogether his face was merry, homely and fine. By the time he opened his eyes again and looked at her, she felt as easy as if they were old friends. She noticed that his brown eyes still held traces of fear as a rabbit's mild eyes do, even as it eats out of one's hand.

Otis settled down just above the survivor's head and began his long drawn out tremolo of a howl.

Sarah shrieked at him, "Stow it, Otis! You've got it wrong. This man is going to live . . . *live!*" She threw a piece of driftwood at him. Otis yelped, retreated and launched into another eerie, quavering death howl.

"Can you talk?" Sarah asked the survivor. "Are you all right enough? It's important that we witness together what we both saw, you understand me?"

He nodded, his eyes full of intelligent agreement. He began to say something. His voice gurgled with salt water which he modestly swallowed. "I'm doing very well for a human barnacle." His smile deepened the wrinkles beside his mouth. Had this funny, likable little man been chosen to live? she wondered. Or was survival left to the same chance that governed the flight of a gull feather in the wind?

"I'm with you," he said. "I hope there are other waterlogged witnesses."

"Only you."

"Oh God. The captain and his wife?"

"Dead."

"The whole crew?"

Sarah nodded. She leaned closer to him. "Before the wreck, your captain followed the light of another ship—so he *believed*."

He nodded.

"You know now that it was a false light, a Mooncusser's light, here on this beach."

"Yes." He nodded, his eyes quick with agreement.

"So you can testify to that! You saw it too! A dipping swaying light here on shore, leading you to the reefs. You'll stand beside me and bear witness?"

"Of course."

The survivor's eyes suddenly glazed over with horror. His adam's apple bobbled desperately. He whispered, "Not now . . ."

"We can talk about it now, because I *know* about it. I saw them in action." Sarah wondered at the change in him.

Someone cleared a throat behind her, a small

sound as full of menace as a shouted threat. She looked up. Peter's servants had formed a circle around them. The cook's hideous clean hands hung from his sleeves like bleached chicken feet. The groom's face looked more commonplace and terrible than ever, an ordinary but diseased ship's hull.

Sarah looked slowly from one to another. Hilary, the fat man with piercing eyes, stood to her left, next to Wylie, the man she had seen climbing aboard the *Challenger.* Young and supple, she remembered his perfect profile stamped indelibly with evil. Beyond them came Thankful Cassidy striding across the sand until she blotted out the rising sun.

They all looked down at the frail survivor as if he were a fish that should have been dead long ago but still flapped in the hold.

"God help us," said the survivor. He struggled weakly and got to his feet.

Sarah jumped up and broke through the circle, but her screams for help were lost in the noise of the crowd. The ship's hull was finally breaking up and the wood-hungry Cape people disputed over the spars and boards that washed in. Zenas was arbitrating.

Despite the noise, Peter heard her cries and came running. She raced back to the circle of men with him but before she arrived she noted that Otis was quiet, his howling broken off short with a whimper.

Mrs. Cassidy, her back turned to them, was kneeling over the survivor. He was still lying on his back but his face had sand all over it—just his face, not the rest of his wet body, as if he had managed to twist his face around like an owl and grind it into the sand.

"Stop!" Sarah screamed as the big woman lifted the survivor up, supporting his head with one hand.

"This poor little man is took real bad. I'm going to put him in my wagon and get him to the doctor," Mrs. Cassidy announced. "Don't worry, Mr. Garrett, sir. You and your lady just go on with your business. Trust me to take good care of our only survivor." She gave a repellent motherly smile, her big upper lip hanging down over the lower one.

"Stop her!" Sarah cried out. "Peter, don't let her take him away, she'll kill him!"

*"Sarah!"* Peter's voice was sharp. "You are making a serious accusation."

A patient smile came over Mrs. Cassidy's features. "Lucky it's only old me as understands nervous girls," she said. "Now don't you trouble yourself, sir. I'll take him right to the doctor's house. Doc's in Truro tonight but I'll leave him with Mrs. Doc—that is if it ain't too late. The poor dear looks very white. He don't seem to be coming out of it right."

"Peter," Sarah looked full at him. "If you fail me now . . ."

He nodded gravely, accepting her ultimatum. Embarrassed but firm, he said, "Mrs. Garrett has been watching over this man. She will continue to take care of him. I'll carry him up to the house."

The men were silent. Mrs. Cassidy looked at Sarah. The early morning sun outlined the wiry hairs around her mouth. Suddenly she smiled, showing her granite teeth.

"That's all right, sir," she said pleasantly. "Humor your lady. It don't pay to get her mad, does it?" She handed her burden to Peter and then it could be seen that the little man's neck hung as limp as a wrung chicken's and his eyes stared into the sun without a flicker.

"Oh, dear Lord," said Mrs. Cassidy. "He's gone, the poor soul. I was afraid of it. Well, others need me more than that poor man. May God have mercy on him." She clucked her tongue loudly and wagged her head. "Well, boys," Mrs. Cassidy said to circle of men, "it's an ill-fated ship for sure. No survivors to tell the tale. None of us will ever know what happened out there, more's the pity."

She turned away and the silent men fell out of the circle one by one and followed her.

"But he *wasn't* dead a few minutes ago!" Sarah shouted after them. "He spoke to me. He was very clear about what happened."

"Must have been his last words you heard, mam," Comstock said. They turned back as if at an unspoken signal and stood silently around her as they had around the survivor. Peter walked on ahead with Mrs. Cassidy who carried the survivor over to lay him down beside his fellow corpses under the bluff.

Sarah paid no attention to the circle closing in around her. She was watching Mrs. Cassidy adjust the little survivor until her victims lay in as neat a row as any exhibition of a hunter's trophies.

She thought of his merry adam's apple and the grooves laughter had worn beside his mouth. The other bodies were unknown tragedies and Sarah was awed by them, but the little survivor, who didn't survive, was as human as herself. How could he be dead? Yet there he lay in the hollow roar of the breakers, limp as seaweed on the beach. Never again would he shave carefully around the little thing on his cheek or make light jokes of clinging

194

like a barnacle, or swallow sea water rather than offend a lady. She felt sure that despite his small size, he had been a man, someone with inner strength. Overcome with sadness and shock, she began to cry. "He was all right," she wailed. "He was talking to me."

The circle of men closed in. "Must have been his last words," Comstock said. "Tell us what he said."

"You saw to that, you and . . ." Sarah began.

"She doesn't mean that," Peter broke into the circle. "Now leave us." The men stood motionless. "Go on about your business," Peter added sharply.

"What did he say to you?" the groom asked.

Sarah lifted her head. Revenge him, she told herself, revenge him as well as the others lying beside him and countless more back through the years.

She looked from one staring brutal face to another. Behind them a few people had gathered to listen. Now was the time. She must do it or be known to herself as a coward and an accessory to all their future crimes. Speak out, loud and clear, she implored herself.

"I'll tell you exactly what he said and what he promised," she said, but her voice was not strong against the hubbub on the beach. She cleared her throat and tried to call out the accusation as she had sounded the alarm in town.

Thankful Cassidy broke into the circle. "What's this?" she asked. The morning light sharpened the pitiless lines of her face.

"She's going to tell us what he said before he died," one of the men told her.

"Well, well," said Thankful. They all stepped in closer. Was it the red sky reflecting in their eyes or

195

did they give out red rays of their own?

Sarah's throat closed as if it had been gripped. She could almost hear the bones in her neck break under Mrs. Cassidy's twisting hands. It has to be done, so do it. She told herself that to put it off for a better time is to find a rational excuse for fear. There is no better time. Do it!

"All right. First he made a joke, calling himself a human barnacle. People don't really joke unless they are in full possession of their senses. Then he agreed to . . ."

Mrs. Cassidy, that expert in fear, gave her a probing look. "A joke?" her deep laugh boomed. "Half drowned and his neck broke and he made a joke?"

They laughed with her, loud in relief.

"That's not all," Sarah said. But the men's laughter, led by Mrs. Cassidy, as if she led an orchestra of ha, ha's, increased until Sarah could not raise her voice above it.

Thankful, wheezing with laughter, jerked her head at the men. "Come on, men, times a-wasting." One side of her mouth lifted in a fleering smile, as if to say, That bad moment is over.

Sarah called after them and to any who would listen. "He talked about the *wreck*. He knew why it happened!"

Thankful tapped her forehead. "Oh, for sure, my dear. Some day *you* may have a little neck trouble and we'll see how clear you can talk. Well, ha, ha, take care of your missus, Mr. Garrett, sir. She'll make better sense later. She's a tired skittish girl. Come on, men, there may be still a few lives to save out there. Some who cling to floating spars come in late. Maybe we can save one who can talk sense, not

196

like the poor little fellow with the bad neck. or . . ."
She jerked her head back at Sarah and gave another
tap to her grooved forehead. "Let's go. There's still
work of mercy to be done."

# Chapter
# sixteen

Move carefully on this planet.
There are breakable beings here
and the one you shatter
may have a glaze
that cannot be restored!

Peter took Sarah to the shelter of the cliff. She clung to him, her face contorted, tears gushing from her eyes. "I failed. I failed!"

He put his arms around her. She let him, explaining in a sobbing mumble, "Right now I would cling to anyone, even you."

"You are crying for the little survivor?" Peter's voice held no surprise at her treatment of him.

"Why shouldn't I?"

"You didn't know him."

"I *did* know him. He was a fine man. But these tears are for me. I've let a mighty moment go by me. I should have *prevailed,* made myself heard by the people standing in back of your Mooncussers. They were listening to me for once. That was the time. As long as I live, I'll remember and be afraid to look behind me because something will be following me, the shadow of a worm—myself." She covered her face. "Don't let me see that line of bodies. I've betrayed them all."

"Sarah!" Peter spoke sharply. "That's nonsense. You had nothing to do with this wreck and it's all over now."

"Over? Never for me." She shivered.

Peter picked up one of the jackets, his own, that had covered the survivor and tried to put it around her shoulders. Sarah threw it off.

"Let's go home." Peter suddenly picked her up in his arms. The sand dragged at his feet and she could feel his heart pounding against her as, for some reason, he made an attempt to carry her to the rope ladder.

"Put me down," she said in his ear. "I'm a big strapping girl and you are tired from having assisted at the murder of a ship full of men."

She slipped down and they stood at the foot of the rope ladder staring at each other. Peter saw a tired, beautiful girl, whose salty lips were drawn down with strain but were too full and curving to be bitter. The salt spray clung to tendrils of hair at her temples. Peter shivered with cold and with love for her.

He held the rope ladder as she began to climb, then followed her. When he was shaken by a sudden racking cough, the ladder swayed and grated against the sandy cliff.

*"Stop it!"* Appalled by her own sharp voice and the contempt in it, she looked down at him. "I'm sorry, but a mass murderer has no right to do anything as commonplace as coughing!"

Peter, stifling his cough as best he could, looked up at her. "You really hold *me* responsible for the dead sailors?"

"I hold you directly responsible for the action of the Mooncussers. You hired them. It is your fault that sweet little man is dead."

A closed stubborn look came over Peter's face. "There is no proof that my men are Mooncussers. I saw nothing but their efforts to retrieve the bodies. However . . . . I do admit that some things are suspect, but if it should be true that they caused the wreck, what makes you think they would not have been in action on the beach if I had not hired them? Am I responsible then for all their past misdeeds? Be reasonable, Sarah."

"I don't *want* to be reasonable!" Sarah, with this perfect female reply, looked out over Peter's head where she could see Zenas carried on the shoulders of a yelling crowd. Zenas had now become first citizen of Wellfleet. As he looked up at the rope ladder, he cupped his hands and shouted at Sarah, "I'll get myself out of this pretty damn quick." But his gray eyes were alight with excitement as he let the men carry him to the nearest carriage and then, singing and shouting, they followed him across Cape, all the way to the tavern.

Sarah let go of all regret at not having sought him out and told him who had murdered the little survivor she had rescued. Zenas would have called them to account at once and some dark night Zenas would . . . . disappear. It would be too great a loss. There had to be another way than putting Zenas at risk and she had to find it. She climbed the rest of the ladder to the tower, and there an idea began to take shape.

She stared out of the window thinking about it. Through the sliver of view afforded by the crack in the cliff, she could see a portion of the row of bodies on the beach. The wind ruffled their drying clothes. The rest of the crew was beneath the waves, each with his separate cargo of memories and instincts dissolved into the foam and the mist. She remembered a neat little hawser of string on the survivor's

202

coat, something to take the place of a button until his woman could sew it, no doubt, a tiny thread to tie him to a future that was not to be. He must have had a woman in his life, he was so gallant and courteous in his extremity. But how soon all the small devices of his personality had vanished, along with the boat in which he had been a passenger. She turned away from the window, unable to bear the thought of vivid people dissolving into mist and fading like dreams.

The room seemed intensely private, a cave scooped out above the tumult on the beach. And beside her was Peter, trying to suppress a cough as he reached for the telescope.

She looked at him incredulously. "*Peter!* How can you go on as if nothing had happened? Don't you believe in *anything*—in people, laws, God?"

"I'm busy trying to believe in Peter Garrett, against all odds," he said. "What do *you* believe in?"

"In people, the natural good in them. And in God, of course."

Peter gave a short laugh. "I believe in zero, on both counts. Particularly tonight." He waved a hand at the beach.

"The Great Zero? Poor Peter, you have the most jealous God of all! You must always be slaughtering something on his altar, a random sprig of hope or . . . that wonderful feeling we have sometimes of a loving presence nearby or . . ."

"If I had wanted to marry a missionary, I would have looked elsewhere." Peter shrugged. He turned back to the telescope, adjusting it and scanning the horizon and adjusting it yet again.

Sarah watched him for a moment. "Peter," she said quietly, "I am on my way to inform against your men. You will have to answer for them unless you can prove ignorance of their actions. There I can stand with you. You *are* blind, obsessed as you are by something else."

Peter's face congealed into its old air of chilly arrogance. "And whom have you selected for this announcement?"

"Deacon Handy. I know him and I have reason to think that he will see me and listen to me. When I tell him what the men he recommended to you have done, his own reputation will be at stake. He will of course be merciless with them."

"Wait, there are things to consider first."

"No, I shall not wait. I saw them close in on that fine little man from the wrecked ship. He knew they had swung a false light. He knew, oh he knew. That's why he clung to the boat, but that hell-hag wrung his neck like a chicken, and *you know it!*"

Peter turned away. For some reason he took out his handkerchief and brushed the sand off his boots. His brows were furrowed with anguish. He spun the telescope around and fussed nervously with the lens.

"Peter, haven't we reached a place where only absolute honesty will save us?"

He was silent.

"Who is it that you want to kill, Peter? Who is this enemy for whom you hire assassins and are blind to a massive murder?"

He was silent.

"Oh Peter, what have you done that you must blot out in *him?*"

They looked at each other with set, white faces. Sarah's shot had struck home. She hurled at him, "Are your own lines fouled, Peter?"

Peter's guarded expression left him. His eyes opened wide and she saw how vulnerable he really was. She felt as if she had been treading with spiked shoes on the quick of his heart.

As they stood like statues, staring at each other, someone cleared his throat in the window. They whirled about, Peter drawing his sword as he turned.

The twig-legged young man from the *Challenger* stood a moment, irresolute and frightened, thinking he must have interrupted a fight. When he met Peter's furious eyes, he knew it for sure. He spoke all in one breath:

"Just reporting, sir, like you told me. The privateer's brig, *Windshadow*, is here, anchored in hiding, the third cove on the bay side, just beyond Truro."

Peter stared at him a moment, shocked by the message, Then he ran for the window. "Wait," he called. "I want you to escort my wife to her father's house."

But the young sailor was already rattling far down the rope ladder, wondering where to look for his next job as cabin boy.

Peter stood still, thinking, then gave a strangled cough and whirled about, putting a hand with fingers like hot wires on Sarah's arm. She could feel the morbid heat of his body and knew that he was burning up. He had stripped off his jacket to put it over the survivor and in his excited, overheated state that was enough to bring him down with a fever.

"It's definitely not going to be safe for you to be here," Peter said. "Go at once. Take the gelding to Wellfleet."

He ran to his guns, loaded one and thrust it into his belt. Sarah followed him. She had a strong feeling of something nearly finished. She took his hand and held it tightly, wanting to speak to him direct and without anger.

"Peter, I don't understand what you have done here or why. But I do understand fear, the kind you are running toward in order to end it one way or another. Fear as I felt it, was a kind of horror that seeps from the mind down over the nerves and we are made ready for it by an earlier fear. Mrs. Cassidy put the knife of fear into me earlier and, when she came back, the place began to bleed of itself, causing my voice to grow weak while the moment for courage and action passed and I squeaked into the wind when I should have accused them all with a stormy voice that rallied the beach. I failed myself. I failed the dead!"

Peter nodded, his eyes softened. "I know. It was a bruise on a bruise."

"Peter . . . I don't know what you are about to do but I apologize for the terrible things I have been saying, right as they may be. Because I said them in anger without any—compassion. I just want to tell you now . . . that I *do* know what it is to fail myself, that I'm sorry for my harsh words. I'm not so fogged over with pride as I was before that experience on the beach. I'm afraid . . . Oh Peter, I'm afraid for you, for us! Forgive me right now for my harsh words!"

"If there is to be a forgiving, I ask for it. I regret having put you in such a . . . I love you. Now I must go."

"Go. I know now that there is only one kind of safety. Mine would have been in speaking out, being heard. Yours is not to cower but to go and meet him."

Peter gave her a quick hard kiss. "You are right. There is only one kind of safety."

Sarah's eyes were deep with sadness. "So I'll do what I have to do and . . . you do what you have to do . . . and . . ."

Peter nodded. He ran past her. He was no longer listening. She saw that his face was exalted like that of a man possessed by his own high courage.

# Chapter seventeen

The layer of cold
that congeals his eyes
are frost crystals
from his heart.
To ask for pity
is absurd.

Sarah leaned out of the tower window, trying to calm herself by watching the changing patterns of a flock of gulls in flight. When she realized that they were wheeling and gathering densely over the row of dead bodies, she shuddered, closed the window and ran down to her room.

She threw on the fashionable riding habit she had bought in Salem and stepped up to the mirror to adjust her new amber hat. No need for plumes on this hat, rolled high on one side. Her thick blond hair was decoration enough. But was the hat and pleated neck ruff too jaunty a frame for her tired face? Never mind. Better to dazzle a bit for this particular visit.

When she left the house and swished across the bearberry in her long skirt, she felt glad of Otis's wheezing company. The fat old dog was dear to her and she had come to trust his psychic gift. She would have stopped to pet him but did not dare hesitate.

It seemed likely that the men would still be down on the beach guarding their stolen loot. She could see no one near the stable.

The stolen gelding, to her relief, had come back to his stall on his own. Abandoned by whoever had taken him, the horse still had his bridle on. They stared at each other a moment as if silently agreeing that it had been a terrible night.

As she led him out of the stable and made several false tries at mounting him, a sound of men's voices came from nearby. They were saying something about hitching up the carriage to transport their goods.

Otis gave a snarling bark. Sarah flung herself up on the horse, grasping his mane. One of her short boots fell off in the struggle to stay on. Leave it. Any delay could be fatal.

A hoarse yell and a whistle came from near by. The gelding, prodded by Sarah's jolt of fear, started off at a gallop that nearly unhorsed her. She lay flat on his back clutching his mane with one hand, the reins with the other and managed to guide him to the sandy road that led across Cape. She rode in a panic of haste until they were halfway through the woods. Only then did she slow the gelding into a trot.

The woods were lonely. Dark scrub pines reached across the narrow road. She thought of Peter riding through here, coughing, burning with fever and intent upon purging his integrity—while back on the beach, the gulls hovered greedy over the dead.

As she neared the end of the woods, her thoughts fixed on her destination, she slowed to a walk and made some attempt to fix her attire. She could hide the bootless foot behind the other one in Deacon Handy's parlor and still look respectable enough for her words to carry weight. It was too bad that she had not chosen a more gracious way to refuse his offer of marriage. But, after all, she had only been following Zenas's maxim. He had always told her, "Look 'em in the eye and think, You're as good as I am until you prove yourself a damn sight worse." The Deacon had ruined himself with her by patronizingly listing the degrees of her rise in status as his wife. She hoped that by now, her rude refusal had lost its sting.

Sarah adjusted her ruffled stock and settled her hat as the gelding carried her out of the wooded road and into the busy port of Wellfleet. As she approached the Deacon's square white mansion, she felt confident that he would be home. It must be midmorning by now; so old and corpulent a man would no doubt be taking his ease.

Deacon Handy was at home and at this moment busy at his desk. From day to day, he jotted down bits of unrelated information about people in his parish. When enough notes had accrued, he clipped them all together, first in one order then in another, until he had reached some equation that satisfied him. Not only did this hobby provide him with scholarly thrills but it was useful in many other ways.

Peter Garrett's file was a stubborn puzzle. The Deacon slipped the latest item on top, something Sam had extracted from a very thin young sailor off the *Challenger* whom he had found in a tavern drinking himself into slovenly speech in what seemed like an effort to dull the memory of a bad experience.

Sam had a drink with him and learned that he had carried a message to his master, and, very unfortunately, jumped right into a blazing row between him and his lady, almost as bad as breaking in on them rolling around in bed together. So he might as well start looking for another job right now.

Sam, knowing how intrigued the Deacon would be with this information, had indicated that another job would be no problem. He could fix him up. The young sailor readily told him that the message had stirred up his master to the point of strapping on his guns and running out of the house. "Saw him run by me to get his horse. Before that he yelled out of the window when I was on the rope ladder. Wanted me to take his lady into town. Getting rid of her, eh? I thought, but I pretended not to hear. I'm no servant—a sailor is a cut above."

He embellished this point, infuriating Sam, a servant himself, who decided against procuring him a job even as he promised one to the young man who, on the strength of it, must produce the message itself.

Sam copied it down as told; and brought the scrap of paper to the Deacon who studied it carefully.

Why was the brig *Windshadow* anchored somewhere near Truro and of what interest was this to Peter? The *Windshadow* was a rich, active privateer's brig. Why would Garrett gallop off to visit her? The young fool was way out of his depth, a minnow among game fish.

The Deacon put away Garrett's file and leaned back in his chair. He made a church steeple of his finger tips. So the *Windshadow* was anchored off wild country, eh? Captain Collier was here for a purpose. The Deacon pursed his purple lips. A woman? He might be offship right now. You'd never catch the *Windshadow* off the reefs on a dark night—the captain was too experienced to run afoul of a welcome party swinging a high lantern on a mast. But . . . The Deacon smiled. A landing party might be arranged in that wild cove off Truro. A freebooter could squirrel away a hold full of treasure—line of duty of course.

The Deacon's mind shifted from these pleasant thoughts of gain to the disturbing question of Peter. Why would he be challenging so perfect a fighter as Captain Collier and risking a lifetime of bedding Sarah? The thought of Peter, realizing in person the many daydreams of the middle-aged Deacon, was enough to bring on the first rumbling of nervous indigestion. The gold trinkets on his vest leaped with the agitation of his stomach.

To cure this discomfort with cheerful activity, he took a ledger from the drawer of his desk and took a look at last night's transaction according to an estimate brought in early this morning by one of his men.

"Let's see," the Deacon mumbled. "Five cases of fine Spanish sherry, seven of champagne, one of Napoleon brandy off the top for me, plus one third of the value of all the flotsam . . ."

The front door knocker sounded, interrupting his pleasant accounting. Sam was away again, eeling around town, listening, watching and making notes on the little pieces of paper that gave the Deacon such an enjoyable hobby. He pushed back his chair and moved his vast person to the door.

"Oh!" He put a hand on the curve of his vest to quell the agitation there. "Sarah Mayo! Well . . . come right in, my dear."

One sight of her here, near him, and all his vengeful malice over her refusal of him began to drop away. Her physical presence jolted his old glands and quickened his heart.

Sarah gathered up the long skirt of her riding habit and stepped into the spacious hall. She walked on tiptoe to disguise the loss of her boot, gave an unnatural smile to disguise her dislike of the man and, then, impatient of so many disguises, said, "Riding a horse unsettles me. It is still a novelty."

"Dear girl, you rode all the way from the backside to see me? I am flattered. Come into the library and rest."

"Give me a sail, any day," Sarah said. "No matter how rough the water, it's my element." This was going to be easier than she thought. The Deacon's welcome was so warm . . . *too* warm?

"I quite agree." He retained her hand, bowing over it. "But I am grateful to any conveyance that brings you to me."

"Are you alone? I have come to talk to you, sir, about a very important matter," Sarah said.

"*You* may see me alone at any time, dear girl." The Deacon controlled his excitement until only the faintest bell of lechery rang in his voice. He would forget her old discourteous reply to his proposal of marriage. This was a shining new day; *she* had come to *him*. Why? Was it money? He hoped so. Most of the lower Cape borrowed from him at one time or another. Perhaps young Garrett was at the end of his financial rope. What luck if so. He glanced at her splendid riding habit—cost a pretty penny. He noted too that her hair was disheveled and that her hat might have been put on more skillfully. It would take Zenas's daughter a little time to get used to the grooming of fashion but she was still the most beautiful woman he had ever seen and he was a traveled man.

The Deacon led Sarah to his library where he seated her with all the care of a portrait painter, so that when he sat at his desk he could easily see the outline of her figure in her tight riding habit.

Sarah hesitated, deciding how to begin, but the Deacon was in no hurry to talk. Her physical presence here in his office thrilled him. He savored the way her hair sprang up and away from the center part and turned in loose, untrained curls on her forehead in one of those new cuts which she had not known how to handle, but nature had done it artfully. A bridge of freckles over her nose delighted him. Gold highlights in her curling eyelashes made him hold his breath. A fresh fragrance came from her person. The Deacon, relishing all this like so many voluptuous little springs, felt them become a torrent. He half rose from his chair to go over to her when she began to speak.

"Deacon Handy . . ." She cleared her throat and made sure that her bootless foot was well hidden under her long skirt. Then, angry with herself for bothering with such trifles at such a time, she placed both feet in plain view. The gesture released her. Fixing her luminous eyes full upon the Deacon, she told him her version of last night's shipwreck.

While she talked, the Deacon's arms and legs grew cold with the shock of coming loss. She had come to him, the feast was here, but like a banquet in a dream, it now faded before his eyes.

His breath fluttered unevenly in his throat while he mourned the passing of his old sensual day dreams, along with his sudden new hope.

"Answer this carefully." He poised his pen above a piece of paper and slowly wrote the roman numeral two. "Are you positive that your husband gave no credence to this story of yours?"

"Yes, of course I'm positive. That's why I came to you. Otherwise Peter would be here. His mind is closed. He is . . . preoccupied."

"Do you think in time he might come to see it your way?" the Deacon asked in measured tones.

"Peter does not *want* to believe me. If I pound away at him he may come to realize. . . . But now, he is too intent on . . . I doubt if he really listens to me. But what *difference* does this make? My only concern is that *you* believe me."

"But your version of the unfortunate wreck may germinate and grow in his mind."

Sarah gave a little cry of impatience. "Surely we are straying from the point! Peter rejects the crime. And it is the crime itself we should be discussing."

Deacon Handy looked down at his pad. He crossed out the number he had written before and replaced it with the single digit, *one.* He added meticulously, "for now" after it. And he began to take his farewell of Sarah. His stomach grew numb with sorrow.

"So," he sighed. "We must take extreme measures. I see no other way." He looked at her fixedly as if memorizing her face.

"That's right, sir," Sarah said quickly. "I am relieved to hear you say this. Extreme measures *at once.*"

"Yes." The Deacon sighed again. "At once."

His lachrymose sighs puzzled Sarah. With his eyes fixed so sorrowfully upon her, he reminded her of a beached sea turtle.

"I can't say that I blame your young husband for refusing to credit such a fantastic story. Are you quite sure, my dear, that you will not agree with him finally and come to believe that you have misinterpreted events and . . . so . . . let the whole matter drop?"

A bird of hope began to sing somewhere in the Deacon's mind. He poised his pen ready to cross out the digit he had written on the pad although his better judgement called him a fool.

For some reason, the marking of roman numerals for this sort of business suited the Deacon. It had a tombstone dignity.

"Think it over, my dear. Suppose that two sound men, your husband and myself, urge you to wait and let us gather more evidence to make sure that this is not merely a woman's fancy."

*"Fancy!"* Sarah was outraged. "A woman is as capable of bearing witness as a man. I have seen the men mooncussing and I can swear to the murder of the last survivor by *your* men, the men you recommended to Peter—or by Mrs. Cassidy herself. A terrible mistake has been made! I expect you to take quick action, sir, or I have no recourse but to go to the Governor."

The silence in the room gathered until it became oppressive. Deacon Handy's eyes glared at Sarah tragically from under their heavy eaves. Only his hand moved as he wrote a note.

Sarah stirred restlessly.

"You came straight to me?" he asked with emphasis. "Only me?"

"Yes, of course. Why?"

"And, when you leave here, you will go directly home to the house on the dunes?"

"I had not planned on it."

"It is necessary." His voice was sad and mea-

218

sured. "Go directly home to the house on the dunes and talk to no one on the way. We must not alert the men. You owe me this favor. You have asked for my help and, although I find it hard to believe that my stalwart shipbuilders are Mooncussers, I will investigate. I promise you that."

Sarah sighed with relief. "Thank God something is going to be done! At first I thought you were against me."

The Deacon looked down at her narrow, bare foot and imagined its even fringe of toes becoming the delicate bamboo toes of a skeleton. He shuddered, stood up and, leaning over his desk, drew in several breaths of the fragrant air that had touched her person.

He put the note he had been writing in an envelope and, as if he presided at a somber rite, slowly lit a candle, melted sealing wax and stamped his ring on it with an air of grave finality.

"So that's that," he said. "As for Peter Garrett," he shrugged. "We will not worry about him until later, my dear. One of you is all I find it convenient to handle at present." He gave a cold, sad chuckle.

Sarah looked at him questioningly. "I don't follow you, Deacon."

"Ah, but you will. You and I are both going across Cape. You start slowly on the main cross-Cape road and I will take a short cut that will bring me ahead of you. Now . . . since Sam is not available at the moment—he is checking out a crate of wine that washed in at Nauset beach last night—will you be so kind as to drop this note off at Wreckers' Tavern?"

He handed her the sealed envelope. "No need to go near its foul door. Just give it to anyone lounging outside. As you can see it is addressed to Abraham Cassidy himself. I intend to have him over there when I question the men, who do, after all, frequent his tavern. He knows them better than I. And there is that little awkwardness about his wife and the survivor, isn't there?" He spoke in a remote voice as if his thoughts were elsewhere.

"*Awkwardness!*" Sarah cried. She suppressed the rest of her comment—after all, he was taking action. But she felt that something was not right, a dislocation somewhere.

"Do you ride fast, my dear?" he asked.

"Why yes, I have, why?" She thought of that ride to alert the town last night and again this morning when she left the stable.

"Then don't ride fast this time. Amble along. It's best if I get my business over before you arrive. There could be language unfit for even Zenas's daughter." He looked at her sideways. "But start as soon as you have delivered the note."

A stubborn look came over Sarah's face. She had intended to visit with her father. Now that the Mooncussers would be captured, she would tell him everything. He would be proud of her. She felt annoyed with the Deacon's allusion to her father's vocabulary, remembering how valiantly he had used it in getting his lifeboat along the clogged road.

The Deacon failed to notice her expression. The bonfire into which he had tossed all his voluptuous fancies seemed to have spread to his blood. His collar was tighter than ever and his head ached alarmingly.

"I repeat my warning not to talk to anyone about this. You and I don't want to warn the guilty, do we? Or feel like fools if they turn out to be innocent?"

"They *can't* turn out to be innocent! But I agree not to talk—that is, to anyone but Zenas. I intend to visit my father."

"*No*," the Deacon spoke emphatically.

"Why not?" Sarah was indignant. "I certainly will."

Deacon Handy found her flash of temper stimulating. He reached out to touch her, but drew back with a sad shake of his head. His swollen jowls wilted the points of his collar while his stomach churned in an attack of dyspepsia.

"I may have put it too strongly, my dear. I meant only to spare you, but I am afraid that our local hero, Zenas Mayo, has been carried home from a tavern and put to bed. So much celebrity was his undoing."

"Oh." Sarah accepted this at once. It was only logical. The little cottage would be filled with his stentorian breathing and would smell like a moldy wine cellar. She would not go there, but she felt disappointment that was out of all proportion to the event, as if this was a serious setback for her. "Well then," she said, very reluctant, "I'll have to see him later."

"You may in time," said the Deacon, somewhat mysteriously, she thought. "So my dear, ride back home slowly through the cool woods and I will go on ahead and call on you at your cottage to report."

"Wouldn't you like a signed statement from me now?" she asked.

The Deacon stood up. "Later," he said. He could no longer bear to look at Sarah, young, beautiful and whole. "Goodby, my dear. I'll take care of it all. You just follow my instructions. Deliver the note, then go back to the ocean side in a leisurely amble. Everything is out of your hands now. Your worries will soon be over."

Sarah stood up, then hesitated. She felt something awry, an undercurrent that tugged at her mind, but it was impossible to know its direction.

The Deacon said goodbye to her again, holding her hand a moment while he rubbed his thumb over her fingers. He seemed to be feeling through the flesh for the bone. He gave a sickened smile. "Goodbye," he said for the third time.

Sarah gave him a surprised look. "Goodbye, sir." She swept the skirt of her riding habit up over one arm and the lines of her back and her pretty bottom, as she went out the door, gave the Deacon one last melancholy twinge of lechery.

From now on, he thought, life would be savorless, for there was no one like her or like the way he imagined her in his bed, full of deep emotion, laughter and sweet bitchery.

He sat down heavily at his desk. Tears swam in his impacted eyes. He now understood that despite his fury at her rejection of his offer of marriage, he had loved her for years. Through his layers of heavy flesh and heavy evil, he had cherished this one, higher emotion.

Through the open window came the scream of a gull, wheeling high above the walk on his roof, a scream like that of a frightened woman.

The Deacon's whole person gave a convulsive leap of nerves. And somewhere inside his head, the thin wall of a vein prepared to break. He felt a heavy stuffed sensation around his heart and a premonition of physical change. But despite his genuine grief and the ominous warning from his body, he saw no reason to change his plans.

# Chapter eighteen

*Form without horror*
*is the hawk's eye*
*barred and cruel.*
*As he rends,*
*he follows the law*
*designed for him.*
*The man who rends*
*and therefore fails*
*his own higher design*
*is formless horror.*

he weather was warm, foggy and enervating. Sarah took off her coat. Her hat slipped back on her head and her hair clung damply to a forehead on which the last twenty-four hours had traced faint lines. She had a desperate feeling of having made a mistake somewhere, set something in motion that was hidden and terrible.

She rode up the hill to her old home, but after staring about with large vague eyes, she decided not to go in to the heavy air of Zenas's fermented breath. She felt lax and somewhat weak—hunger probably.

She had almost forgotten the Deacon's letter and looked at it curiously. A faint inner voice advised her to break the seal, but she brushed it aside. The voice was no more than a gnat's whisper, but it persisted. Why had he sealed it? Oh well, it was beneath her to sneak a look at someone's private letter. Surely he had sealed it to safeguard it from prying eyes at the tavern.

The Deacon had made sure that his message contained nothing that would interest Sarah. His message asked Abraham to start now for the backside to meet him, and on his way, stop off to get some fresh-water bass for him in the bottomless pond. And, if he should chance to meet Sarah Mayo who would be coming that way, would Abraham please escort her to her destination.

Sarah yawned in the sultry weather, tucked the letter in her pocket and let the gelding walk slowly to Wreckers' Tavern. An old man was rinsing his mouth with a dipper of water. The drops of water on his white beard held her attention as she handed him the letter and gave him some money to bring her some bread and cheese and a tankard of beer.

Sarah ate and drank without dismounting and left the unsavory neighborhood of the tavern feeling refreshed but sleepy. The long night with no rest gave her a strange, floating sensation. As the gelding plodded slowly along the forest road, she found herself longing for the cool breath of the ocean. Mist was settling into the hollows everywhere and even the birds seemed subdued by it. They announced her arrival with a few lazy notes and were silent.

The gelding's somnolent pace and Sarah's fatigue all made her inclined to delay her appointment with the Deacon. She gave an involuntary shudder as she imagined herself making sworn statements with Mrs. Cassidy's eyes flaring red as she looked at her. It would be best if she could doze off, get just a little rest before that ordeal.

The gelding's snort of alarm made Sarah jump. A square, bandy-legged man appeared around a turn in the road, going ahead of them as fast as he could walk with his back bowed over with the weight of a rusty anchor and a coil of rope around one arm. He must have come in from a side road. He turned to face them and, still bowed down with the weight of the anchor, blocked the road.

It was Abraham Cassidy. He must have received the Deacon's message and, while she was eating her lunch, left at once for the backside. But . . . why the anchor?

Sarah had always tried to avoid encountering this hideous man. What had he done to so destroy all goodness in the human face? It was impossible to imagine him as a baby or a boy. What child could wear even the promise of Mr. Cassidy's expression?

He must have been running, for he was breathing hard and his dingy clothes were stained with sweat. Sarah made an effort and addressed him politely.

"Good afternoon. May I please pass by?"

She felt such a horror of his company that she longed to touch up the gelding and gallop at him, forcing him into the brush, but the thought of falling off in his path frightened her.

"And a very good afternoon to *you*, Mrs. Garrett, isn't it?" said Mr. Cassidy, very polite. "Glad to see you taking your time in this hot weather. That's what I'd do if I were lucky enough to be riding. I'd amble along and enjoy the scenery, I would."

Mr. Cassidy's face seemed to have no share in his affable speech and his eyes chilled Sarah's spine despite the weather.

"I don't want to be detained, so please let us by." Sarah fixed her eyes on the little hole on the side of his head where an ear used to be. She speculated on his reaction if she told him he might go trawling for it as it bobbed about in a jar off the coast.

Mr. Cassidy stepped aside. "Well, take it easy on a day like this is my advice. I'm off into the woods myself for a bit of pond fishing. A man gets hungry for fresh-water bass now and then. I'll see you when you round the road by the pond. Maybe I'll have a little present for you." He would have gone on and on with his horrible innkeeper's cold loquacity if Sarah had not interrupted him.

"I thought you were bound for the ocean side," she said.

"And fish for fresh-water bass in the ocean?" He gave a chuckle that sounded like ice cracking.

Sarah knitted her brows. "Why the big, heavy anchor?"

"It might come in handy." Mr. Cassidy turned away abruptly and went into the woods. In a moment the underbrush hid his bandy legs and his bowed back.

Sarah wondered why he had lied. Of course he was on his way across Cape to meet the Deacon. Why had the mention of the anchor driven him away and how could that subhuman-looking creature have a finicky palate for fish or anything? It all seemed strange and somehow sinister to her. Why had he darted into the woods when he had been walking on the road before?

She halted the horse. The pond was close to the road around the next bend or two. She would be bound to see him again. She felt a strong aversion to this. Why not wait here awhile, give him time to get off the road, then prod the gelding into a fast gallop and whizz by him.

While Sarah deliberately idled on the road, Abraham Cassidy went loping through the woods as fast as he was able with the great weight of the anchor on his back. He took short cuts through the woods that would bring him back to the place where the pond adjoined the road. Then, heaving and wiping away the sweat that ran down his low forehead into his eyes, he swung the heavy anchor off his back and kneeled down to tie the rope to it, the rope that would anchor Sarah deep in the bottomless pond, halfway to nothing.

At that moment he heard a horse pounding along, coming fast. Abraham swore at having to rush his operation, and furious at Sarah for speeding up the road, he jumped to his feet, still panting raucously, and stood blocking the narrow road with his bow legs far apart.

It was not Sarah. The horse was coming up from Truro along a road that cut across the Cape road, a black horse ridden by a big man with a vivid face and easy grace. When the stranger hit the crossroad he turned toward the ocean side and, seeing Abraham blocking his way, he pulled up his horse and put one hand on his sword.

Abraham recognized everything in one glance. The brown curling sun-bleached hair worn long. Muscular dimples, perfect teeth and strong piercing brown eyes.

"Captain Calvin Collier, in person!" Abraham shouted. And he began a freshet of small talk while he planned how to kill him. "Well, well, after all these years," he said. "You never can tell what's going to be washed up on the beach these days or what's going to sink into one of our bottomless ponds yonder."

"You recognize me. How unfortunate for you, my poor fellow." The captain twitched one shoulder in irritation. "I've come ashore on a quiet little business trip. I'm in no mood to be noticed or hold a conversation."

Abraham pulled out a long knife. "And so it will

230

turn out to be for you—a very quiet little trip."

Captain Collier jumped off his horse and drew his sword in one bounding gesture. "Who the hell are you?"

Abraham's hand went up to the place where his ear had been.

The captain gave a bellow of laughter. "It's One Ear Cassidy! I understand you have been boring all of Cape Cod with the story of how you lost your ear and everyone wishes that I had finished the job."

While the captain roared with laughter, Abraham lunged at him with all his tired, sweating weight behind his knife.

Captain Collier leaped aside like a well-disciplined dancer and turned to jump on his horse. He had no appetite for killing; his reputation was in error. He was an enormously successful privateer making up in seamanship and daring what he lacked in brutality. What bloodlust he had was directed toward Peter Garrett.

He was a superb fighter, however, and when Abraham threw a boulder that knocked him off his horse, the captain picked himself up like a cougar.

With an expression of regret, he drew his sword again and stood looking at Abraham. "Why not put this match off?" he said. "The weather is poor."

Abraham cut short this offer to save his life with a furious charge, his knife held ready.

"If I must," said the captain as he ran him through, arresting forever all Abraham's unsavory projects.

The captain stood for a moment looking down at Abraham's white face. So full of life himself, the sight of death usually depressed him but somehow this death gave him a sense of a pattern fulfilled.

231

He pulled Cassidy off the road and left him lying by the pond.

At first the many voices of the pond and surrounding trees and bushes hushed, then they grew used to the presence of the dead man and nature went on with its rhythm of coupling and death. A hawk's ridged talons seized a fish and dropped it, leaving it flapping beside a snake, lumpy with frog.

It's all a form, a design without horror, thought the captain. Only the dead man, made in the image of a higher law and failing it, is hideous.

As Cassidy lay there with his head resting on a large fungus that grew from a rotting log, Captain Collier thought it a pillow to match the face. No undertaker could have laid him out any better, he decided as he turned away.

Nevertheless, it was not until he came in sight of the ocean, and found a place under a dune to wait for dark that he began to look like himself again, vigorous and full of hard cheer.

# Chapter nineteen

*We did well, my love.*
*Slow growing passion*
*is a century plant,*
*risking ruin by blight*
*before the centennial*
*blossom appears.*
*Our sudden love may end*
*like fireworks*
*in crisp sparks*
*but we hold*
*the arching memory*
*of how the sky*
*did marvelously bloom!*

The road became a shadowy tunnel. When the gelding ambled slowly past the pond, Sarah sighed with relief to find no one there. An odor of blood hung on the heavy air. A deer, she thought, or some other large animal fresh killed. An uneasy feeling came over her and she urged the gelding into a faster pace.

As the foliage grew lighter and became mostly small scrub pines, Sarah felt an irresistible urge to lie down under one of them and sleep just for a few minutes, and then she would be on her way. The Deacon had said to take her time while he investigated the criminals.

Just a *few* minutes' sleep would be so sweet—the long, tragic night, the fear, the two long trips across Cape, had exhausted her. Her nerves had been wound so tightly that she had felt no need for a rest but now the soft mist relaxed her and the urge to sleep was so strong that she feared she might fall off her horse. If she curled up out of sight . . . back here . . .

Tying the gelding to a scrub pine well off the road, Sarah lay down on the pine needles. "Warn me if anything . . ." she said to the munching horse, and was fast asleep in a few seconds.

Sometime later, a hawk screamed once from a dark hollow back in the woods. The sound ripped the air around Sarah. She sprang to her feet looking wildly around for a moment until she oriented herself. She had slept too long. Soon it would be dark! It had seemed all right to come back to the ocean side on the Deacon's request but not at night! The Deacon himself would have left by now, having finished his questioning of the men. Suppose he had found no evidence to back up her story? Her spine chilled at the thought of their vengeance here in this lonely place.

She mounted the gelding for safety. It was easier now, she was used to him. She reached down and stroked his neck, taking comfort from his warm, rippling muscles. They had been through a lot together and the horse had become like that familiar friend in a nightmare that one clings to as the others drop away.

The horse, hungry and thirsty, started up briskly for his stable and would not be denied. Sarah pulled hard on his bridle but he tossed his head and went faster. "Stop!" she cried out in a muffled voice. "We're going back, back to Wellfleet." But she could in no way force the gelding from his pull toward the stable. They were now at the dunes that flanked the ocean before the cliffs began their towering eminence.

If she could not force the gelding around, she would walk, run, anything. After all she had done her best, summoned the town to the wreck, gone to the Deacon, it was now time to save her skin.

As she prepared to slide off the gelding's back, he

snorted with surprise and pranced sideways. A man was leaning negligently against a high dune, his legs crossed and his arms folded. Sarah gave an involuntary scream at the suddenness of his appearance. But she realized at once that this was no Mooncusser.

He looked like a life-sized portrait framed there against the dune, all style and dash. While she stared, he was also staring at her as if in shock while his arms slowly unfolded. Shaking his head as if to collect his thoughts, he bounded forward to help her control the horse.

With his hand on the bridle, he said, "I have seen you before, coming out of the mist." His deep vibrant voice made this a declaration of fact. He paled slightly as he looked up at her.

Sarah hesitated, shrugged. "It's possible. Wellfleet is a busy port. But I have never seen you."

She would have remembered even a fleeting glimpse of this man whose intense air of masculinity was arresting even to a citizen of a whaling port. Who was he? A swaggering younger son of a great English house who had stolen all the family vitality as well as its silver and gone to the devil? A dashing freebooter, equipped with Letters of Marque from at least three countries at once?

"I have been trying to turn my horse around. I'll be obliged if you will start him back on the cross-Cape road," she said.

The stranger ran his hand down the gelding's neck. The horse stood still, appreciating this knowing hand.

"You are late," said the stranger.

"Late?"

"By ten years and a number of lesser women."

Sarah gave him a distant stare but her mouth betrayed her amusement. "I was unavoidably delayed." At once she knew it was a mistake to start bandying words with him.

"I'll run him through," said the stranger.

Enough, thought Sarah. No more playful jokes with this vivid man.

"Goodbye." She lifted the reins.

"Just leave your horse here in the courtyard," he said, "and come have some wine on my terrace overlooking the water. We'll talk over old times."

"Old times?"

He gave a laugh that rolled about the dunes and made them seem warm and inhabited. "We will begin our collection of old times now."

"Sir, you are a stranger to me." She made her face stern.

"Maybe so, but I'm a compelling stranger."

His laughter sounded familiar, full of zest and joy of living. It reminded her of . . . of . . . she could not trace the fleeting memory. But as she lingered here, she realized the intensity of her loneliness. Surely that was all that held her—the warmth of a friendly human being after so much terror. Surely that was all.

Sarah looked down at his big, well-shaped hand resting near her knee. He was like a sea breeze, insistent but with a warning of hurricanes. She looked curiously at his clothes—a habit, just as she always noticed the sail and fitting of a boat. His fine shirt was torn open and the ruffles hung to one side. He will rip them off, she thought, as he had the sleeves above his brown arms. His breeches were faded and tight on his agile looking thighs and the leather carving on his boots stood out, rimed white with salt. He had style. He was like a ship built for racing and fine company moored among ruffian brigs. Sarah liked style. She had first been attracted to Peter because he had what she thought was style, but this man had the real thing. Style must come from within first, and only then decorated with clothes. But why had she thought of ruffian brigs?

She felt drawn to his whole person with the pull of an undertow. Her awakened body leaned toward him very slightly and involuntarily.

He noticed and smiled directly into her eyes. "Dismount, why don't you?"

"Oh no . . . I can't do that. I'd be well on my way by now, but you are charming my horse."

"I see." He gave her a laughing look.

Sarah's willpower and judgement trailed off somewhere and was lost. She looked down at the gelding's head. All she had to do was lift the reins and gallop away. Even if the horse took her to the stables, and she trudged back to Wellfleet, she should go. Do it, she urged herself to no avail. Go . . .

The stranger, reading her irresolution, suddenly put both hands around Sarah's waist and swung her down. He caught the gelding's reins in a scrub pine and led Sarah to the high dune.

"This is ridiculous!" She was breathless for a moment. "I can't stay but a minute, just to rest my horse."

"Of course, he needs a lot of rest." He smiled at her with all the power of a man who consults only himself in all things.

"What happened to your other boot?" He kneeled down. "Let's take this one off. You list like a boat in a storm."

He pulled it off and Sarah moved her bare toes in the sand. In a moment she would be on her way.

"I lost one boot on my way to the Deacon's," she said absently, remembering odd things about that visit.

"A Deacon? You are lucky to still have on your riding habit," he laughed.

"He is a respected, older man," she said with dignity.

"Ah!" He shook his head. "Then it's worse than I thought. Better sit down and rest."

"No, I really have to go now."

"Where?"

She was silent. Where indeed? She had not worked that out. Peter had gone, possibly to his destruction. She felt a pang but, if she had followed and made some attempt to save him, he would with justice never have forgiven her. He had found his courage and it was his to squander. To wait for him, possibly forever, in that house on the dunes, alone, surrounded by murderous men was unthinkable. Go home to Wellfleet in a panic? If she had to, but she felt averse to showing the whole town that she was back home again so soon after her fine marriage. If Peter was dead, that would be differ-ent—a widow. But God knows she did not wish him dead. If he returned, then she would return. Well, in a few minutes she must get started for *somewhere*, but the warm mist was not conducive to vigorous decisions. It was like that lax, dreamy sensation of

239

sailing over the gulf stream.

"What to do?" The stranger looked into her face.

She stared at him a moment in the fading light. His face with its male vigor and its curly optimism pulled her as the moon pulls the tide.

He put an arm around her and drew her back to lean against the side of the dune with him. Sarah broke away from him. "You have formed a wrong impression of me. If I seem hesitant, it is because I have a lot to think about." She tried to speak forcibly but the words came in a murmur as she went toward her horse.

He made no move to follow her but leaned against the dune relaxed and watchful. "Why have you cut off some of your lovely long hair, your hair that blew in the wind out on Cape Cod Bay?"

She turned back to look at him in utter astonishment. "You saw me, out on the water?"

"Not as I wanted to see you. Your lovely body was covered with wet cloth."

"But . . . I never swim when another boat is near. You couldn't possibly have . . ."

"My telescope has never been so lucky."

"You must have been very far away or I . . ."

"Close enough to remember everything." He followed and, with strong confident hands, drew her back beside him.

Sarah understood at last that she was powerless to order her body on its way. Her entire person identified with this man who seemed a part of the fresh freedom of the sea. She had found another being like herself.

"Are you a mist maiden?" he asked. "When I was a

boy in Cornwall, I used to run away from my tutor and listen to the old sailors' tales. They warned me against mist maidens—to see one is an omen of doom. Ah, but what if there is more than seeing? Suppose I hold a mist maiden . . . like this . . . What then?"

His flexible voice descended to a vibrant hypnotic note. "I accept the omen and . . . . I take."

Sarah's keyed-up body, long cheated by neglect, flared in response to this perfect equation of man, time, and place.

Presently the mist blew away from the dunes and the moon became so brilliant that the beach grass was outlined against the sand. In the hollow behind the dune, the sound of the surf was like the muffled roar of a conch shell pressed to the ear. The whole night passed by as swiftly and easily as the clouds pass before the moon.

Once, as they rested, Sarah whispered, "Who are you?"

"Whom shall we get to introduce us?" The moon etched his smile into pools of shadowy amusement.

"I'll do the honors. I am Sarah Mayo." She drew in her breath, wondering at her use of her maiden name. She started to correct herself, but he was already repeating the name over and over.

"Sarah Mayo, Sarah Mayo, it sounds like distant surf, wind in the rigging, a soft tide against the side of a ship at night. Sarah Mayo, you are very warm-blooded for a mist maiden and, if disaster is your price, I will pay, over and over again . . . like this!"

241

When the morning light invaded their sheltering dune, he kneeled beside her looking into her eyes, his own brilliant and strong. His bold nose and laughing mouth curling up at the corners seemed to her like the familiar face of someone she had known all her life. Was this how it began . . . a deep and lasting love or a short indelible love?

A killdeer plover hovered in the air nearby giving her disconsolate cry; "You fools . . . you foo . . ools!"

Sarah put both hands over her ears. This abrupt passion had shaken her as the surf shakes a helpless boat. But when he put his arms around her again and she felt the driftwood smoothness of his neck and inhaled the clean smell that came from him like fresh sails in the sun, she knew that the delirium of the moonlit spell was over and the solid person in her arms was real. She was lying here on the sand with a gaudy stranger talking poetical nonsense about mist maidens and making wild, passionate love. She looked up at his rapturous grimace.

"You fools . . . you foo . . . oools. . !" cried the plover above them.

A light breeze blew a ruffled branch of seaweed onto her lover's hair, that curly hair of his that now hung over his forehead. The frilled seaweed resting over it reminded her of when she had hung her plumed riding hat on her horse's head just above his forelock. And suddenly, that old enemy of romance, that thread of the ludicrous, betrayed her. It wound through the tapestry of this high romance as easily as anywhere else. A trill of soprano laughter escaped her.

Her lover got up and walked away for a moment, adjusting his clothing. Every line of his body expressed grace and power and he had, with quick perception, unlike Peter, bowed to her change in mood.

Sarah put herself in order and shook the sand out of her hair. When he came back to her, he said, "My laughing lady, you choose a time for your laughter when I can't join you. Is that fair?"

How could she share such a ludicrous image? She shook her head, smiling at him, and prepared to leave him.

He held her face in his hands. "Next time we'll know for sure."

"How can there be a next time?"

"How can there not be?" he asked.

"But this is . . . almost mystical. Two people meet as if there were no time in back or in front of them and they . . ."

"Do the only correct thing to do in such a situation."

"I mean, sometimes nature herself conspires and the unusual becomes quite . . ."

"*Unusual?*" His laugh made the plover dive upward again.

Sarah got up. "It is unusual for *me* to have spent all night lying under the dunes with you, and then, just to say goodbye seems . . . seems . . ."

"Folly, of course," he said. "It will not be goodbye. Among other things, your laugh needs discipline." He pulled her close to him but her body was stiff, almost formal. He let her go.

Sarah walked away but more and more slowly.

She knew nothing about him—who he was, where he came from and, above all, why they had been together all night. If she left him now, so casually, what did it make of her? A wayside wench, lying with a compelling stranger for the brief pleasure of it? Suppose she did meet him again with the purpose of putting this whole affair in its true light, whatever that was. Then, they could say a proper and regretful romantic goodbye. But somehow that picture was not altogether pleasing to her.

She looked back at him. He held out his arms and gave a confident smile. "Come back." His entire magnetic person pulled at her.

She hesitated, her legs felt weak with remembered desire. With a physical wrench of her body, she went over to the gelding.

She looked back at him. "Tomorrow," she said, surprised by her own words. "I mean that. If I do come here tomorrow, it will be to talk for a while, explain, understand ourselves and perhaps say goodbye—in short, round things off."

He laughed heartily. "What nonsense you talk! I'll be here waiting and we'll round things off thoroughly." He looked out at the ocean a moment. "It might be that I love you."

He put one hand on the sharp grassy edge of a dune and vaulted over it. He was gone as suddenly as he had appeared.

Sarah got on the gelding and rode away. He pulled strongly toward the stable at first, but a revitalized Sarah tugged at him with authority. "No, not that way. We can't go home, especially *now*."

At last she convinced him and they rode back

across the Cape toward Wellfleet harbor. It seemed incredible that, after this experience, life around her should be the same. What had happened to her must have been a spell brewed by the warm night, the moon and the ocean. A demon lover? But he had spoken of love. Do demons love? Are they vain and virile? Do they yell with laughter and smell as fresh as the sea wind? She laughed aloud. No, he was real, and there was no way to excuse herself.

Her thoughts touched on Peter, delicately skirting the question of adultery. Had he met his enemy? Suppose he was lying dead somewhere even as she . . . a clutch of grief came over her. Not a mighty grief she realized, but to her relief it had the grace to be there.

When her hand rested on the doorknob at Zenas's house, she stood motionless a moment. The house was empty. She knew that instinctively. Zenas made his presence felt, awake or asleep.

She tied up the horse and brought him a bucket of water, some dark bread and apples and pulled up a little mound of grass for him. He looked at her suspiciously.

"All right, I've done my best for you, take it or leave it." She gave him a caress on his velvet nose.

As she ran up the narrow stairs to her bedroom and threw herself down on her bed, she felt weightless as if she were wandering in a dream. "I love," she whispered. "I love with my whole being, for the first time!"

Could it be that this stranger in one night had become her universe? She had, of course, sinned— but what *was* sin? Cruelty? This was not cruel.

Endangering someone? She had not done that. Deceit? Ah yes, as far as Peter was concerned, but she would tell him the truth and . . . depart.

She reached up and felt sand on her pillow where her back hair was resting. Drawing out a few grains, she held them in her hand and stared at them. Bits of shell and rock ground by time and tides from other shores, where people in past centuries had lain and felt this ecstasy for each other. And for each it was different.

With a feeling of mysteriously belonging to a vibration of love that girdled the earth now and then in past time, Sarah fell asleep.

# Chapter
# twenty

*Gentled by love,
troubled by mystery,
hounded by death,
we are unraveling
very slowly
to the central spool.*

aptain Collier was also troubled by mystery. A strong emotion and sense of well-being had blotted out the obsessive revenge that had brought him to this place on Cape Cod.

When Sarah surprised him, he had been waiting by the dune for nightfall when he planned to attack young Garrett, skewering his hired assassins on the way if need be. But now . . . he felt gentled by Sarah Mayo and the impulse was no longer there.

As he stood by the bluff watching the early sun rise over the waves, he tried to motivate himself by thinking of young Garrett's physical person which he found so loathsome, possibly because it was totally different from his own. That fine dry, blond hair, his bewildered, vulnerable eyes when he forgot the disguise of his sailor's squint. His long fingers and censorious nose which he brushed for reassurance with the edge of that Goddamned clean handkerchief. His head held high on a long neck and his oil-can shoulders. *Araghhh!* But it was no use counting the ways he found him repulsive. The vengeful tension was gone. The romantic echoes of this love—and he admitted love—had canceled out violence.

He buckled on his sword but, for the time being, he knew he was gentled. He had sailed over the Gulf Stream with its tepid languor with many a lovely lady and eventually set sail for the nearest port to rid himself of what had become a clinging nuisance. But, with Sarah Mayo, a man could sail over the Gulf Stream or any weather the ocean of life provided, sail on . . . and on . . .

He sat down, sifting sand through his supple fingers. Like most men of quick instincts, he collected physical details and formed opinions from them. He recalled a certain amused look in her eyes at the end, a look that went ill with lovemaking. Then that leap of laughter when the wave of passion was mounting in him. He frowned. Laughter was fine in its place, but a woman laughing when she should be half fainting with love, pleasure, fear, anything but amusement! Sarah was a mystery like the sea. A man could explore and never come to the end of questions.

The captain got up and walked restlessly back and forth. Next time, he'd discover more. He was ready for the next time now.

"I'm hungry," he said aloud.

With a sudden leap of activity, he jumped over the low dunes and found his black horse. He cantered off toward the harbor, his hungry, thirsty horse flattening out into a run. The sun shone brightly on the captain's muscled arms and made caves of his strong, grooved dimples.

The sun shone just as brightly on Abraham Cassidy's body lying with his feet in the pond. His eye sockets were already empty and his face half eaten.

249

As the captain stopped to water his horse and let him eat the green grasses by the pond, he took a look at his victim and reflected that the man looked better as carrion than he had when alive.

On his way again, his horse refreshed, the captain whistled through his teeth as he rode along. Today he felt that all the elements of his life were beginning to draw in and close about him like a drawstring but he resolutely kept his thoughts on his lady of the dunes and looked ahead with a light spangled joy, to their next meeting.

A little further down the road, he came upon Symonds, riding cautiously, looking to left and right. He shouted with relief when he saw the captain. "Captain! I've been looking for you all night." He pointed to the lantern that swung by his saddle.

"What are you doing here, Symonds?" The captain was very displeased. "Why aren't you on the *Windshadow* in charge?"

"What are you *still* doing here, Captain? The men left the taverns long ago and are on the brig."

"What of it?" The captain yawned.

Symonds slowly shook his head. Even his pessimistic nature couldn't help admiring this boundless confidence in a star that had faded more than once. "We can't trust them alone on the brig," he said. "You must have skewered that young whelp by now, so let's take a short cut to the cove. I've used up precious time looking for you."

"Not so fast. I haven't even tickled his hide."

"Christ! Then get it done fast . . . now!"

"I'm not in the mood today." The captain yawned again. "Tomorrow, perhaps."

Symonds kicked his horse's sides and then held

him in until rider and horse seemed to prance with fury together.

"What are you doing?" the captain laughed.

"I hardly know!" shouted Symonds. "Listen to me . . . *Will* you listen to me? This young pup will ruin us all over again. Let me run him through for you. *I'm* in the mood!"

Captain Collier took Symonds' horse and forced him about. "Go back to the nearest tavern and bring me some meat and wine and a few bottles of good champagne suitable for a lady. Bring it all to the big dune at the ocean end of this road."

"So it's a woman detaining you!" Symonds pounded his brow in despair. "Captain, don't throw away the *Windshadow* with all its plunder! I tell you the crew want the open water. They don't like being anchored off shore. It makes them nervous. They have already fought off a boarding party of land rascals. Somebody betrayed our hiding place. Our men killed a few of them, enough to cause some trouble. They want to weigh anchor *now!*"

"Congratulate the bastards on a good fight and tell them to wait there one more night."

"They will—but only if we get to the brig first and make them do it."

"By God, they'd better wait!"

"What will you do—run over the water and give them hell?"

"I'm hungry!" the captain shouted. "You know I would be recognized in the taverns. Go get me something to eat."

Symonds looked at him a long moment. "You may be full of power and luck but this . . . oh my God . . . it's stupid, Captain. Stupid, *stupid!*"

The first mate turned his horse and rode back

along the road, then with a rending sensation in his chest, Symonds tore away the habit of obeying Captain Collier and turned his horse off at the Truro road.

He'll be back, thought the captain with a laugh, and, supremely confident, he went back to the beach where he stripped and went in swimming. Plunging through the rising surf, his bare buttocks looked as powerful as those of a centaur. When he emerged, stripping the foam from his body, he pulled on his clothes and ate double handfuls of ripe beach plums.

The captain then stretched out under a pine tree where he had a clear view of the beach and the sky. More than a morning breeze was beginning to rise and the pine branches above him swayed and bent, groaning in a wind that had shifted to the east. He could smell a storm behind it. His men would never sail out on deep water on a dark windy day like the one that was coming. Not without their captain's seamanship at the wheel.

Captain Collier smiled at the dunes where he had lain with his lady and thought of her snaking the sand out of her hair. He gave a satisfied laugh and drifted off to sleep.

The birds called back and forth over him. In the woods, bats slid down their invisible bannisters. Now and then the captain, sleeping heavily, gave a loud snort that sent them into a panic, but the birds came back along with several field mice and a fox. The captain was less alien to the earth and air than most intruders.

# Chapter twenty-one

In the late evening
of the heart,
a memory of love
flashes
like heat lightning
and we think it is morning.

Zenas had been out fishing since dawn. After he docked and sold his catch, he dropped in at his favorite tavern where one liquid testimonial after another was offered to the new town hero, who accepted each award manfully.

His howling laugh resounded in the tavern until at last his admirers, unable to keep up the pace, fell away or down and Zenas was left alone.

Ordering lunch, he asked two barmaids to assist him in reading the obscenities carved on the heavy wooden tabletop, but they whinnied like mares and left him, their rumps tingling from his enthusiastic pats.

Zenas, more than a little drunk, sat pursing up his lips and smoothing them out. It was at this point that the door of the tavern opened and a woman came in. She selected a table near him, and gathering up her skirt until her full bottom was outlined, she sat down. Zenas was thrilled.

"Rum," she ordered. And when it came, she smacked her lips and swooped the glass up and over her large bosom without spilling a drop. She turned to face Zenas, shocking him to the very roots of his past—for she was the image of his wife!

Zenas's glass dropped out of his nerveless hand as he stared at her through a fog of rum. His dead wife come back to haunt him as a drinking companion? How unlikely, knowing her! Then who in hell was she?

"Hello, Zeeny," she said.

Zenas's mouth dropped open. It *was!* But no, it couldn't be. Would they crown his wife's puritan brown hair in heaven with a rolling breaker of perfectly dyed hair? His wife's eyes had always made him uncomfortable with their deep soulful expression, but this woman's eyes were merry and pleasingly hard.

His wife's mouth had tightened to a ray of wrinkles, but not this full mouth that even now was opening to a peal of laughter.

"What's the matter, Zeeny?" she asked. "Don't you know me?"

For some reason he smoothed back a lock of hair that had fallen over his seamed forehead.

She looked him over. "You are thinner and a good deal more drunken, but you still look like a fine man to me."

"Would you mind telling me," Zenas lowered his voice, looking at her askance, "who the *hell* you are?"

"Hope Bemus, of course. Your sister-in-law."

"Well, I'll be damned," he said.

Of course it was Hope, the girl who had marked him out for her own long before he took that boat ride with her sister. When they came back, he remembered how hotly she had accused her sister of poaching. "Well," Zenas repeated. "I'll be God-damned!"

"Your damns are getting monotonous," she laughed. "I'd prefer a not-so-brotherly kiss."

Zenas got up and went over to her, regretting his rum-soured breath. His feet were a bit unsteady but his mind was as lively as ever. Danger, it warned. This plump charmer wants everything.

Shut up, he told his better judgement, and he sat down close beside her. The perfume she wore mingled with his breath like a rose floating in rum. He gave her the kiss as ordered.

"Where the hell have you been all these years, Hope? We lost track of you."

"Oh, here and there. I married with some and tarried with some." She lifted a plump arm that glittered with fine bracelets and patted a curl.

"Crazy wench," said Zenas, "wearing all that junk here in this rough port."

She gave the satisfied laugh of a rich, fat woman. "I can afford to lose it," she said.

"Go to Wreckers' Tavern and you'd lose your arm along with it."

"I would *give* my right arm for you, Zeeny."

Zenas's fine grizzled head jerked upright. He gave her a piercing look. "I'll be damned . . . why?"

"I took the packet boat from Boston to the Cape to find out why, Zeeny."

"The hell you say—after all these years?"

"I've had you in the back of my heart all the time. You spoiled every romance for me. Finally I decided to come take a long, hard look at you, Zeeny, and free myself, but it seems to be having the opposite effect."

"I've got one damned Bemus sister after another, like a school of sharks chasing me!" Zenas gave a howl of laughter.

She laughed with him. "Maybe so, but I'm a *live* shark, Zeeny. Very much alive. If we can't be honest at our age, we never will be."

Zenas moved in closer and Hope met him more than halfway. "I loved you first but Serenity got you . . . first. It is all very simple."

Zenas poured himself some of her rum. "Christ damn but you're a straight speaking woman!"

"Straight acting, too," she said.

"Yes." Zenas was both scared and delighted. "I can tell that, all right."

They had several drinks, talking easily like the well-met boon companions they were. Finally, Hope put her glass down hard and said, "Times a-wasting. My packet boat sails in a few hours. The captain wants to get out ahead of the big storm brewing."

"So do I." Zenas put a hand on her staunch thigh. "God knows I never sailed right into one before tonight."

Hope threw back her head and laughed. Both her pretty white chins pulsed like a frog's throat. "There is only one Zenas. I ought to know—I've spent half a lifetime trying to find another one."

"Hell's tide!" Zenas was appalled at the thought of this sordid search. "I'm nothing to find at the end of a rainbow."

"Ah, but I have been more fortunate than most because I was looking for something, a quest, not just bowing my shoulders to time and events. I looked everywhere—frontiers, wars. Plenty of brave men, oh yes, but most men can be brave on demand. Real *men* are like genius, scattered in unlikely places."

"Goddamn," said Zenas mournfully. He felt hooked and gasping on the line. "Why didn't you look on the Cape?"

"Would I have found another Zenas here?"

"Damn close."

"But compared to you they all seem watered down."

"I could do with a little watering down." Zenas picked up the bottle of rum and poured it into their glasses.

She gave her full-bodied but discreet laugh that seemed always somewhat melancholy and reminiscent. "It must be that nothing ever quite matches what you loved when you were young."

She drank reflectively. "I am a very rich woman, Zeeny, rich in experience, friends and less important, gold. I could buy and sell Father if I knew where he was and if I could collect him after I bought him."

Zenas threw back his head and laughed with her.

"So here I am." She touched her glass to his. "With the handsome Cape fisherman that my sister married right out from under my heart. I must confess I sailed in here half hoping that you would be an old Cape Codder with a face like an oyster. It would have been the joke of a lifetime . . . on me!"

"But I am just that," said Zenas.

"Or you might have been a drunken old fool."

"I am," said Zenas. "Let's drink to that."

The old drunken seaman, Jeremiah, who had been pressed into service on Zenas's now famous cross-Cape journey with the whaleboat, came into the tavern. Avoiding the stern eye of the proprietor, he leaned against the wall and took a note out of his pocket. He gave a hiccup and tried to bring the words into focus.

Had he written this message to someone, or

scribbled nonsense? Sometimes when he was very drunk, the real truth, the key to everything, would hover just behind his tongue. He felt sure that he could put it down in one significant line. But whenever he passed what he had written across the bar to be read, people said it was gibberish. The barmaid would yell with laughter and ask if it was a proposal of marriage, adding that she would say yes as soon as he captained his own ship again.

Jeremiah, who had the outraged eyes of a captured bird—and he was in fact, captured, by alcohol—peered down at the words he had scrawled. It had seemed important at the time he had written it. Wasn't it something he had overheard in Wreckers' Tavern? He had made a note of it and written, "For Zenas Mayo," on the outside. He unfolded the paper but could not focus his eyes on it. He looked around for Zenas and lurched over to him, holding out the note.

"Oho, one of those," Zenas laughed. "Found the key to it all again, eh, Jeremiah?"

"Must of wrote this one when I was almost sober. Not too scrawly, take a look." Jeremiah hiccuped.

"What year was that?" Zenas knew all about the old fellow's notes and had never been able to make a thing out of them. He crumpled this one and put it in his pocket just as the tavern keeper advanced upon the old seaman and frogwalked him out of the bar.

On the way out, Jeremiah called back, "Take a look, Zenas. Something about Sarah." But his voice was drowned in the angry shouts of the tavern keeper, "And don't come back, you old sot!"

Zenas turned back to the gaiety and companionship of Hope Bemus. The very freedom that he found during his marriage had become a dragging anchor of late, although he put on more sail in the taverns to ward off loneliness.

They sat happily together, saying whatever occurred to them. "Tell me about Sarah's husband," Hope asked.

"A proud young bastard from Boston, eccentric as a bat at high noon."

She put her hand over his. "Who isn't eccentric?"

They drank on, airing ideas that had been folded up and put away like private papers. Now and then they slapped the table in delight. It seemed that, in all important ways, they were alike.

They ordered food and ate it in a floating, timeless mood. More rum followed to settle their stomachs. Zenas could hear the ships creaking in the rising east wind and the gulls splitting the air with cries of storm warning.

"I'm not a cozy man," Zenas said, "but I feel as cozy as all hell now!"

What a woman, he thought. A lady like her sister, but she doesn't mince words. She holds her liquor like a man and has all the comfortable, easy ways of an experienced woman. She looks like a fat-bottomed pear, hung on the branch a little too long but all the riper for that.

Hope's plump hand came over and rested companionably on his knee as she began talking to him in a new urgent voice.

"Time's a-wasting," she said, "and life is waiting for us all over the world." She gave a large and generous gesture.

"It's here, too, but hell's bells, life never waits, it *attacks*," Zenas said.

"Well, yes, it's here just as there is a world in a

drop of water, but who wants a drop of water? Pass the rum!" She laughed. "No, really; do think about it, Zeeny. Africa, the Indies, Egypt, Greece, everywhere. You love boats—we will *have* boats, any size, and sail the oceans of the world. I have plenty for both us."

"Goddamn!" Zenas stared into this plan with wonder.

"Well said!" Hope leaned over in the shadowy corner where they sat. She affirmed her offer with a kiss. They went on affirming until Hope drew herself up with an embarrassed look around. She pulled a jeweled watch out of her bag. "The packet leaves pretty soon now. I came here to cure a chronic disease of the heart, but it's too late. It has spread all over!" She leaned toward him. Her hard, merry blue eyes deepened.

Go ahead, Zenas told himself. This is what you should have had in the beginning. This is your girl. His stern eyes filled with light. "But I have the habit of solitude," he said.

"Lose it!"

This is a flood tide, he thought. Take her, with all her experience and her old, old love.

"Embark with me, Zeeny, chart your course for love and laughter. We've lived too much to take life seriously. The boat sails in an hour."

"Goddamn but you're a fine wench! A wise, warm, laughing wench." His hand slid down her shoulder to her arm and encountered her diamond bracelets. Some of the joy went out of his face. He drew back.

Hope stripped the bracelets off her arm and dropped them casually in her bag. "What's the matter with you. Money is only a servant. Put it in its place, never let it get the upper hand." She kissed him. "Now," she said. "Go on, what did you say I was?"

"Wise."

"What else?"

"A fine warm wench."

"That's correct," she said. "And I'll be all the wenches you ever had and a lot more."

"Why, hell," he said, "this might be love!"

"Why, hell," she said, "it *is!*"

They sat looking into each other's eyes for a long moment, then they began to laugh with helpless delight.

"Time for one more gulp of rum," she said, "and then we will roll aboard the boat."

"And into bed," said Zenas.

"Goes without saying." Her laugh had a pagan, tipsy lilt.

In perfect rapport, they finished their rum, then strolled arm in arm down to the docks. Zenas looked for and easily found old Jeremiah who was by now so far gone that he had forgotten having given Zenas a message.

Zenas scrawled a quick note to Sarah. "Take this across Cape to Sarah Mayo," he said. "And there'll be a bottle of rum waiting for you. Says so in my letter."

The old seaman started off in a vague zigzag course. "He'll get there sooner or later," Zenas said. "Drawn like a bee to honeysuckle, he'll find that bottle."

Hope led Zenas to the packet where the captain was already putting up sail. "He'll never leave in this wind," Zenas said.

"He's made a bet on the speed of this trip with a lifelong enemy in Boston. He'll leave," Hope said.

Zenas and Hope climbed aboard. The packet boat weighed anchor and began to glide out of the harbor despite every sign of a dark, stormy night. As they stood hand in hand on the stern, watching the lights of the harbor dwindle, Zenas feared that his old life would dwindle like the receding harbor.

Hope looked at him with a sensitive, unsure smile. "We can visit Sarah often," she said.

He clasped her hand. "Now and then," he said. "We will have our own life as she has hers."

But his heart did swell with memory. A thousand cords of habit that tied him to the harbor were being severed. Not only the little Sarah with skinny legs, a band of freckles across her nose and a flute-like giggle, but off-shore whaling, the taverns and echoes of old laughter, the lobster pots wreathed and encrusted and the sorrowful voices of the gulls.

Hope, aware of his emotion, was silent.

Zenas put a hand over his uneasy heart. It was time to leave all these oldtime joys. He had walked the same path from tavern to tavern too many times—and here was Hope, earthy, loving and capable of holding a long, long love. Life would be good with her.

A paper crumpled beneath the pressure of his hand. Old Jeremiah's drunken scrawl. Well, just to round off the farewell, read it and throw it in the bay, watch it float back home to the taverns.

He opened it out, smoothing it against the rail: "Heard tell the Mooncussers are after Sarah."

Zenas swore into the wind. "I will have to go back." He showed Hope the note.

She looked at him with shocked eyes. "Yes, of course, right away. I'll pay the captain to

263

turn back."

"Won't work," Zenas said. "Wind's against him and he has a bet on."

A wave slapped against the side of the packet driving spray up into Zenas's eyes. He put his hands on the rail.

"No, no," Hope cried. "Zenas, you will never get ashore!" She held him.

"Come back for me!" He pulled away from her.

"You *know* I will. Oh Zenas, live, *live*."

As Zenas hit the water and began to swim with nervous speed, he could hear her calling out over the wake of the packet, "Zenas, live . . *live*. . . ."

Zenas pulled for shore with his old, strong powerful strokes. He figured that he was opposite Truro or a little further down Cape. The wind was against him but what the hell, he was a good long distance swimmer or he used to be . . . . used to be . . .

It was not until he drew in his breath in gasps that shipped water that he understood that Zenas the strong swimmer was beginning to fail. He was not the Zenas who could command his body and it would obey and it was possible, really possible, to die here in the water!

Was he on a course charted for nowhere? Heading for the shores of youth that had washed away long ago? Was the tide set against age? Swim slow, old man, he told himself, swim easy. Point for the shore that's still there.

Damn his drunken heroics! He tried to float. The lights of the packet rolling in the high waves were still bright. He imagined Hope, leaning over the rail, trying to see him and still crying out, "Live, live."

Damn fool, he cursed himself. Could have taken

one of the small boats and made it to shore. Had to be virile, had to jump in and start ploughing through the waves like a young feller. Damn fool! Life finally stretches out a hand to you, a hand loaded with everything you ever wanted, and you refuse to accept payment. The debt has been canceled now. Life owes you nothing more. Just a chance to get the Mooncussers before they get Sarah. Give me that one chance and I won't ask for anything more . . .

He started swimming again, slower and slower, down into the trough of one wave up on the crest of another. It was clear to him that his chances of survival were fading, but his old mariner's body was feeling for the turn of the tide. If he could hold out and go in with it, without struggle or loss of strength . . .

A wave slapped him in the face, forcing water into his mouth and nose. He let himself drift a moment, upright in the water. At that moment he could feel it beginning to happen, imperceptible to anyone who wasn't tuned to the ways of water. But Zenas could feel the draw of the tide around his legs, feel it begin to change.

He lay on his back and managed to drift with it. Now and then he sculled quietly with his hands, resting all he could.

"Just overlook me, Death," he begged. "Forget I'm here. I'm a part of the sea, going with the current."

At last he felt himself grind against the sand bar. It took the rest of his strength to crawl out of the water.

Afraid of falling asleep on the beach, he put a broken shell under his head for discomfort and lay there resting for a few moments.

In the distance, he could still see the lights of the packet boat. He raised one heavy arm and gave a salute. "You threw me a line with that word . . . . That Goddamned magic word, a word to moor yourself to . . . *live!*"

# Chapter
## twenty-two

If you could twist the heart
of a cruel man
until its acid dripped out
and melted his bones
and he went screaming to Hell
begging for the moisture
of his own tears
which dried up long ago,
would you?

Sarah slept through the day. The sun was nearly gone and the crickets and grasshoppers had an evening sound when she finally awakened. She sat up abruptly as memory rushed in like a forceful tide.

Where was Zenas? The house echoed with emptiness. She went through the house getting reacquainted as if she had been away for years. After eating some fruit, she discovered a bucket of fresh clams and set about making Zenas's favorite clam pie. He must have been here to leave the clams earlier in the day. Surely he would see the smoke in the chimney and come home.

She could not talk to him about Peter, whom he hated, or tell him how her love had leaked away until the hold was empty. Nor could she tell him about love's sudden recovery with the man on the dunes. Zenas was a mighty sinner himself but she had no intention of discussing her wanton behavior with him. She only wanted to be with him and hear his voice. It was probably safe now to tell him all about the Mooncussers and her own horrible experience with Mrs. Cassidy and the murder of the little survivor almost in front of her eyes. It would be pointless for him, as new chief of the lifesaving crew of Wellfleet, to rush in now when the Deacon had it all under control.

The Deacon's servant, Sam, was at this moment looking up at Zenas's chimney where smoke had not been seen since Sarah left home to get married. Curious, he darted up the hill to investigate and saw Sarah out in the windy grape arbor, anchoring a redchecked table cloth with four stones at the corners. Sam watched her place a bowl of flowers in the center. She was making it festive for someone. He did not wait to find out who; that Sarah was still among the living was news enough.

Sam started on a run for the backside. He was half way through the forest and his breath was coming in quick panting gasps like the breath of a small animal, when he saw Wylie, his perfect, cold features outlined against a rock as he leaned against it. Sam stopped at a safe distance from the long sharp knife that Wylie was using for carving a bit of wood.

"What happened to Cassidy?" Sam asked.

"How do I know?" Wylie replied. "He's gone, that's all. Nobody has heard a peep out of him."

A peep, Sam thought, was an unlikely sound to issue from Abraham Cassidy at any time, particularly now. Sam had a hunch that he was dead. He had never failed the Deacon before.

As Wylie stood up, Sam shrank back slightly. He understood criminals, they were men who had broken something in themselves like a mainmast and they were wounded within and therefore fierce like any other wounded animal. Sam felt at home with criminals but feared a whole man—like Zenas, for example. But Sam also feared this newcomer, Wylie, with his empty eyes. The sockets of a skull's eyes had more expression.

So, well within the shelter of the woods, Sam told him what must be done.

Wylie nodded. "All right," he said. "Leave it to me." He blew the wood dust off his long, shining knife and put it in his pocket as he walked down the sandy road toward Wellfleet harbor.

All along the way, the birds sang as sweetly to Wylie as they did to anyone else.

At a little distance from the grape arbor, Wylie halted and stood watching Sarah place a large pie on the table. Wylie kept his hand on his knife and a bright, empty smile on his face. He liked to pause and stare when there was time.

The current of life in people was such a mystery. Death he understood very well. A body became all of a sudden a large jellyfish, hard to pick up. But life! What made the body so tense and lively only a moment before? A year ago in Bedlam, he had pondered this mystery before he escaped, but the inmates there seemed not so much alive as full of the frenzied gestures of the dying.

Wylie stared fixedly as the girl in the arbor waved eager flies away from a large pie. If he touched her, she would spring up quick and tense, full of that strange life force that left a body he had stabbed, and yet, he could never *feel* anything rush out along the blade of his knife, try as he might to solve the mystery. Killing was easy, like spearfishing—a struggle, a trophy, but what *was* it that went out of the body? Wylie shook his handsome head slowly. One thought such as this had sufficed him for

270

years.

Sarah put the finishing touches to the table for the festive, welcome-back-together, dinner she planned.

She had a lost, uneasy feeling and suddenly realized that she craved company but there was no one in all of Wellfleet that she cared to see. She had been too proud to make a friend of anyone who looked down upon Zenas, which had eliminated all of prosperous Wellfleet, and others were too uneducated to share her thoughts.

Where *was* Zenas? Enjoying his new celebrity with a long spree? She might have guessed.

Sarah's hand fell to her side. The clam pie was getting cold and she might as well let the flies climb over the brown crust. She watched them twiddling their front legs together in a kind of grace before dining. "Go ahead," she told them. "No one else is coming."

The wind was rising in the east, another storm off the coast. That explained the brooding airless warmth of last night. The storm had been gathering, hushed for a spring.

Sarah looked around. She felt suddenly miserable sitting here in the darkening shadows by an empty house. A stern expression came over her face. Maybe it was meant to be empty because she was trying to go back in time for comfort. She was steering for a backwater, setting her compass for nowhere. She must get on with her life.

"What am I doing here?" she cried aloud.

"What?" Wylie said.

Sarah started, she laughed briefly. She had imagined a voice saying "What?"

"Zenas?" she called out into the dark. "Is that

you?"

Wylie put his hand on his knife. Silent as the shadow of an owl, he came to the door of the arbor and stood in the dark, looking at her. These pre-pleasures were too soon over with.

A sudden thundering knock on the front door of the house made Wylie hesitate even as he entered the arbor. He withdrew behind a pine tree.

Sarah ran to the door and greeted old Jeremiah with some disappointment. "Hello, Jerry. Zenas isn't here. Did you look in the taverns?"

"For you." He thrust Zenas's note at her. "I been all the way to the backside looking for you. Sobered me up, too. I got to fix that. I worked up a powerful thirst, ho, ho!"

Sarah smoothed out the crumpled paper:

Setting sail tonight with my girl, your Aunt Hope. I'm hooked, my dear, right through the gills and damn glad of it. Be back to see you before long. Give old Jerry a bottle. Love Z.

Sarah read it three times. Both old Jeremiah and Wylie waited impatiently for her to finish.

Finally the old seaman cleared his throat. He took a chew of his red beard. "Big storm blowin' in on the backside, kind of weather for a drop of demon rum to ward off all the other demons, eh, my dear?"

"Did you see my father leave?" Sarah asked him. "Is it too late to . . ."

"Yes, left on the packet boat. Now about that rum, my dear."

"Tell me, did you see *her* . . . I mean the woman with him?"

"Yes. Getting mighty thirsty."

Sarah had never seen her Aunt Hope, but it seemed impossible that her father would fall prey to a replica of her mother! She went to the cupboard and took out a bottle of rum, but held it tightly. "What was she like?"

"Well she. . . . .she . . ." He made a large, round gesture."

"A plump woman?"

Jeremiah sucked in his cheeks and looked at the bottle. "How can I remember? I'm too thirsty."

"Think hard, Jerry. You were drunk, of course, but you must remember *something*."

He winced. "Now if I had a few pulls out that bottle as promised me by Zenas, I might remember real sharp."

"Oh, all right. Take it."

The old seaman seized the bottle and edged toward the door.

Sarah pulled him back. "No, you don't! Tell me about her."

"Well, she put me in mind of a bellbuoy, round and with something steady about her. She had a real loud laugh. You might call her a bellbuoy with a diamond necklace."

And Jeremiah was gone into the night.

Sarah went back out to the arbor and stood a moment looking at the attractive table she had set. "When I really need Father, he has flown the coop or the Cape." She gave an ironic laugh at her own predicament.

Wylie took his knife out of its sheath and prepared to act. He was quite used to people laughing into the night and talking to themselves. It almost made him homesick for Bedlam—Now what was she doing?

273

Sarah took the flowers from the table, stuck them in her belt and suddenly shouted into the night, "All *right,* sail off with your love, the buoy with the diamond necklace! I am going to *my* love."

With a speed that took Wylie by surprise, she darted into the house, took up Zenas's gun, then ran out to the gelding.

Wylie, a few seconds too late with his knife, stood still in the dark and watched her ride away down the hill. He was relieved by his failure—not because she was a beautiful woman, that made no difference to him—but for some time, his nostrils had been quivering with the aroma of clam pie, his favorite dish.

At first the air had been heavy and deep with it, then, as it cooled, the smell grew thinner and more threadlike, but still called out to Wylie and to scores of rapturous insects who flew in upon the slender path of fragrance.

Wylie sat down at the table, swept away the flies and cut himself a wedge with his long knife. Too cold, just as he had feared. He took it to the kitchen where the fire was still glowing in the little wood stove. He sat whittling on a piece of wood, until the pie was warm. He ate slowly, savoring the exact proportions of onion, potatoes and clam. He had a fancy palate.

When the last bite of light, flaky crust had dissolved in his mouth, he decided not to kill its creator. But suppose someone else did! Wylie's thoughts came slowly. He wiped his shapely mouth and thought about it. He would protect her—yes, keep her safe.

He put the remaining half of the pie on top of the stove where it would keep warm for her. He could be very thoughtful. He had always been tender with his mother and he now thought of Sarah as a mother who made good-tasting things to comfort him.

Wylie stood for a few moments at the top of the hill, looking around. The whale oil lamps were lit all over town but the boats were dark. Even here in the harbor, the strong wind was tilting every mast. There would be a high surf over on the ocean side and a dark night. That meant there might be something doing tonight, some real sport. Wylie enjoyed taking apart the innocent-looking contraption the men carried to the beach. It looked like a mast and could be used either as a fake mast for swinging a lantern to fool a ship or as a ladder to board what was left of the wreck when she struck the shoals.

About one fourth of the whole length of the mast could be pulled out. That part held the rungs of the ladder attached to it by hinges so that when it was pulled out, the rungs also came down and out of the hollow part of the mast to form the ladder. The other end of each rung was inside a runway which was attached to the opposite part of the mast. The runway ended at the proper points so that the rungs were at right angles to the mast and thus were supported. The ladder could be closed by pushing the side back into the mast and the rungs would move up into the hollow part of the mast.

Oh, it was a sweet invention, thought Wylie. He loved to swing the great mast with its lantern on the tip, loved to fish with this bait as much as he loved the action in the waves when they had caught their huge fish.

Wylie ran his tongue over his teeth, dislodging a morsel of clam pie. He had better follow the girl.

275

Mrs. Cassidy or someone might get to the creator of this pie unless he protected her. He put his hand on his knife handle. A few bodies more or less wouldn't make much difference tonight. It looked like a fine night for fishing.

As he loped along the shortcut through the woods, he thought about Mrs. Cassidy and how her thick white skin, as full of pores as a sponge, offended him. She had made his knife tingle when he first met her a few months ago in Wreckers' Tavern. He had cosily gravitated there soon after his arrival on the Cape, after his escape from Bedlam and his kidnapping aboard a whaleship to complete the crew.

Whenever he looked at Mrs. Cassidy, it put him in mind of carving blubber on the whaleship. Wouldn't it be nice if he ran into Mrs. Cassidy now!

But when Wylie came through the woods and rejoined the cross-Cape road, just as he had expected, he found someone posted there looking down the road. Word must have got around that the girl was on her way. There must be no mistakes this time.

Wylie circled around through the heather. The girl would have to be saved to comfort him with pies, to be a mother. He came up in back of Zeke, the cook, who waited. His big hands, his best weapons, hung free and ready by his side.

Wylie's knife struck him with the speed of a lizard. Zeke's bucktoothed face turned gray-white but remained charged with evil as long as his face lasted.

Sarah heard the thrashing sound and a bubbling cry but put it down to one animal overcome by another more ravenous one. She was more accurate than she realized.

A northeast wind sang through the bearberry and heather and tested the suppleness of each blade of beach grass. Clouds erased the moon and the rumbling crash of surf shook the air as Sarah came to the end of the cross-Cape road.

She was nearly blown off her horse, but clutched at Zenas's gun as old Jeremiah had clutched the bottle. She was a good shot, having been taught by Zenas and, even if she couldn't see to shoot here, the gun felt comfortable in her hands.

Dark as it was, she knew instinctively when she had come to the dune where they had been together last night.

It was deserted!

It had never occurred to Sarah that he would not be here waiting for her, no matter what the weather. She bowed her head down before the wind to absorb this shock.

The gelding plodded on for a moment, then suddenly shied sideways, rearing up and throwing Sarah from his back.

# *Chapter twenty-three*

Living dents me
here
and dents me
there,
but I am nimble
they have not found
the place. . . .
so far.

arah landed in the soft sand and rolled away from the horse's hooves. He had been startled by a small fire sheltered in a cave dug out of a dune.

There, with the flames lighting his face, was the stranger. He was scowling into the darkness with no trace of the gaiety she remembered. He bounded to her and picked her up in his arms.

"Where were you?" he shouted above the wind. "I was about to put the ocean between us."

A swirl of wind filled the air with sand. They ducked their heads, and he put her down in the cave he had made in the dune. He bent to kiss her but she drew away.

"What now?" he said. "I have waited here for you when everything I owned was at stake. I have waited beyond that."

"We must talk," she said.

"You don't understand. My being here now is the summit of folly . . . of love. We'll leave together and talk all the truth you want when we are on the water. We'll have a lifetime of chatter when we are not better engaged . . . like this . . ."

"No! Don't you see, we can't just . . . we behaved

last night as if we were not in the world at all."

"Fine, we'll do that now."

"But we have to find out about each other. We both have this . . . this shining memory of last night and we may have to fold it away . . ."

"Fold *us* away? What kind of a lovely fool are you?"

"I don't know—I keep discovering a new kind every day."

"Then let me inform you, multiple fool, that I know why you came and why I risk my life which I prize to meet you here. It is because we . . ."

"No, don't say it! You don't know me. First of all . . . I didn't tell you the truth. I am married. My name is . . ."

He pulled her to him. "Who cares? We'll talk later, on the water." He kissed her with a passion that waned as she remained cold and still in his arms.

"You will spoil the other night," she said.

"Nothing can."

"But there must be another way to know each other. Don't you *want* to know who I am?"

"No."

"Then tell me who *you* are."

"I'll tell you when we are out on the water. Now it might jeopardize you to know."

"But we are not out on the water. We may never be. Let's talk the truth now."

He released her. "Whoever you are, I want you. But go on—waste our time in gibble-gabble. Tell me who you are."

Sarah drew a deep breath. Somehow she felt that to reveal her name was going to be explosive—why, she had not as yet understood. She had won, but in a female reaction, she dallied a bit, almost sorry now. "All right. I'll begin. Although I don't know exactly who I am at this moment. I'm either a fisherman's daughter content to wench on the sand with a stranger, or the child of a fine Boston lady who finds lovemaking not to her taste unless it has other graces such as good talk shared."

He burst out laughing. "You speak as if you had a clear-cut choice of qualities. You are a composite, thank God." He took her in his arms again. "To be all wench would be a disaster equalled only by being all fine lady."

He kissed her. "You are Sarah Mayo, and you came here to meet me a second time. Let's have no more of this 'who am I' folly. A split mast is useless."

She was quiet a moment, hiding the easy buoyant sensation that spread its warmth through her.

"You felt nothing when I kissed you?" The hint of stricken male ego in his voice made something in her heart go out to him. She held out her hand. He clasped it, saying, "So be it, I'll trim my sails to suit the wind. You want me to talk, I'll talk."

He began with an exaggerated patience but his voice soon grew impassioned. "After you left here last night, I felt as if I could stand lightly atop the surf. My heartbeat shook me and my mind was stunned with the memory of the light in your eyes when you awakened in my arms. My ears still heard your little private trill of laughter that comes, I must add, at unseemly times. My hands still felt curved as if they held a body smoother than driftwood polished by the waves."

His flexible voice dropped to a clear, quiet note. "I am more of a man yet less of a man. I feel tenderness for the first time. But you are crying now . . . why?"

"With relief," she said. "I know *why* now. The vein of poetry in you, the . . . the cadence of your voice . . . the . . ."

"I'll give you a different cadence now," he said. "I went to sleep here, waiting for you. I somehow thought you would be back during the afternoon. Judging by my own feelings, I did not see how you could stay away.

"When I awakened, and my first mate had not arrived with the food and champagne I ordered for us both, I felt something give way inside, I knew what it was before I jumped on my horse and ran him to the cove. My men had stolen my brig. Mutiny!"

He picked up a piece of driftwood and broke it apart for the fire, bulging the muscles on his arms and chest. "Bastards!" He gave a bright cruel smile. "I'll catch up with them."

He put his hands on her shoulders and their heat burned into her. The fire shot up in a shower of sparks revealing the stubble around his jaw and his vivid, magnetic face. "I never discuss my plans with anyone. I do now, only because I can't drag you over the heather. You'll have to gallop willingly beside me."

"No!" she cried.

"What is that word? I never hear it." His hair blew in the wind and his grooved dimples were deep.

He is wild, Sarah thought, wild with grief over the loss of his ship and maybe with love.

"I don't know the man who asks me to gallop beside him."

"That didn't trouble you last night for much more than a gallop."

"Nor do you know who I am . . . So I . . ."

283

"I don't care who you are. Sarah Mayo is all I need to know." He held up a hand to test the wind. "Time will be on my side tonight. In this storm they can't round the end of the Cape . . . fools to try without me on deck." He twitched his shoulder with impatience. "We must act, not sit here introducing ourselves. Come, I have a fortune in a London bank. We'll buy ourselves a fine boat."

"What holds you here?" Sarah asked. "Leave, why don't you?"

He looked at her somberly. "You know full well what holds me here. I am not leaving alone."

Sarah met his gaze. She sat motionless.

He gave a sharp, exasperated sigh. Holding out his hand to her he said, "If it must be, then take my hand and we'll sail quickly back over the past. It's against the wind and the tide to go back, but we'll embark."

Sarah took his hand. She held it in a firm, warm clasp.

"I come from the coast of Devon," he began. "The son of a drunken squire. My mother, a sensitive lady, read every book in his library, then, when she came to the end of them, died one night, I believe of acute boredom, while her red-faced man snorted in alcoholic slumber in his wing chair by the fire.

"My education was the only thing upon which they agreed. I was prepared for any high office I cared to pursue but I was wild as a gull in a storm—as revenge upon them, I thought, being unable to see the first and only real victim was myself.

"I sailed through my youth as close to the wind as possible, then took to privateering. I am not obscure, having turned the tide of many a battle by preying on enemy ships, Navy as well as merchant ships." He gave a vain grimace.

Sarah's head jerked back in surprise. "In other words, a pirate. I should have guessed."

"Call me a privateer in the employ of several navies."

"What do you mean?" Sarah's voice was stern. Her hand dropped away from him.

"I am the arm of two navies," he said. "There can be no recognition, thanks or medals, we must take our chances, but the recognition from several governments is munificent. We see that it is, in advance." He waved his hand and gave a careless shrug.

"It's almost the same as piracy . . ." Her voice choked over the word. She turned her shocked face away. "Your conscience must be as thick as a sea turtle's shell."

"Look." He drew out a gold tooled leather envelope that was full of large bills and drafts on a London bank. "We are rich. We'll buy a fast ship, take her into Jamaica and get a fresh Letter of Marque from the Governor. From that moment, Napoleon's luck begins to turn."

He threw back his head and gave a vigorous yell, broke it off and seized her around the waist. The very thought of action turned him into the fiery, compelling man of last night.

"You'll have a castle in the Indies, a hundred servants, peacocks in the garden, pearls in your hair and we'll make love all night long and eat melons by perfumed fountains. And *then*, my love, we will talk about our passion in the best soul-searching New England fashion. How's that?" He gave a confident swagger.

"I am married," Sarah said.

"Lose him in a thousand miles of our wake."

"You would have me leave him for you, a pirate who has done countless, cruel, briny murders?"

"You persist in calling me a pirate? As for *cruel* . . ." he was sincerely outraged, "very seldom do I take life. Murder is forbidden on my ship except in self-defense or to turn the tide of battle. Never for lust or discipline. I am cruel only as nature is cruel, not wantonly but with form."

Sarah, shocked and sorrowful, got up. "Good-bye." She turned away, stumbling a little.

He bounded after her, taking her roughly by the arm. "What folly, to have to plead a case, convince a stubborn woman before I take her away! Listen then." He spoke with rapid, furious eloquence.

"I am a thousand times more kind than a court of English law. There, a citizen can prove his neighbor guilty of a small misdemeanor and have him pilloried. They nail his ears to a board that lets his head and arms protrude as a target for kindly law-abiding, civilized people who can be relied upon to stone him until he is blind.

"Yes indeed, how pleasant it is to be law-abiding, especially when a law that covers forger or the treason of a wife to her husband—and take note of this, Madam—provides in its mercy that the lady must be hanged until nearly dead, then drawn and quartered on a stone block, the entrails to be pulled from the criminal's belly and burned before her eyes. A difficult sentence, for the just and civilized law you seem so fond of demands that she be still alive during the burning."

Sarah murmured something and tried to pull away but he held her fast. "*I* am cruel, bloodthirsty?

Forty thousand law abiding people went to see two men and a woman hanged last year. It was a festive outing with mirth, dancing and fornicating in all the alleyways." He laughed abruptly. "Yes, where I grew up any clergyman could denounce a man, woman or even a child for an offense against decorum and have them stripped from the waist up and whipped from Aldgate to Newgate until, the kindly law says, 'the body be bloody'. I hope the Christ of these clergymen rewards such zeal? I survived that bloody journey when my father had me denounced for defying him. I survived only because I was an unusually sturdy ten-year-old."

He let go of her arm and ripped the front of his shirt down further. "See, the scars have grown with me, keeping pace with my determination to keep off dry land where such things happen."

Sarah gave him a horrified look. "I won't listen," she said violently. "It must be false."

"Why? Because it is terrible?" he laughed. "But you and I will be on the sea, Sarah Mayo, where most of the rending takes place by nature, under the water."

"I refuse to become a part of all this evil and cruelty," she said.

"Miss New Englander, you already are. The same tide laps in us all. It is a longing to see punishment done for crimes or mistakes that we feel capable of performing ourselves." He shrugged. "We punish ourselves through others. It feels better that way."

Sarah thought of her father. Despite his potential, he had insisted on becoming a drunkard to punish himself and his wife for their union. And then her mother in her turn used her powers of contempt to punish Zenas for her own mistake in marrying him.

287

And I, she thought, have been punishing Peter because I stepped aboard the *Challenger* that night, a mistake of every degree!

"Punish," she said. "A horrible word! I hate the very sound of it."

"But revenge is clean." He looked up at the black stormy sky impatiently.

"Revenge or punish, I fail to see the difference."

"Enough talk. We'll leave now and take the *Challenger*. Why not? She's a fast racing sloop and I have a right to her. He owes me a ship. Can you sail her with me? We'll pick up a crew in harbor or kidnap whoever is on her."

Sarah's jaw dropped. "Did you say the *Challenger*?"

"Yes, it's time to go." He tightened his grip on her arm. "I came here to the Cape to maul an enemy and I have tarried too long on the dunes with a lovely woman until the vengeance was near drained out of me. I'll content myself with his sloop."

At last it came clear for Sarah. She should have guessed it from the first. This man was Captain Dear Friend! She stared into the night, shocked and cold. She had lain with her husband's mortal enemy and betrayed this man as well by not informing him of her real name—a double betrayal.

"I have changed my mind about talking," she said. "Nothing can be gained by telling you who I am."

"Right," he said. "I have already talked too much. I bore even myself. We have better things to do than wrangle over your puritan scruples which are, after all, come-lately."

He drew her to him. "Time Waster, chatterer."

She slipped through his arms and moved away,

beyond the ring of firelight to hide her face.

"You see, you can't leave me," he said.

"I must know about your enemy, the one you came here to . . . to maul," Sarah said out of the darkness.

"We haven't *time* for all this! Anyway a stronger emotion has dimmed my feelings for him. You ask about my life, my enemy, and announce that you refuse all comment on your own situation. Come, my love, forget all this nonsense. Let's be on our way."

"How do you know that your . . . enemy has not surrounded himself with vicious guards? I would think he may have." There, she thought, beyond that I cannot interfere.

"It would be like him." He sat upright, frowning into the fire. "Will you leave me if I tell you about him?"

"Tell me," was all she would say but she drew close to him and to the fire.

He spoke quickly to get it done. She sat absolutely still, listening it seemed with her entire body.

"We were looking for water and turtles in the Galapagos and there he was, marooned by his crew who had turned pirate, marooned until his flesh had shriveled on his long proud bones. There was not much left of him but that cursed look of high-mindedness on his face."

Sarah nodded to herself. Who else but Peter?

"Sometimes I go back in time," he said. "Back . . . far back to that day when I first saw the cursed white handkerchief, that symbol of his that he had rigged up on a pole. It was a hot day and even now I can almost smell the tar melting in the cracks on deck. His signal was so small on that distant island that I might have mistaken his flag of distress for a gull and sailed past . . . oh happy dream!"

"Why do you regret the rescue of another human being?" Sarah's voice was muffled, as if her hands were over her face.

"Regret? That's a squeak of a word. I wish I had left him rotting on his island until nothing was left of him but a stinking shimmer of integrity, nothing that couldn't be fanned away by a gull's wing!"

Sarah sat up straight and looked out toward the black water where even the whitecaps were invisible. No need to ask him to name the man with the long proud bones and the shimmering integrity.

"We took him off." His voice was grave as if he described a multiple disaster. "We fed him and dressed him in the best we could find aboard—my own clothes. But the men had an instinctive distrust of him. One day he found out the business of the brig, as we took a merchant ship—line of duty, she was supplying an army. But he, having been marooned by his own crew, had a hatred of anything that smacked of piracy. Although we took off the captured vessels armaments to bring to the country that gave us our papers, we of course sweetened our crew a bit with some extra items.

"Our rescued New England puritan denounced us roundly for it. The crew would have killed him, but I saved the life of this fastidious young man. Why?" he shrugged. "With a gentler career I might have been something like him but not so priggish. The men would have tossed him overboard when I slept, but I saved him from them only by making sport of him so that they let him live as an entertainment."

Sarah remembered the night aboard the *Challenger* when Peter had taken a sudden dip into the past and described a nightmare filled with fiends, the stench of turtles in a hold and a roaring laugh.

"Go on." Her voice vibrated like a stringed instrument. She felt impelled to fill in the spaces, to know it all.

"We should have cut him up to feed the turtles in the hold." He twitched one shoulder.

"But what did he do to you? What *could* he do in his position?"

"I let him off at the first port we touched. He stood listening as I guaranteed him to my worried men. I had saved his life a score of times. He was a gentleman with a code of honor and I was impressed by his discipline under stress and also by his damned high-minded look which he wore as he strode off my boat. I had the privilege of seeing that look once more as he stood up in one of your New England courts to denounce me as a pirate. Before we could leave port, he had us seized. As he informed against us, he kept flipping the edge of his damned informer's nose with his handkerchief. He had seen my look, and fear makes his nose run, the rheumy bastard."

Sarah could see Peter perfectly well as marooned, and comporting himself on the freebooter ship with poise at all times—but oh, not informing on his rescuers, not informing on the man who had saved his life over and over! She had received so many shocks now that she felt numb.

"We may have taken a few trophies for ourselves here and there in the line of our naval duties," he went on, "but Garrett had most of my men hanged. He used to walk by the jail and stand staring at me, fearful that I might escape hanging. He knew what would happen if I did. And I *have* and it *will*.

291

"He would stare at a portion of my foot or arm through the bars and walk on. He was afraid to meet my eyes again. You see, the cold young prig had put the dark side of himself safely behind bars. That's the way it is with punitive measures. Someday there will have to be something better, more humane, and sensible."

"What happened then?" Sarah asked in a small voice.

"The King's Navy pulled some wires and had the sentence changed. I am too useful to hang. They knew that, while I lived, no bars could hold me and. . ." he shouted into the wind, "so did *he* know that! Nothing can hold me not when I can smell his blood somewhere on the wind. I was gentled by love, last night, but now that I have brought it all back to my mind . . ."

"What are you going to do to him?"

"I'll throw his eyeballs to the gulls, I'll . . ."

"Give it up!" she cried. "Give it up and go away because . . ."

"As well tell me to give up breathing," he broke in. "After all the time it took me to escape, get at my treasure in England, buy a brig and procure fresh Letters of Marque, he owes me a fortune in time alone. I hate like a brother. Damned high-minded prig! He is the other side of my coin, what I might have become had I cleaved to the letter of the law."

Sarah shut her eyes and let the sandy wind tear at her face.

"You have had your revenge," she said quietly.

He shouted down her words unheard. "Come with me! We'll sail his boat out with the tide and bring her to harbor down Cape this same night and I'll come back for him. I'll bring a trophy to nail to the bowsprit, a lock of dry blond hair and a white handkerchief. Then we'll sail her out over deep water and exchange ships with the first likely brig we overtake, in the line of duty, that's heavy enough to carry cannon—Sarah, where are you? Answer me! Sarah!"

He snatched at the darkness outside the circle of his fire. "Answer, you witch, you mist maiden! You bewitched me into telling too much, into raising my blood lust, my vengeance. Sarah Mayo, Sarah Mayo, where are you?"

He ran crashing into a high ridged dune for the dark was now total, nothing could be seen.

Somewhere in the night, she called out, "You have had your revenge!"

"Come back," he roared into the wind.

Somewhere in the night, the snort of a horse and the soft clopping of hooves on sand was Sarah's only answer.

Captain Collier stood still. The wind blew sand into his face. For the first time in his life, he had confided in a woman, made himself vulnerable, and she had left him. Furious and pleading in turn, he called into the wind until sand grated in his mouth.

He listened to the sonorous beach below, then with a wrenching movement of his whole body, he stamped on the fire until it was out, threw himself over the dune and started down the side in an avalanche of sand. Even that was not fast enough.

Down on the beach, he tried to outrun his anger at his enemy and his frustrated desire for Sarah, but the sand delayed his feet and the unseen spray of the surf cooled him down.

Hatred left him as if a red glaring eye had closed. Now his entire being called out for Sarah. He shouted her name aloud in the wind and the waves seemed to echo in a hollow roar: "Sarah Mayo Sarah Mayo Sarah Mayo."

# Chapter
# twenty-four

*We are measureless*
*within our box of bone*
*that holds a tempest*
*and a galaxy*
*of equations.*
*Compared to us,*
*the ocean is no deeper*
*than a saucer.*

Sarah and the gelding bowed their heads to the flying sand. Keeping the tumult of the waves on their left, they progressed slowly through the windy black tunnel of the night.

A rip-tide of emotions filled Sarah. Her lover's murderous hatred seemed as terrible as Peter informing on the man who had saved his life. As for herself, she had done a thorough job of betrayal all around. A complete score. No right action occurred to her now, only to go to the house on the dunes and attempt to save . . . prevent . . .

In between the rhythmic thunder of the waves, Sarah heard a cracking of bushes behind her. It could be her lover following her but it might not be. In any case, the gelding was too easy to follow. Even in the storm his snorts could be heard and the rattle of his bridle as he shook his head, longing for the stable.

She slipped easily off his bare back and felt her way to a dune beside the cliff. Within the next few moments, the gelding gave a neigh that was half a scream of pain and pounded away at a dead run.

Sarah could hear someone cursing and running

after him. It sounded like the pock-marked groom, Comstock. Sarah ached for her friend, the gelding, who had become dear to her and was now wounded, knifed probably by Comstock, who was after her. But why? Why were these men still here? The Deacon should have removed them by now. What had happened? Had they convinced him of their innocence? Had he gone back for the militia, or—unthinkable—was he indifferent? Even more unthinkable, was he himself involved with the Mooncussers?

As she tried to recall anything about his reaction to her visit that would indicate this, she heard voices down below her on the beach, calling to each other. Of course . . . it was a perfect night for a Mooncussers' strike.

Far out beyond the reefs, the glimmer of a ship's light was just barely in view. "Lord have mercy on that poor ship and all hands aboard!" Sarah whispered.

If she saw a lantern swinging down on the beach, would she have mercy enough to shoot out the light? Or would she save her own skin and lie safe in the dark while a good ship was wrecked on the shoals and the crew slaughtered?

As if by appointment, a light began to climb over the dark resounding beach. It stopped mast high and began to sway and dip like a ship in high seas. Now and then in its disciplined dance, the beam flashed on the taut faces of the men below, highlighting deep furrows from nose to mouth as they looked from their light to the faint light out on the water. They had the dedicated look of artisans engrossed in delicate work.

Each of the men took his turn at supporting the

mast and each took his turn at the ritual of pulling on the rope which gave the light its deceptive rise and fall. Each man looked as if he believed the decoy would fail unless he performed the mimicry in an exact fashion. They were as silent as fishermen when the catch is near the bait. Some clasped their hands in mock prayer.

Sarah could almost feel the pull of the message from the false light to the ship out on the water whose light now seemed a little nearer to the shoals.

She loaded and prepared the gun in total darkness, then leaned it on the dune and lay flat on her stomach. Sighting along the barrel to the bright, swinging lantern just below her, she knew she could not afford to miss. They would be upon her. No time to reload, no second chance for her or the storm-tossed sailors.

If only the lantern would be still a moment! She followed its dip and swing and waited for a time of transition from one team of Mooncussers to another, when the lantern might hang still for a second or two.

Looking out at the ship, she whispered, "Trusting fools!" They were coming in closer, there was no doubt about it. Soon in this heavy sea it would be too late to warn them.

Sarah took quick aim and fired. The lantern shattered, dropping bits of glass and flame down on the men who held the pole. Shouting with surprise, she could hear them make a rush for the cliff.

Sarah dropped the gun and ran full speed in the direction of the house. Keeping pace with her panic was a feeling of hard courage. At least I've done

298

something here that I can be proud of, she thought. I have spit in the very eye of fear and made a damn good shot too, as father would say!

The climb up the cliff delayed the men as she raced by them. If they had any brains, she thought, they would climb up further away by the house and cut me off. She ran a little closer to the edge and saw that some of them, carrying a lantern, were running up the beach to climb the crevasse.

Terror pumped new speed into her but not enough to pass by the place where they would climb. It was impossible. She looked around. The woods? Where?

At that moment, Otis's furious deep barking came from the edge of the cliff as the men tried to climb over. The lantern showed Otis guarding the cliff with quick darting bites. He was too wise to close his teeth on one of them and be knifed by another. One of the men yelled with fear and pain as Otis snapped at his face.

Sarah ran toward the faint glimmer of light coming from the house. Thank God, Peter must be home! She flung herself against the door but it was locked. How much time could Otis give her? So far, judging from his snarling barks, he was holding his own.

She pounded on the door. "Peter!" she yelled. "Let me in! Oh hurry, hurry, let me in!"

Peter ran down the stairs and flung open the door. Sarah jumped inside then turned back. "Otis," she screamed. "Come!"

The sounds on the cliff stopped as the men, realizing that they were too late, retreated to the beach. Otis came racing through the door and sat down, looking up at them with an air of proud achievement.

Sarah slammed and locked the door. When she turned to Peter, his face seemed oddly unfamiliar to her, as if a great deal of time had gone by for each of them.

Peter threw his arms around her and gave a rapturous laugh that amazed her.

"Sarah! What could be better! I was just coming to Wellfleet to get you."

Peter, with his joyful smile, seemed to have escaped from his cage of nerves and was moving freely in the outside air. "It's a good sign that you are here. Everything is going to be fine from now on."

He led her up to the tower room where the wind, persistent as water, howled around the closed casement window and the surf sounded through the room as if it were a hollow shell.

How young he looks all of a sudden, thought Sarah, feeling old and infinitely sad herself. Peter's features seemed unlocked almost back to his boyhood. He failed to jump when a handful of pebbles flung against the window made Sarah leap convulsively.

"Peter," Sarah's voice was low, even. "Someone is out there on the dunes, trying to get our attention."

Peter shrugged. "Let them try. *You* have all my attention."

"Peter . . . It could be Captain Dear Friend!"

"But all that is *over*," he said. "His brig is gone. He either changed his plans or . . . he is dead." He took her by the arms and in his excitement shook her slightly.

"Don't you understand? He came here to the Cape and, of his own volition, went away. He has changed his mind. Too much risk, or he is at last bored with the chase. My charging at him has shifted fate somehow. His unsavory crew may have done away with him. Whatever the reason, it's all over and we are free to love and to be together without secrets or fear from now on."

God help me, thought Sarah. How can I tell him that I came back only to try to save him? She looked at him in wonder. He seemed real at last, now that she knew all about the fear and possible shame that had motivated him, knew but would never understand how he could have informed against the man who saved him, then, fearing him, wanted him to hang.

"Peter, we have to leave here, *now*, race to the barn and ride to Wellfleet, if it is not too late."

"Don't worry about anything. We're *going* to leave. I'll put the house up for sale and we'll sail away tomorrow on the *Challenger*."

"Mr. Garrett, sir," called a voice halfway up the stairway.

"Mrs. Cassidy!" Sarah gasped. "How did she get in? Has she a key?"

"Not that I know of," Peter said.

They went to the doorway and stood looking down at the large woman who seemed to fill the stairs. She had halted only because Otis stood in front of her, snarling and rumbling, his short yellow fur standing up along his spine. But Otis did not cause the look of shock and horror that came over Mrs. Cassidy when she looked at Sarah. She went back down a few steps but, when Sarah spoke, she regained her stolid appearance.

"What are you doing here, Mrs. Cassidy? Looking for another lamp?"

301

The act of courage it had required to shoot down the Mooncussers' lantern had been germinating in Sarah like a seed and she looked boldly at the woman. She congratulated herself but at the same time remembered a bit wryly that she had Peter and Otis beside her.

Mrs. Cassidy said, "I was surprised to see you here, Mam."

"Why?" Sarah asked, her voice hard.

Peter stepped in front of his wife. "How did you get in, Mrs. Cassidy? You are intruding." His placating manner was gone. He had no further need of it.

Comstock's pitted face appeared behind Thankful Cassidy. "You didn't believe me. There she is," he said.

"You get down and tend to your business below," she murmured to him.

"The door was open, sir," Thankful turned back to Peter. "I was just coming over from the harbor side alooking for . . ."

"The door was locked," Peter's cold voice broke in. "I told the men to go. I have no further need of them. Everyone is paid up generously for the next two weeks. Do you understand me? Go home, all of you. Mrs. Garrett and I want no more of you on our property."

"Lord, how fast you talk, sir. Can't get a word in," said Mrs. Cassidy, aggrieved. "I came here looking for my husband, sir."

She gave Sarah a long wicked look and Sarah felt again a ripple of the old terror this woman inspired in her.

Comstock, who had disappeared below, now called up from somewhere near the front door, "It takes a little time to get underway, sir, and it's a

302

good—I mean a very *dark* night, sir. With a thankyou for all your generous pay, we'll leave in the morning."

"No!" Peter called down. "You will leave now. Go tell the others. I want it well understood."

Comstock went out the door. His violent oaths could be heard outside.

Mrs. Cassidy glowered at the dog who blocked her way and kept up a low slavering growl. She raised one of her big clumping boots as if to kick him, but Otis gave a convincing lunge at it. Sarah would not have been surprised to hear Mrs. Cassidy growl back at the dog.

Thankful addressed herself to Sarah. "What have you done with Abraham?" She gave a fleering smile. "I've heard tell as how you're a very good shot with a gun."

Sarah looked at her with amazement. "Abraham Cassidy? What have I to do with him? I passed him yesterday evening by the pond in the woods. He was going fishing in the big pond."

"Fishing!" Thankful Cassidy gave her a long, knowing look. "That's a good story, a very good story. It's not that I care much what happens to the old hulk, but he is mine and, if anyone is going to put a hook through his gill and troll for sharks, it'll be *me!*"

Sarah gave a cold smile. "I don't know what you are talking about, but a medal for public service should be given to whomever disposes of either of you!"

I must be mad, Sarah thought. Would I dare say this if I were down at the bottom of the stairs?

Thankful raised her booming stormvoice. "So you won't tell me where you stowed him? We know you

303

have a gun and you know *how* we know it."

"What is all this?" Peter asked.

"Mrs. Cassidy is annoying me," Sarah said.

"I'll do more than that first chance I get," Thankful said. "I can stow people away forever, too."

"That's right," Sarah said. "And I have seen you doing it."

Thankful gave her another long look that resembled that of a malignant sea monster—a moray eel, Sarah thought. Finally the woman turned and clumped downstairs, slamming the front door behind her.

"What was she talking about?" Peter asked. "You have made a vicious enemy there."

"She has a very dangerous enemy too. *Me!*" Sarah could almost feel the woman's murderous hatred left behind, palpable in the air. The shattered light must have ruined their night, saved the ship. Sarah was about to tell Peter but he had gone down to lock the door.

When Sarah followed him down the stairs, she found that Peter had set out some bread, cheese and wine. Sarah began to eat ravenously, but, as her hunger lessened, she wondered at her appetite. How could she eat while down on the beach were murderous men probably making a business of wrecking a ship, killing the crew. How could she eat so heartily while a man inexorably bent on revenge was coming through the storm to Peter?

Those stones thrown at the window could not have been from him, or he would be here now. One of the Mooncussers must have thrown them, hoping that she would lean out, her head framed by the light to give him a perfect shot.

Tired of thinking, weary of emotion, she flung herself down on the couch and listened to the storm. The wind had risen to a gale. Pray God the ship had turned away in time. Distant rumbles of thunder sounded above the boom of surf. Lightning cracked across the waves as if whipping them to greater frenzy.

To Sarah, feeling alone with her rip tide of emotions, the ocean now seemed shallow as a saucer compared to the measureless depths of one human being.

In the hall she could hear Peter hammering a board across the front door. That was just as well, since the Mooncussers seemed to have the key. In a moment she would get up and call out to him to make sure that Comstock had not stolen their spare sperm oil lamp. In a moment, yes, she would do that; it was important. She doubted if they could make do with a household lamp out there but they might try—she must make sure . . . but the long ride, all the emotion, fear, wind, wine and food had made her drowsy.

She drifted away and dreamed of going back to her lover on the dunes with Peter in tow. "You see," she explained to them both, "God help me, I can not bring myself to throw either of you back in the water to drown!"

As she lay sleeping, she looked beautiful but worn, like a figurehead that had been through weather.

# Chapter twenty-five

Her heart was piping
its first tune,
a tender green melody
like a blade of grass
growing in granite.

After a while, the incoming tide lapped over the sandbar close to Zenas's face. The shell began cutting into his scalp and he awakened, cursing and strong enough for anything.

He got to his feet and walked up the beach, estimating that he was somewhere between Truro and Provincetown.

After some miles of walking, he found a tavern that was run by a friend. "I need rum, a horse and a gun, in that order," he told his friend.

As soon as Zenas arrived in Wellfleet, he located old Jeremiah, shook him out of his usual drunken stupor and took him down to the dock to douse his head.

"It's no use, Zenas, All I can remember is hearing the word being passed in Wreckers' Tavern that Sarah Mayo was in the way. You know what that means! But they must have changed their minds."

"How do you know that, Jeremiah?"

"I saw her, she was home at the old house, safe and sound. She give me a bottle but it's all gone now, more's the pity." He sucked in his cheeks.

Zenas with a great sigh of relief fixed the old

fellow up with the only tonic that could help him now, more drink.

At home, he found a piece of clam pie still warm on top of the stove. No one but Sarah could have made it. He supposed that she had waited for him and then dined alone, apparently with good appetite. It was not likely that a girl in mortal peril would eat half a clam pie. Anyone as close to the elements as Sarah would feel uneasy if in danger. Well, he'd go across Cape and see for himself. She must be home with her husband by now. He'd take a look around for Mooncussers while he was at it.

Zenas relaxed and dressed his sinewy body in dry clothes. He wolfed the rest of the pie, feeling no pang at having missed Sarah's visit. After all, this night he had paid in full with everything he had, for any past neglect of Sarah. For her sake he had abandoned his woman, survived a dangerous swim and come home to a lonely house.

Lonely, hell! The house looked downright alien to him now. Hope's laughter rang in his memory, lilting, pagan and wise. He had swum away from life itself, back to a habit, an empty shell of life. He was ready to sink all Mooncussers in the bottomless pond single-handed.

Zenas got back on his horse and galloped along the cross-Cape road to the other side. He stood a moment getting his bearings in the dark. A windy night, moonless with a rough lee tide. Made to order for the Mooncussers' siren light.

He dismounted and lit his oil lantern. With the cliffs so near, it was safer to lead his horse. He turned the flame down to a flicker protecting it from the wind with his coat.

He progressed slowly, keeping the sound of the

breakers on his left. Thunder growled far out on the water and a flicker or two of lightning—too far away to ruin the night for Mooncussers. If the thunder storm were nearby, one vivid flash of lightning would reveal the whole area and their pole and light to any ship approaching the shoals.

Zenas reached out into the night and beckoned to the storm. "Come in closer to shore where you can do some good," he shouted.

Mrs. Cassidy, stationed on top of the cliff as a lookout, heard his voice. She turned around and saw the spark of light coming from his lantern. She ran to the edge of the cliff. Down below, the men were carefully swinging the sperm oil lamp, an indoor lamp Comstock had procured somehow to replace the shattered one. It was hard to maneuver. They were concentrating.

She threw some stones down, hitting them harder than was necessary.

"Look out, you heavy-handed bitch! It's our only lantern," one of them called up in a muffled voice.

"Put it out," she called.

In a few seconds all was dark except for the dipping light on a ship heading straight for the shoals. The evil tension of the Mooncussers was almost a palpable force on the dark beach, pulling at the ship.

Fearful that the ship's peril might be seen by the man on the horse, although he was not near the edge of the cliff, Mrs. Cassidy felt for the brick that swung in a stocking under her petticoats.

She could no longer see the spark of light. She listened for the soft *clop clop* of a horse's hooves but the storm made that impossible. Finally her acute hearing located the whinny of a horse as

Zenas's mount sensed the presence of other horses in Garrett's nearby stable.

Once Thankful Cassidy had located the horse, it was easy to follow the creak of leather and slight jangle of bridle in the dark.

Zenas had seen nothing of the activity on the beach below. The Mooncussers were well hidden from the road in the shelter of the cliff and he had not looked out over the water where the ship was headed direct for the dangerous shoals. He had been preoccupied with preserving his lantern and looking for a light in Sarah's house, to orient him in the howling dark.

Zenas jumped as the dead-white face of Thankful Cassidy appeared in the small beam of his lantern light. Her head seemed to float like an unsavory blob while her black shawl merged the rest of her person into the night.

"Hell's gale!" said Zenas. "What are you doing here, Mrs. Cassidy?"

"The same to you," said Thankful. The coy smile that creased her face as she recognized him filled Zenas with dismay. That anyone so repulsive had a warm personal feeling for him, gave his cast-iron stomach a lurch of nausea.

Thankful came closer to Zenas and gave a sigh that could be heard above the howling gale. "I'll confess that I'm a-looking for my poor husband that has been missing these last two nights, God rest his loving soul."

"Congratulations," Zenas muttered.

"That ain't in order yet." Mrs. Cassidy gave a sly smile. "I ain't sure he's dead. As long as I'm out looking for him, I thought I'd bring a little cheer to the boys that works for the young off-Cape furriner.

311

I brought a bottle or two from the tavern but now that I've found *you,* why the hell with *them.*"

"I'm busy." Zenas was very curt. "Better get back to your tavern. It's a rough night out for a woman."

Struck with the surprise of someone considering any night too rough for her, an open-mouthed expression of wonder flitted across Thankful's face.

Zenas turned away. He wanted no more mysteries. He had enough of them inside himself. A wicked woman should stay that way and not go mixing things up. This terrible woman had no right to go all mushy, feminine and coy.

"But I'm in safe harbor now," she advanced a few paces, "with you here to protect me, Mr. Mayo . . . Zenas."

Zenas dropped back but Mrs. Cassidy followed. Her plan to knock him out with her stockinged brick before he could see the ship or the beckoning lantern on the beach was by now abandoned. Thankful Cassidy's heart was piping its first tender green tune, like a blade of grass growing in granite.

Zenas recoiled from her with great energy.

"If it's Abraham you're worrying about, he is probably dead," she said. "Anyways, I got no more feeling for him than for a sand flea—never had, the one-eared bastard. But if anyone is going to have the satisfaction of killing him, it should be me. Somebody cheated me there. Don't go away, Zenas, stay here a while along with me."

"I don't give a small slice of Goddamn about your husband," said Zenas.

Thankful, misunderstanding, quivered like a boat hitting a rock. "No more do I," she simpered.

Zenas prepared to bolt but, with a longer stride, Thankful came up to him face to face.

"Don't go." She lowered her foghorn voice to intimacy. "If you're on your way up yonder," she jerked her head toward the house on the dunes, "to see your girl, Sarah, why the little lady is home safe and sound with her hubby who is busy right now nailing up boards inside the door. Now that don't sound very hospitable does it? Guess you can't get in, so let's you and me keep each other company."

"How do you know he's nailing the door shut?" Zenas asked.

"I was just there a-calling on them to see if they knew where Abraham is, because if the old bastard is lying dead somewhere, I want to feast my eyes on him."

Zenas turned down the wick of his lantern against the wind and prepared to leave.

"Stay with me awhile. The night is a fierce place for a lone woman." She gave a hypocritical whimper.

"Some women are more fierce than any night," said Zenas.

"Don't leave me here all alone. Let's have a little business chat. I can offer you a handsome sum of money."

"You . . . offer me money? Goddamn it, what for?"

"Why not? You must have known when they gave you the office of life-saving and made you head of the beach patrol, that a lot more than that would come in with the tide, so to speak."

Zenas stood still, his hand tightening over the handle of the lantern. "For instance, a few tokens from grateful Mooncussers?" His voice was deliberately noncommittal.

"Now, Mr. Mayo, who said anything about Mooncussers, grateful or otherwise? I'm sure I didn't."

313

She gave a sly giggle that sounded like the gurgling of tide-water in a hollow cave. "I just thought as how you might be looking for a profitable side-line."

"Doing what?" Zenas asked.

"Well, seeing as how Cassidy has most probably cashed in his chips, or he would be around tonight all hotted up with . . . well, that's neither here nor there. Seeing as how he *ain't* here and I always thought as how you were twice the man he is . . ."

"A damn low estimate," said Zenas.

Mrs. Cassidy made the night hideous with her appreciative laughter.

Zenas took no more steps backward. When the Cassidys and their friends had once been accused of mooncussing, Deacon Handy had reluctantly dismissed the charges for lack of any evidence other than the appearance of evil. However, given a grain of fact, Zenas and his new beach patrol crew could do the rest. He forced a receptive smile.

"Well, well. Go on, you interest me, Mrs. Cassidy."

"Call me Thankful." She was too close to him now. Zenas tried to hold the lantern between them. Lighted from below, her face seemed huge, her nostrils tunnels.

"Just a little side-line for you. You could work it right in with your life-saving work."

"How so?" Zenas asked.

"Well, it's the same kind of thing. You're dealing with human life, only with a different attitude. More . . . well . . . like Abraham used to say, 'Some save, others spend.' "

"What do you mean?" Zenas asked. He knew full well but he wanted to hear it from her.

Thankful put a hand on his shoulder where its heat burned through his clothes despite the cool

314

wind. "Can I trust you? I want to. I'm hungry for a real man."

Zenas forced a smile. "You've been on starvation rations in the tavern." He put his lantern down.

That was enough for Thankful, with another bray of laughter, her heavy arm went around his neck and she sat her square body against him.

Zenas tried to put his arm around her but his flesh refused this terrible order from the brain. Give her a little encouragement, enough to make her tongue wag. You don't have to make the supreme sacrifice, he reminded himself, but still his arm refused.

Thankful Cassidy pressed against him. "I'll share everything with you. If the one-eared bastard shows up, he'll wish he hadn't," she whispered with a hot blast of her fetid breath in his ear.

"Share what?" Zenas asked.

"All my property as it comes in."

"From where?"

She leaned on him heavily. "All you have to do is protect our property."

"How?"

"Make sure that there won't be claims and lawsuits—*you* know."

"How do I do that?"

"Come on, Zenas, loosen up. I'm not asking you to do anything unpleasant. I'll cut up the bait while you sit in the shade." She pressed a kiss against his averted face. Zenas felt his flesh crawl away from the spot in ripples.

"What do I do exactly?" he asked hoarsely. "Be quick."

"That's exactly it," she said. "*Don't* be so quick. Don't come ripping through the crowd on the road with your new beach patrol and your life-saving crew. Let nature take care of things before you get underway. When the next cry goes up, 'Ship ashore and all hands perishing,' you just rest back, say Amen, and have another drink for the road. At the same time you can tell the money in your pocket to move over and make room . . . a crowd is coming."

"You hell hag!" Zenas yelled. He felt thunder in his brain, lightning in his nerves. He longed to trample on her and throw her away as he would a reptile. But he controlled himself and only hit her, with a force that would have sent a normal-sized woman flying to the ground.

Thankful rocked a little but stood her ground. Zenas put out his lantern and merged into the darkness.

"Where are you, Zenas boy?" Thankful called in her coyest voice. She was used to violence and considered it a voluptuous prelude.

"Zenas," she roared above the wind. "You naughty boy, I know you want me to come find you! Where are you? Give me a little hint. I have more, much more to offer you."

As she continued to call out to him, her booming voice began to change and hold a note of doubt.

"Zenas . . . Mr. Mayo . . . Answer me."

She turned this way and that, bellowing in progressively colder and more threatening accents.

Finally she was quiet. She had said too much. Zenas would have to go. "My foolish heart," she said aloud, pressing her hand on this tender organ. The best man on the Cape too, she thought bitterly. Goodbye, Zenas Mayo, but business is business. For once she took no comfort in the phrase.

At that moment, a carriage came slowly around

from the end of the cross-Cape road and turned to come over the heather toward them. Its light revealed the narrow figure of the Deacon's servant, Sam, sitting up in front.

Thankful gave a yell of surprise and ran to the carriage.

"Shut your big oven door of a mouth," said Sam. His manner was brazen, his voice harsh. Not a trace of the squirming lacky was left in him.

"What?" Thankful looked up at him incredulously.

"You heard me," said Sam. "And get your ugly face away from me or I'll . . ." He drew back his whip and gave a hard laugh.

Thankful, stupefied by the change in this craven little man, looked in the carriage window. The peak of the windstorm was over now but the fine carriage quivered and shook as the Deacon's great bulk floundered around inside.

Zenas, standing nearby unseen in the dark, saw a hand reach out. The carriage lights shone on a triple bulge of chins and a ghastly face. Zenas edged closer. Deacon Handy here . . . at this hour!

"What brings you here, sir?" Thankful Cassidy asked. Zenas had never heard her use such a respectful, groveling voice. She added, "We have everything well in hand, sir, you may be sure of that."

What could she mean? Zenas came closer. A strange remark from Thankful to the Deacon.

Deacon Handy stared out of the carriage window at her with tragic, beseeching eyes. His face churned but his mouth hung open in a queer one-sided way. Uncouth sounds came from it.

"What did you say, sir?" asked Mrs. Cassidy, awed.

The new cocky Sam spoke up. "Stupid here paced the floor half the night, then he fell down with a crash and I found him like this. He croaks a while, then he grinds out a few words. He told me to pile him into the carriage and drive here. Pile is right, the old fool! But I did it. Always wanted to watch the sport down on the beach."

Sam leaned out and lightly flicked the Deacon's face with his whip. "So here we are, Stupid," he said.

"Stop that!" said Thankful. "Why, how can you treat him like that and calling him . . ."

"It's a favorite word of ours, like a password," Sam laughed. He nudged the Deacon hard with the butt of his whip, "Isn't that so, Stupid?"

Thankful seemed unable to take in the extent of the Deacon's indisposition. She came up close to him and bellowed as if he had been stricken deaf.

"Got your message all right, sir!" She bobbed a curtsy that sent Sam into a gale of laughter.

"You picked a good night for our fishing, sir," yelled Thankful. "And we've got a big one on the end of the line right now. Your share should be very satisfactory, sir."

Zenas had heard enough. He had urgent business in town. This was a case for the militia. He eased away, found his horse, then let him out into a run for Wellfleet. Sarah was safe enough with that ass of a husband nailing his house shut.

As Zenas galloped along, the whole pattern of Mooncussing on the lower Cape fitted together like the scales of a fish. He had known all along that someone powerful was protecting the Mooncussers but it had never occurred to him that it was the Deacon! Now that he knew, somehow it was no shock at all. Those pious bastards were the worst.

Meanwhile the Deacon's haggard eyes remained fixed on Thankful Cassidy, while his lips struggled and writhed in an effort to speak. Sam, as sprightly as a mouse playing over a dead lion, gave a free and easy laugh.

"Well, don't stand there staring at him," Sam said. "Get back to your business. *He* don't care any more about the action down on the shore, do you, Stupid?"

"My God," said Thankful. "What's wrong with him? I know every variety of drunk there is and he isn't one of them." She finally accepted the fact that something irrevocable had happened to the Deacon and addressed herself to Sam.

"He's been took bad, real bad," Sam grinned.

"But, my God, what will we do now?" asked Thankful

"What do I care?" Sam said.

"Get him to a doctor."

"He won't have one. He wants to ride back and forth over this road looking for something. You'd think he had a fortune in gold hid along here. Maybe he has. That's why I go along with him."

"He's saying something," Thankful pointed at the Deacon's face as if he were no longer human.

Deacon Handy's mouth worked and brought out the words, "Stop . . . Cassidy."

"Cassidy!" said Thankful. "I'd like to get my hands on his freckled hide, myself. What do you want with him?" She yelled into the Deacon's face, the better to make the stricken man hear.

Deacon Handy's face quivered as if shaken by the wind. When he had felt the approach of death, something became clear to him. His money and his power were vanishing with his life but whatever love he had managed to feel, remained with him. The last of his strength was focused on this.

His flaccid jowls had become so heavy that they dragged the lower lids of his eyes down, showing a broad edge of inflamed red. After much struggle with his drawn down mouth, he brought out the words, "Sarah . . . Sarah Mayo . . ."

Thankful yelled at him, "No, it ain't done yet, sir. Cassidy disappeared, then Wylie had a go at it but something prevented him. I must say, I don't like the way the smooth bastard follers me around with one hand rubbing the handle of his knife. He ain't normal like the rest of us. So then, sir, we put Zeke on that job, but *he's* disappeared too. It's like mysterious."

"Arah . . ." croaked the Deacon. "Not . . . kill."

"I'll get to it myself, don't worry, sir. I'll get her."

"You don't need to be polite any more, does she, Stupid?" Sam again flicked his whip across the Deacon's congested face.

The Deacon reached up a slow hand and brushed at the whip as if a fly had annoyed him.

He was entirely obsessed by his message. His hand came out of the carriage window and grasped Thankful by the shoulder. He looked at her earnestly from his red-rimmed eyes as he slowly and thickly told her, "No . . . No, don't . . . Sarah . . . Mayo. Not . . . ever . . . ever . . . kill."

Thankful yelled with the pain of his grasp. "Oh *what* is he talking about?" she cried out to Sam. "His voice is so queer I can't make head nor tail of it. Is he trying to change orders on us *now?* It's too late, she knows too much. Or is he mad because it ain't done yet? I swear I can't figure him out. Let *go*, sir, don't hang on like that."

"You learn slow," said Sam. "Calling him 'sir.' You don't have to take orders from him! He's lost the use of his legs. I had to drag him out to the carriage like a sack of meal and believe me I did, bumpedy bump. He can't move."

Sam twisted around to yell at the Deacon. "All right, for the last time, where's the money hid, Stupid?"

"Sarah . . ." said the Deacon earnestly.

"Make him let me go," roared Mrs. Cassidy in a panic.

"He's dying. Hit him," the Deacon's servant said. "Hit him in the face, he'll let go."

Thankful took his advice.

"Save Sarah Mayo," mumbled the Deacon. He had at last put the right words together.

However, Thankful had gone and so had Sam, who at last had his fill of the sport.

Deacon Handy remained alone, abandoned on the dunes, looking out over the edge of the carriage window. Now and then he croaked a few words into the wind.

# Chapter twenty-six

The pain I give
I will inherit.
The tears I cause
I will shed.
To injure you
will maim myself.
From all such cruel
involvement,
I will deliver me.

When Peter came back upstairs, he bent over his sleeping wife. "Wake up, Sarah. Those ugly people are locked out now for good. In the morning, if they are not gone, I will throw them off our land. You are beautiful and I love you. Wake up, Sarah, our life begins *now*."

He looked at her with rapture. Sarah opened her eyes and thought that she would rather never awaken than be the one to remove this joy from his face.

"But I must do it," she said aloud.

"Must do what?" He sat down on the couch beside her, laughing.

"Warn you that . . ."

"No more warnings. We are free. I feel it . . . know it! With this day comes an unshakable conviction that I am free of him. I no longer feel that strange tie that was like being bound to him. I am sure of this, Sarah, sure! I feel a change coming for me. A total change. What else can it be but freedom? I feel almost drunk with it!"

"I beg of you listen to me. Let me speak." Her eyes were full upon him, candid and sad. The pupils appeared to flutter as if with pain.

"It's you who pays no attention to *me*," he said lightly. "I'm stepping into something new, free, and unfettered."

Sarah was silent a moment. Finally she shuddered and began, "*He* has not sailed away . . . or given up."

"What do you know of my enemy? You have been brooding. Forget him, Sarah." Peter's voice was confident. "We are both free of him."

"I can never be entirely free of him," she said.

"Why not?" He looked at her in amazement.

"Because I know him."

"You! How could you know him . . . where?"

"Last night on the dunes. He is out there now. I . . . saw him again . . . tonight."

"What! You *met* him? You, alone, and in danger! I never should have let you go out. I was off like a fool, following phantoms while my wife was in danger!"

"I was in danger," Sarah said. "But not from him."

"What do you mean?"

"The danger was here," she touched her chest, "in me."

Peter looked at her attentively. His face became grave.

"I was riding the gelding through the mist at night. I . . . felt alone."

Peter was so silent that he seemed not to be breathing.

"Have you ever been so alone that you feel there is no one else in the world and the sudden physical presence of another person is a . . . a magnet?" she asked.

Peter was silent, waiting.

"When I met him there by the dunes, something that I had only glimpsed in myself around the corner of my being, pounced on me and became my whole nature. Afterward, this new me went back to its post around the corner but was a little more visible than before."

. Peter said nothing.

"I am not saying this the way . . . perhaps there is no way to say it. But . . . I am not just one person in a box, but a series stretching out to . . . God knows where. For what we Sarah Mayos have done, I am deeply sorry. Oh, what's the use! I can no more explain what happened than . . ." She made a helpless gesture.

"What are you trying to tell me?" he whispered in horror.

"Yes," she said. "I did."

Avoiding her eyes, Peter went to the window and opened it wide. He stood before it, letting the gale and the rain lash him. When he turned back to her, his face was cold, polite.

"I'll leave this open," he spoke in a remote voice. "We will be expecting a visitor before long." He sat down in an armchair and crossed his battered Hessian boots. His guns were on a table out of reach.

"Peter." Her voice was sad, flat. "You must be prepared to protect yourself."

"Why?" He watched the sand build up in the angle of the window sill.

"Because he is coming to kill you."

"Yes?"

"Although . . ." her voice grew faint, "when he sees me and realizes who I am . . . I didn't explain, he does not know, not yet. When he sees me here, he . . ."

"May think himself revenged enough? He is."

Traces of his earlier delight stayed in Sarah's memory, making him seem the more shocked and empty now. She felt as if she had killed something trusting and hopeful.

They were silent a long time. Then Sarah began timidly to tell this controlled young stranger at the other end of the room that nothing was absolute.

"It is possible, I think, to love one man and at the same time be strongly attracted to another if the circumstances are . . ."

"Love in duplicate?" he asked, "or perhaps in triplicate? Do go on."

She was silent, then, after a few moments, asked hesitantly, "Is it—is everything gone, over . . . for us?"

"If you mean fear, of course, for which I thank you."

"I mean love." She touched his arm.

"Don't touch me." His voice was even.

"But . . . how can your love end in a moment? It can't *be!*"

Peter turned his face to the window. The wind billowed his torn shirt and opened it to his waist. He closed his eyes and let the wind beat against his eyelids.

Sarah's face winced in a pattern of grief that was all for him. "Why don't you rage at me, threaten me?" she asked, wanting to release him from this cold numbness.

"Why should I?"

"Because of love . . . past love is it, Peter?"

"It is not past. It will always be with me, at the

327

hour of my death and perhaps beyond." He said this as if stating an established fact.

Sarah raised her arms to him but let them drop. "You can't think of dying now . . . I can't let . . ."

"Nor do you want *him* to die, may I remind you."

"Peter . . . can we *will* this to be put aside as a . . . a stumble, a lapse? Can we clasp hands and demand a fresh start? Surely it is up to us."

"Your affair by the dunes was an interesting way to make a fresh start."

Sarah's features turned white and drawn. She had been offering herself in all generosity, crushing the protest in her heart, crushing the vivid memory that lodged there.

Otis came snuffing up and down the crack of the door. He gave a whine that led into an eerie howl. It swelled in volume until it seemed to reach beyond the barrier of time.

"Otis has been far ahead of us all along," Peter said. "If events go against me, please put Otis outside the house before you leave with your lover. I would prefer not to give my chief mourner such an exhausting concert schedule. Or does he howl only before the event?"

Sarah went up to him. "Peter, please stop this. Talk naturally. I am your wife."

"Are you? Then let's talk about something else. For instance my feeling of being freed, severed from the past was accurate, wasn't it? I will be, shortly. The dunes are close by."

"You are invoking . . . asking for . . ."

"Life is quite simple after all." Peter stood up and brushed her arm aside. "There is nothing else but courage."

Sarah drew a deep breath. She reached for the

perfect words to return what she had taken away—
hope . . . joy . . . but she waited too long and when
she said in a low voice, "It may be that there is
nothing but love . . . the rest is unimportant," it was
too late.

Otis filled the room with his barking. He snarled
and pawed at the door as the rope ladder outside
the window grew taut and ground against the sill.

Sarah and Peter stood motionless as they
watched the straining rope ladder protest the
unusual weight it bore.

"Defend yourself. Oh, Peter, defend yourself!"
Sarah's voice was like a tendril of wind.

Peter gave her a long, grave look and, at that
moment, Captain Collier came in through the
window.

"Well met, dear boy," he shouted as if the wind
still howled around him. Then his face smoothed
out with surprise as he saw Sarah.

The three people stared at one other, silent with
shock, each in the eye of a private storm. Even the
Captain's incredible vigor was stilled.

I must help, save, stop, thought Sarah, but she
felt powerless and the air around them seemed
stale and metallic with their exhaled stress.

At last Captain Collier, wet with rain, twitched one
massive shoulder, then bowed. "Good evening. Mrs.
Peter Garrett, I presume?"

Sarah spoke slowly as if her thoughts crystalized
with each word. "So our actions have drawn us to
this moment, like three magnets . . . No, that
sounds pompous. What I'm trying to say is . . . what
happens from now on, we are free to . . . to decide.
Could we try some deeply truthful talk, then go
away. . . in three separate directions and leave each

other alone from here on? Would that . . . be a solution?"

She saw by their faces that she had been absurd. She raised her hands and let them fall.

"He knows?" Captain Collier asked her.

"Yes," Sarah said.

The captain gave an echo of his old hearty laugh. He sat back on the window sill in a negligent attitude that seemed to cover coiled springs.

Peter went over to his gun on the table. He looked at it curiously.

The captain's black eyes were huge and stern as he looked at Sarah. "This was the first time I ever put myself in the power of a woman and of course, it is the last." He reached out, picked up the gun and flung it out the window in back of him with a stylish ease that was infinitely insulting.

"Shall I kill him now?" the captain asked as if to himself.

"You can try," said Peter. "Down below. You go first, I will follow." His manner was punctilious.

He has nothing more to fear, thought Sarah.

"How nice we are," said Captain Collier. "No disorder in front of our lady."

Sarah said, "Fighting can't free us of each other and it might be that not even killing each other off can free us."

"True." Captain Collier gestured upward to the lowering windy sky. "Nobody knows what the arrangements are."

"But if there is some—some truth beyond the facts that we know about each other, perhaps that might . . ." Sarah went on trying. At least they were not fighting, not yet. When they did, the outcome was only too clear to her. Equally clear was that

330

Peter's death would be upon her conscience forever.

"Each to his own fact," said the captain. "My momentum of revenge now rules me. Peter wants to get rid of his guilt and fear with one brave gesture. You want to undo the damage you have caused to our hearts. So it goes." He leaned back against the window frame.

"You may be right, but not for Peter. He is different, now." Sarah said.

"I do not require a defender," Peter said.

Sarah's voice was distinct against the storm. "Haven't we all damaged each other enough to call it quits now? Damage binds us to each other."

"Nor do we need a philosopher," said Peter. "If you are trying to talk away what must be done, it is useless. Let's get on with it, Captain."

The captain was staring silently at Sarah. He thought of the times he had seen her. First, through his glass out on the bay—a vapor, a mist maiden of ill omen—then on the dunes riding out of the night into his arms. And now here, a beautiful young woman with a tired face and luminous eyes, who said words that delayed his cleansing fury. If she had screamed, lied and cringed, he might have killed them both and been free. Instead she had made him look inward, away from action, inward where he loved too well this woman and his brig. In a flash of intuition, he added Peter's name. It was possible that through long concentration on him, he had grown to know him with the intimacy that only an enemy or a lover could feel.

The captain exchanged a long look with Sarah. It was possible that she had ruined his life. He would never see her like again, so his enjoyment of women would wane and with it his male power from which came all his good fortune and his vigor. A trace of superstitious horror constricted his features.

Peter moved restlessly. "Captain Collier, stand up and defend yourself."

"Eh?" The captain started as if he had forgotten Peter's presence. The effect was the perfect insult. "Why should I stand up, dear boy, when I can kill you from here with a fly swatter? Ugh, your heroic posture, your sickening pride! Have you been knighted for informing?" The captain hesitated, gave a short laugh and said in a curious voice. "But after all, dear boy, I am fond of you in a strange reverse way. As a hunter is attached to his prey, when after a long hunt he raises his gun and almost with regret . . ."

Peter took a short sword off the wall.

Now at last, thought Sarah, Peter is the way he wants to be. Cool and aggressive in the face of death. Ridicule is a kind of death for him.

As if the pressure here in the room was too much to bear, her vision shifted from the larger outlines of tragedy to trivial details. She noticed a split seam on the captain's thigh and his well-shaped gentleman's hands, clean as fresh sea sand as he scratched a forearm full of mosquito bites, a legacy from two nights in the open. *Scratching!* At this moment of high drama and peril! But we are all slaves of this bodily business which went on in spite of everything. Despite love or murder, they must still take care of various physical necessities. She, for instance, was even now removing a grain of sand that had blown into one eye and her throat burned with thirst. There were other urgencies. And who could tell what the two men were suppressing of a like nature?

332

Here they were in a room together while a storm raged outside and in their breasts, until they were beside themselves with emotion while at the same time . . . as if to illustrate her thoughts, Sarah suddenly sneezed.

"Dear boy," said the captain. "Lend your lady that famous handkerchief of yours that wears a groove in your nose."

Sarah's old enemy, the bright thread of the ludicrous that ran parallel with everything, sprang out of the fabric here and overcame her. She laughed. A slight stream of sound at first, then, as if swelled by a river, it burst into peal after peal of ringing feminine laughter. She pointed, helpless to explain, to them then to herself.

Both men were incredulous, then offended.

"Is she hysterical?" the captain asked.

"No," Peter said. "She does this. Something amuses her inappropriately . . . in times of . . . of stress."

"Ah, yes . . ." The captain remembered only too well.

The two men were momentarily together, their hatred cauterized by the belting ridicule in her laughter.

Captain Collier was the first to acknowledge it. He jumped to his feet. "Damn us and our fool's talk! There is more truth in her laughter than anywhere. Let your courage recede to low tide again, dear boy. Goodbye, Sarah. I would know how to stop your laughing."

He flung himself over the sill to the rope ladder and before he left, looked in at them. "I'll leave you alive to enjoy your laughing lady but, by God, I'll take your boat. All I want now is a ship, the wind at

333

my back and the night sky. My course is marked out. I'll find my brig. No sea is big enough to hide her from me." He vanished from their sight. A moment later, on the ground below, he stood motionless, staring at the window where the ferocity of his deep carved dimples still seemed to linger in the air.

At that instant, a loud cracking noise rose above the storm and the crash of thunder. It was the unmistakable sound of a ship breaking up.

# Chapter twenty seven

*Without the benefit of the artist, tragedy invents itself!*

Sarah and Peter ran downstairs. Peter wrenched the board off the door and they raced to the edge of the bluff. The beach down below them was lighted by flares set up by Peter's men who had been joined by others, partners from the town.

Far out, crashing and grinding against the reefs was a wrecked brig. Her light swung wildly on the mast, then was obliterated in the water.

The thunder was overhead now. Streaks of lightning showed the men on the brig the whole panorama of their folly. As a vivid flash lit up the scene, the men aboard could be seen trying to launch the whale boats and arm themselves at the same time.

Savage, exultant shouts rose from the beach as a huge breaker seized the helpless brig, lifted her off the rocks and the strong lee tide hurtled her straight for the beach. She struck with a grinding shivering crash.

Ragged yells came from the raffish crew as they jumped from the hull into the waves, swords drawn. Their wet guns were useless but they knew what awaited them from the Mooncussers standing waist high in the water to greet them. Only their own ferocity could save them.

"My men!" Peter shouted. "My men are out there in the water fighting the survivors!" He groped for the rope ladder leading down to the beach.

"Peter!" Sarah cried. "Don't go down! They will kill you!"

He turned to look at her, that was all.

"Peter if you go down there, I have a strong feeling that . . . you will never come back. Is that what you want?"

He looked at her, his eyes somber. "And if I do come back?" He shrugged, pulled away from her and started down the ladder.

At the edge of the water, Captain Collier was already striding through the waves to his brig. His face was foolish with bereavement. The *Windshadow* was his child. Many of the timbers and spars had felt the caress of his hand before going into the structure of the boat.

"You bastards!" he yelled into the wind. "Mutiny, would you, without a decent navigator in the crew. You've wrecked the best damned brig on the water, following a false light. Damn your thick skulls!" But he drew his sword and joined his crew in the fight.

"Pirate gold," the Mooncussers yelled. "Get the gold!"

"Kill 'em all!"

Sarah, following Peter to the beach, heard Thankful Cassidy's deep voice boom above the surf. "Kill 'em. There's a bounty on pirates. Don't miss a one but don't waste time. Hurry . . . *hurry,* men. Zenas Mayo was *here.* Speed it up! I say Zenas Mayo was here and he'll bring back the militia. Hurry up with what you have to do."

When Captain Collier saw the caved-in side of the *Windshadow* he felt as if his own ribs had given way but he stood fast before the bowsprit repelling every attack with his brilliant swordsmanship and his vigor.

A group charge of Mooncussers got in under his guard and as he grappled with two men, Comstock's sharpened boat hook hovered above him ready to split his head.

Peter rushed out into the water and before Comstock could aim his boat hook at its moving target, Peter ran him through, the first man he had ever killed. He leaned against the hull of the *Windshadow* a moment.

Captain Collier had seen. He threw Comstock's corpse at his two remaining attackers and knocked them underwater where, unnerved by Comstock's pitted face leering up at them below the surface like a huge diseased clam shell, the men came up at a disadvantage and were easily dispatched by the captain's sword.

A huge breaker tore off a part of the *Windshadow* and carried it ashore damaging some of the Mooncussers in the water. This freed Captain Collier to look at his brig—the second one he had lost because of Peter.

His anguish and fury centered on Peter as the flares on the beach lighted up that long, proud face.

Peter understood the captain's look. "Now?" he asked.

"Now." The captain nodded. He came toward him slowly through the surf and the debris. His sword was held firmly, his arm clamped against his body to steady it.

Peter's sword wavered above the surging water. He put his back against the hull of the *Windshadow* to steady himself.

"First, why did you save me?" Captain Collier asked.

"I . . . don't know."

"To even the score?"

"Maybe."

One of the sailors set off a fuse to shoot the one remaining cannon near the bow. As the fuse lit up the small area around them, it became, for the captain, the signal for a flare of understanding that illumined his spirit.

"Stop where you are," he said to Peter. "We are a single line with a hooked fish at either end. It is time to cut the line, not each other."

Peter looked directly into his eyes and saw the hard kindness there. Something gave way, moved aside in his mind and he held out his hand.

The captain, holding his sword firmly against his left side, grasped Peter's hand with his own right hand. They stood a moment quietly looking at each other, their hands clasped.

At that moment, the last cannon in the *Windshadow* fired. The shot was useless, too high. It went over the heads of the Mooncussers. Then the rest of the powder in the hull exploded. The impact behind Peter's back threw him forward against Captain Collier's sword.

Peter looked up at him as the blade penetrated his chest and nodded once as if he had kept an appointment on time.

Sarah, standing in the surf at the shore line, waited while the captain lifted Peter in his arms and carried him from the fighting to shore.

"I saw it all," she said. "It was the brig that made the decision, not either of you."

"Remember that, and . . . other things." He strode back through the waves to the defense of his crew.

The receding water pulled Peter's blood back into the tide. He was still conscious but he no longer had to squint his eyes against the sandy wind. It had become painless. He opened his eyes wide and tried to hear Sarah saying something to him that was too distant to hear.

Words of love as perfect as the song of a bird came to him but he could not move his granite lips. Something began beating its wings in his chest and in his head. Then it left his body, now a vacant shell lying on the beach.

The wind dried Sarah's face, leaving sand in the channels left by her tears. In the flares set up by the men on the beach, she watched Peter's mysterious mute face and his open mouth where little drifts of sand were gathering. A sand flea explored his left pupil, a strand of his thin, light hair blew gaily in the wind.

Otis came over to sniff Peter's arm where a trickle of blood congealed, but he made no attempt to howl. His schedule, thought Sarah, runs ahead of time. He howls only for death when it waits in the rigging. Its actual arrival is old news.

She stood, saying aloud to herself, "Sarah Mayo, make sure that you do no more harm!"

The fighting raged on in front of the beached *Windshadow*. The crew was large but the Mooncussers slightly outnumbered them. However, the ferocity and greed of the Mooncussers was outclassed by the ferocity and vengeful hatred of the privateers.

Sarah ventured into the boiling surf. Somehow she must tell the captain, warn him that the noise of the cannon and the battling men was bound to alert the Cape for miles around, and that Zenas and the militia would be there any minute. But the action in the water was so fast that she could find no way to approach him. She hovered just beyond the edge of the fighting, waiting for the right moment.

The Mooncussers were avid to sack the ship before she broke up and above all kill the witnesses before the authorities came. But Calvin Collier's vivid face and his deep chesty battle yell rose above the surf as he led his men in savage attacks that even the Mooncussers were too cautious to equal.

He'll be killed! Sarah thought as she watched him fighting with a demonic vigor that could not humanly be maintained for long. As the night and the storm began to give way to morning, Sarah cried out to the dawning light, "Don't give me this day more than I can bear!" But the fight went on as bloody as ever, and the Universe was not prepared to measure out comfort for human needs. The rhythm of the surf would never change by one fraction of a second because of human agony. Gulls flew against the rosy sky and nature went about its business, indifferent to floating corpses.

The young girl in Sarah died that night as she understood at last that it was possible to cry and not be comforted, love and not be loved, suffer pain and not be soothed, mourn alone, feel fear and die without the quivering of a single leaf.

So be it, she thought. I won't ask for comfort. But I can *give* it! Even under the cold eye of nature, nothing can prevent one human from giving comfort to another.

Sarah felt stronger. Her character was energized by this affirmation. She waded further into the boiling surf toward Captain Collier. Wylie, who had been standing guard over her from the moment she came running down to the beach, followed her into the water.

Close to the hull of the *Windshadow*, Sarah saw Thankful Cassidy twirling her stocking with its brick in the toe. Her thick thighs gleamed where her skirt was pulled up and knotted high for easier movement.

Thankful kept booming encouragement and warning to make haste. Leading her men, she advanced fearlessly to the bowsprit. Turning, she saw Sarah's white, contemptuous face. Thankful's eyes narrowed and quick as a shark selecting one swimmer from a group, she made for her, swinging her stocking.

Wylie, who was standing just in back of Sarah, put one hand on his knife and fixing his empty eyes on the thick bare flesh of Mrs. Cassidy's breasts, he launched himself on her with the smooth spring of a weasel.

His knife plunged deep, twice, but he saw nothing escape along the bloody holes, intently though he watched. He must get his eyes fitted for glasses for it was clear that something *had* crept out or flown out because Mrs. Cassidy was now like the other limp bodies in the surf.

Sarah screamed at the captain to listen to her, that he was in danger, he must get out. But he only gave her a brief salute and went on fighting beside his men.

The Mooncussers were performing heroics of greed as they struggled to loot the dying ship. Their arms were already failing from loss of blood and their nerve center was gone with Mrs. Cassidy dead, but they fought on.

The crew of the *Windshadow* had a more elemental drive than greed—survival. Captain Collier's brilliant vigor had saved them so far and they looked at him with the awe they would have accorded a god.

The eastern sky was all light now and Sarah could see one sailor on what remained of the deck on the far side of the fighting. His chained wrists were hooked to the stump of the broken mizzen mast. The sailor would be slaughtered helplessly there by the first Mooncusser who got to him.

Sarah managed to struggle through the waves and climb up on the slanting deck. She helped the sailor raise himself until his wrists were free of the stump.

They slid down the deck together and dropped into the boiling surf where the short, red-haired sailor had trouble keeping his balance with his hands chained together. Sarah helped him retain his footing and led him past the fighting, where he would not have had a chance.

"Why were you chained?" she asked him.

"I'm the mate, Symonds. I tried to stop the stupid bastards from mutiny. Who are you?"

"I am a friend of Captain Collier."

He looked at from under his subtle eyelids. "Oh yes. You must be the same one who caused him to linger here so long that he lost his ship. The same one who changed him from a man to a lovesick

343

fool, waiting on the dunes while his ship was stolen."

"What does that matter now? I saved you, don't forget that. Now you owe me. Save Captain Collier, bring him out of the fight!"

"Why? It's going good—he's winning."

"He will be killed!"

"Not Calvin. You can't get him off the earth or the water that easy. Besides, take a look, he's winning."

"He *can't* win!" she screamed at him. "My father is bringing the militia. And the whole town has heard the cannons. Everyone will be here in a few minutes. If he's not killed, they'll put him in jail, or shoot him. Take him away, hide him! I'll give you my horse up there on the dunes—a fast gray gelding. He may have a knife cut in the shoulder or haunch but he's otherwise all right. Yours for keeps if you bring the captain out now . . . *now!*"

She gave him a little push.

Symonds looked askance at her desperate face.

"*Do* it!" She shook him like a wild woman. "You can sidle in around in back of the fighting. You won't get hurt and you have more influence than I. He won't come out for me. Take him away before the militia shoots him, shoots you both!"

"We'll need two horses. The militia is probably mounted. Stop shaking me, madam, and I'll see what I can do."

Symonds raised his manacled hands to his mouth and gave a shrill whistle that cut through the shouts of fighting men and the roar of the surf.

"Nothing has happened." Sarah said, in despair.

"It will. He knows what that signal means but he'll give a few more thrusts to clear his way out."

In a few moments, Captain Collier did leave the

fight and came leaping through the surf to Sarah and Symonds who stood down the beach at a distance from the turmoil.

The captain held Sarah close to him with one arm and wiped his bloody face on his other sleeve.

"Get these chains off me and we'll be on our way, before the militia get us," Symonds said.

"Not yet, Symonds. Who is responsible for wrecking my ship?"

"All of them. After they put me in chains, they quarreled over the course until the storm came. Then they gave up and followed what they took for the light of another ship, leading the way. The bastards, I tried to stop them!" He gave a grim laugh. "Now let's *go!* It's folly to stand here talking over something that we can settle on the way."

"None of the fools suspected that it was a Mooncusser's light?" The captain's voice was hard and bitter.

"I kept yelling out. I could feel the pull of the devils that swung the light. You can feel their intent, if you listen for it on the wind. Well that's neither here nor there."

"Where is the gold and other treasure?"

"It was in the cabin which is stove in now and washed out by the waves."

"The damned mutineers! I'll make them all dive for it and bring it up with their teeth!"

"If you stand here gabbing much longer you won't be able to do anything. You heard my signal. The militia are coming. *Get these chains off!* We have horses now and we'll find a boat. *Move* before a bullet sinks into that blubber you use for a brain!"

Symonds danced with fury to think that he, the better man, the smarter man, was still and would always be subservient to a natural born leader like Collier. Why was it so ordered? He ran over to the cliff and dashed his chains against a rock to break them, and swore at his bleeding wrists, still chained.

The captain felt hollow and full of losses. His brig, his men—and surprisingly enough, Peter. From concentrating on him, he had grown to know him so well that he had become like a detested but close relative.

His arms tightened around Sarah. She at least was here and his.

"So, Mist Maiden, all those plundering townsfolk of yours who hate pirates for excelling in their own vices, are on their way and we are to cede them the plunder and the spars from the *Windshadow*. Well, so be it. I'll go out and get a new supply. We'd better be on our way."

"We?" Sarah stepped out of his embrace.

The captain gave her a thoughtful look, then ran over to Symonds who was trying to saw his chains off against a rock.

Captain Collier began to pull Symonds' heavy chains apart. His muscles swelled . . . the chain must yield! Everything must yield now, including Sarah and the future.

Finally one of the links opened and Symonds was free. He ran into the surf and took a dagger from a dead Mooncusser.

Captain Collier came up close to Sarah. He did not touch her. "Listen to me very carefully, Mist Maiden." He spoke slowly, his eyes full upon her. "You are mine. You know that. Take the *Challenger* and enough crew to the third hidden cove between Wellfleet and Truro. I will be there, waiting for you."

346

Too wise to let her reply, he kissed her as lightly as the brush of a butterfly's wing.

The captain and Symonds started a vigorous zig-zag ascent of the cliff holding on to brush and beach grass.

At the same time, Zenas arrived near the cliff's edge with a group of armed men and the youths in his life-saving crew. The rising sun gave him a full view of the fight going on in the water beside the wrecked brig.

"Hold your fire, men!" Zenas yelled. "The God-damned pirates are going to exterminate the Mooncussers for us! Let them alone to do it. Pirates are cleaner rascals than our beach ghouls. Now fan out along the cliff, hold your guns ready and keep all those bastards down on the beach. We'll put the leftovers in chains."

Zenas ran over to the edge of the cliff. "I'm going down to make sure they *are* pirates. Could be privateers, but whatever the hell the ragged crew may be, they are killing off the Mooncussers."

Zenas went down to the beach in a half-running slide. "Watch for *my* signal, men," he yelled up from the bottom. "I'll raise and then lower my arm and you fire."

Sarah was still, staring upward, her mouth open in horror. Two soldiers were waiting at the edge of the bluff as Captain Collier and Symonds started to pull themselves over the edge.

"Halt," the soldiers shouted twice.

Captain Collier laughed in their faces. She could hear him roar at them from where she stood. "This is no place to tell a man to halt!" And his big shoulders and arms pulled him easily up over the ledge.

One of the soldiers, not waiting for Zenas's signal, panicked and shot him.

Sarah screamed as blood stained the sand where he collapsed with the impact.

Symonds came over the top further along the cliff. He circled around and sprang on the back of one of the soldiers, knifing him in the throat. As the other soldier turned to fight him, Symonds kicked him over the cliff. Taking the gun from the soldier he had killed, he shot him as he slid down the sand.

Captain Collier was slowly crawling up to the edge of the cliff. His arms were over the edge, grasping the dune grass as he rested.

Symonds ran to him and, taking him by the arms, pulled him up. Sarah could see him quickly tying the bandana from his head around the captain's shoulder.

"He's a fierce little fighter," said Zenas. "Very fast." He sighed. "And he loves his friend. You can see that in the way he protects him. By Christ, I hate to do this but he's killed off two of our soldiers and I'll have to get him."

He raised his gun and quickly shot Symonds through the head.

The captain lifted Symonds in his arms and Zenas aimed at him, but before he could pull the trigger, Sarah lunged and hit the gun a blow that sent the bullet into the bloodstained cliff. She ran over and beat the cliff in a convulsion of grief.

Zenas went to her, tried to pull her away from the sandy slide.

"No!" she cried out. "Why did you have to come back? Why, just at this moment? He could have got away! Don't touch me. You and your men have done this terrible thing. You have shot down my love! I never want to see you again."

Sarah ran past him and followed the captain's trail of blood up the cliff, slipping back and falling forward, holding to anything she could find. Alone with the near certainty of his death and her own anguish, she still carried the memory of Zenas's grieved and horrified face.

She looked back. Zenas stood like an old thunder-blasted tree. A shaft of compassion quickened her heart. If her captain survived, she would not see Zenas again for a long, long time. "Forgive me," she shouted, "I love you!"

Zenas heard, nodded once at her and gave a brief wave. He could only hope that his headstrong girl was going after a real man this time.

Sarah reached the place where the captain, if he was gravely wounded or dead, must be lying. But only Symonds' dead body was there. Thank God! She never looked back but went direct to mount the gelding.

On her way to the harbor, racing the horse and looking everywhere for the captain's dead or exhausted body, she found no trace of him. If he had gone into the woods to die, she could not search everywhere. She had a commitment and would follow it, holding the thought of his vivid person, alive.

Peter's death was tragic but she could bear it. Peter had seemed to carry the essence of death with him always. She could not bear the thought of Captain Collier so full of the very juice of life, lying dead. It could not *be!*

Captain Collier, shot through the shoulder and weak from loss of blood, found his horse tied by a dune where he had left it, and somehow through back woods and no roads, he made his way with his keen mariner's instinct to the third cove between Wellfleet and Truro.

He rested on the beach for the length of time that he thought would measure against Sarah riding to the harbor and getting the *Challenger* underway. The captain had no doubt that she would do it.

Once he slept and awakened with a jump. How much time had elapsed?

He stood up, afraid to sit down and risk more weak dozing. He waded out into the water and shading his eyes looked out through the narrow neck of the cove. He had imagined each sail was hers but now his heart thudded with rapture. For there, what was unmistakably a racing sloop sailed slowly past the cove and turned to come back.

Instead of waiting for a small boat to come through the narrow necked cove, Captain Collier the ardent lover, forgetting his wound, plunged into the water and began to swim out to the sloop, taking powerful strokes with one arm.

All went well until a mist of weakness seemed to gather in his head and eyes. His legs grew heavy and slanted downward in the water, demanding more of his one good arm.

Finally he rounded the point of land that hid the cove. If she did not see him he might soon reach the end of his endurance and will—a concept that was almost impossible for a man of his hard cheer to grasp.

He swam out into the bay but more and more slowly, as the mist gathering in his head and chest slowed him. He was bleeding again, but he knew that she would be there for him, the Mist Maiden, at the end . . . one way or another.

Sarah leaned over the rail. She had rowed out in her dory and taken the *Challenger* and a crew of three with a calm ferocity that made them obey her. "Your master is dead," she told them. "The *Challenger* is mine, my wedding gift. I want you to take her out and sail close by the coves on the way to Truro."

The men looked at her, shocked, uncertain.

"*Now*," she commanded, "or I'll get rid of you all and hire a new crew!"

The men told her that half the crew was ashore and had taken the small boat. Sarah sent a man to shore after them in her dory. He failed to return. After waiting impatiently, she started off with a crew of two working as a sailor herself.

Now leaning over the rail, straining to see into the cove, which was too narrow and shallow to admit the sloop, she damned the mist that hung over the water.

"There!" she shouted to the crew, pointing out a slight movement in the water. "Luff and about, go in as far as we can!"

From that moment on her eyes never left the distant swimmer. As the sloop drew nearer, he grew harder to see. He swam lower in the water. But thank god . . . yes, he was still swimming with one arm.

As soon as they were near enough, she would plunge in and try to help him. She was not good at long distance swimming and it might end by his pulling her down through the waves, which were rough after the storm. As for the two sailors, they were notoriously poor swimmers, the fools! A life on the water but never in it.

Otis put his front paws on the rail and followed

351

her gaze. "Even if you howl," Sarah told him, "I'll defeat it."

But Otis gave no eerie death howl. He curled up and scratched an ear. Sarah could hear the jangling of his collar.

My captain cannot die, because I am pulling him to me, Sarah thought. I am a sea witch, the sea runs in my veins, gulls fly through me, fish swim in my transparent self and my shadow flies over the water to him!

With her eyes always on the distant swimmer, it seemed to Sarah that she had woven a spell and that she did extend over the waves, drawing him to her.

She held her arms out into the drifting mist. . . .